KOSTAS KROMMYDAS

Evora

Where the senses and the heart rejoice

D1736067

With the kind support of

REALIZE

Via Donizetti 3, 22060 Figino Serenza (Como), Italy

Phone: +39 0315481104

Kostas Krommydas

. Evora

To my mother,
in the simplest way, she taught me what it is to love.

Kostas Krommydas

Evora

THICK SNOWFLAKES stuck to my face and my long hair every time I rolled down the car window to clear the foggy windscreen. Even this slightest of contacts with the ferocity of nature invigorated me. There was a time when people worshipped nature, received its beneficial influence with gratitude. Nowadays, most people view it as a daemon, unable to understand its workings. When nature rages, few can grasp that this, too, is part of a necessary primal ritual. A ritual where nature asks us to bow before it, proffer our love and respect.

I had to hurry. The snow would soon block the roads, as happened every winter, and I did not want to end up having to call my father to fetch me in the village snowplow. The old Jeep I had inherited from him could barely struggle up the mountainside in normal conditions, and I could feel the wheels start to skid on the snow. It was time to let go of my emotional attachment and replace this jalopy. I was firmly against mindless consumption, but I needed a new car, although I rarely drove.

Earlier in the day, I had driven to the town of Edessa to stock up on supplies for the village's mountain cabin, which was currently being run by my sister Eva. It had taken longer than I had expected, and nothing foretold that the weather would turn so bad.

If I did not make it to the cabin in time, I would need to call for help. The only other option was to turn back and head home, leaving the two couples at the cabin to spend the night there on their own. They would have little food for one night, but it would not cause any significant problems. I had undertaken the shopping trip to help my sister out, without counting on the weather's sharp turn. Perhaps I had been unwise to offer, given all the other matters I had to attend to. Still, in this community, we all helped out one another.

The snow was coming down fast and thick now, and the wipers struggled to shift it quickly enough, hindering my visibility. The ditches on either side of the road had disappeared from view, and anyone unfamiliar with the route was sure to end up sliding into one of them. The brilliant white veil of snow trapped the lingering light of day, which was tenderly fading, tiptoeing away from the approaching darkness.

I turned on the headlights, but could not see much more than the falling snow. A few meters ahead, I prepared to take the turn I knew was approaching. At the end of the road stood the two walnut trees, imposing and stripped bare save for the fresh snow settling on the naked branches—my sign to turn.

I rolled down the window again and peered up the mountainside; I could just about make out the floodlights beside the cabin. A few more minutes and I would be there. The wind whistled threateningly in my ears. I hurriedly rolled up the window, but the snow had swiftly invaded the car. I took the turn slowly, and once the car straightened, I gently stepped on the gas to go up the low rise of the slope.

As I neared the cabin, the snowfall intensified. The roads were becoming so treacherous, I began to wonder if I would need to stay the night at the cabin. There were only two bedrooms in the little house, but I hoped the two couples staying there tonight wouldn't mind if I slept on the couch.

A small, furry shape suddenly appeared at the edge of my vision and sprang into the middle of the road. Too small for a wolf, too large for a rabbit, it nonetheless caught me off guard. Panicking, I swerved into the oncoming lane to avoid it, and instinctively slammed my foot on the brake.

Wrong move. All my efforts could not prevent the heavy car from sliding towards the ditch, which I knew stood gaping at the edge of the road. My mind froze as I remembered that a small artificial lake lay at the bottom of the ditch, a water reservoir constructed by my father to store snowmelt in the summer. With the snow piling up, I had not recognized the familiar landscape, until it was too late.

Like a skier slaloming down a slope, the car slid toward the ditch, sweeping the fresh snow with it. I had only a few seconds to decide if I should try to jump out, or stay in the car and risk plunging into the frozen waters lying in wait at the bottom.

A metallic clang shook the car, and my world jolted. I realized something had snagged the Jeep's underside, slowing it down and bringing it to a tortuous stop. I swayed and thought I had a dizzy spell, but when I opened my eyes

I saw that the front of the car was suspended in midair. Like a perfectly balanced seesaw, the old Jeep was hovering on the edge of a cement wall, the small artificial lake stretching out ominously below.

For a moment I simply sat there, frozen from shock. Then my thoughts refocused, and I realized I had to get out of the car—and quickly. One wrong move and the car would tip right over and take both it and me careening down into the black, icy waters below.

I unfastened my seatbelt with trembling hands and tried to open the door. My efforts proved futile. The car was jammed into a thicket of bushes—probably part of the reason I had not already plunged headfirst into the icy water—and blocked me from opening the door more than a few inches.

My only option was the window. I grabbed the handle and frantically rolled it down. Cold air and gusts of snow slammed into me, but I ignored the discomfort and focused on climbing up onto my seat so I could slip out the window.

As necessary as the movement was, it was also a mistake. It disturbed the delicate balance I had been perched on. Before I had time to put even my head outside the window, the car dipped forward.

Fear and adrenaline surged through me as I fell back in my seat. There was no getting out now. As the front of the car tipped downward, torturously slowly, I panicked at the thought of what would come next.

Evora

The back of the car was now suspended in the air. My knuckles turned white as I gripped the wheel, as if I could somehow keep the car still. All I achieved was to press on the horn. Its shrill sound exacerbated the frantic beating of my heart.

It all happened in the blink of an eye. The front of the car violently hit the cement edge of the lake. My head smashed into the roof of the vehicle. The Jeep slowly slipped into the water, and in the distance, I thought I heard the faint, high-pitched barks of a dog.

Warm blood trickled down my temples towards my neck, sending shivers through me. The unexpected warmth was oddly comforting. My father's car was slowly sinking into the water, which was gulping it down like a hungry beast.

You have to get out! a voice inside my head kept screaming, but my body was refusing to obey any orders. The knock had paralyzed me. I quivered for a second as I felt the cold water lap my feet. Slowly, my eyelids fluttered shut...

Kostas Krommydas

Evora

A MAN DOVE INTO THE FROZEN WATERS towards the Jeep that had just taken a nosedive

He and his friends had stepped outside the cabin to marvel at the sudden snowstorm at the time of the accident. He had heard the car honk, as well as the loud splash of the car falling. He had located the wreckage thanks to a puppy's frantic barking, which had led him to the right spot at the edge of the lake.

There was just enough light for him to make out the unconscious woman floating in the driver's seat. Ignoring the burning in his lungs and the icy numbness in his body, he reached through the open window, grabbed the woman by her clothes, and pulled her out and up to the surface of the lake.

He kicked his legs hard, trying to keep them both afloat as he slowly made his way to the cement bank of the artificial lake. There, a man and two women stood by, ready to assist him. Anxiously watching the rescue attempt from further up the bank was a small white dog, whimpering in distress, as if he could sense that he had been the cause of the accident.

The man finally reached the edge of the sloping bank. Without wasting a moment to catch his breath, he cried out and pushed the woman into the waiting hands of his friends, who were leaning over the small parapet. They grabbed her by the shoulders and dragged her body through the snow to a small patch of level ground. One of his friends hurried back and stretched out a hand, helping him climb up the bank and over the parapet. The man was drenched and shivering, his breath coming in quick white puffs that lingered in the cold air.

"She's not breathing!" came the alarmed cry of one of the women kneeling by the unconscious driver.

The man pushed himself upright and stumbled through the snow towards the woman stretched out on the ground. He pushed back his friend, who had been shaking the unconscious woman by the shoulders, trying to rouse her. Then, he placed his ear against her mouth to check if she was breathing. No warm breath came. Time was running out.

He knelt beside her, put his palms on her chest, and began to rhythmically pump her heart, entirely in command of his actions. He counted to thirty, pinched her nose, and brought his mouth to hers. Covering her lips with his, he exhaled two deep breaths, trying to force some air into her lungs before it was too late. The cold water dripped from his face onto hers but provoked no reaction.

His two female companions were starting to panic, shouting for help. No one was around, and the snowfall muffled every sound, turning the sharpest cry into a choked whisper. Darkness was beginning to fall over the pristine white landscape. Still, the man refused to abandon his efforts to resuscitate the woman, tirelessly alternating compressions and artificial respiration.

Seeing that the woman's condition remained unchanged, one of the women spoke in a shaky voice. "We should carry her to the cabin. You need to get inside too, Antonis, you're drenched. You'll both freeze."

"We are not going anywhere until she breathes. By the time we get indoors, it will be too late," Antonis said, his breath coming in jagged gasps.

"He's right. Every second counts. If you are tired, I can take over..." the other man said, keeping a close eye on his friend's efforts.

Antonis, determined and angry at his failure to revive her, tilted his head back and howled; a despondent, animal scream that seemed to penetrate the snow falling around them. As if answering his desperate call, newfound strength filled him. He began to press harder, bent down, and once again gave her the kiss of life...

Kostas Krommydas

Evora

I FELT MY LIPS TINGLE AS IF I WERE BEING KISSED. Suddenly, a wave seemed to rise inside me. I woke up abruptly and, coughing and sputtering, started to heave water from my lungs. Hungrily, I gulped down mouthfuls of air, and all at once felt flooded with pain and relief.

My eyes opened and met the worried gaze of a man leaning over me. I was at a loss, my brain trying to grasp what he was doing here. My lungs were on fire, and I kept coughing as voices rang out around me. My body was numb. My mind, even number, struggled to understand why I was here. I tried to speak, but my chattering teeth made it impossible to utter a single word.

"Are you okay?" the man beside me asked, gripping my face in his palms.

Still coughing, I nodded, trying to make him understand that I was at least trying to communicate with him.

"There's no signal here... We should take her to the cabin, use the landline to call for help," said a female voice beyond my line of vision.

"She's hurt her head," the man said, moving his hands to my forehead. "We need to carry her," he added in a determined voice, and tried to raise me to my feet.

No matter how hard I tried, my legs refused to obey me. "What happened?" I stammered, shaking uncontrollably with the cold.

"Your car fell in the lake, but Antonis managed to pull you out," a blonde woman replied, stepping into my view.

I still could not understand much, but when I turned my eyes towards the lake, fragments of memory began to come back. From the corner of my eye, I spotted through the snow the snout of a small, white puppy. It was yelping, as if crying with joy. The image of an animal sprinting across the road flashed before my eyes.

"Help me get her up!" the other man shouted, and they all helped me to my feet, as I was evidently in no condition to stand on my own.

"We won't make it this way. It's best if I carry her and you walk ahead, clearing a path for me," said the man who had rescued me—Antonis.

He quickly hauled me onto his back. Instinctively, I put my arms around his neck, clumsily trying to hold on. Bowed over by my weight, my rescuer struggled up the slope towards the cabin. I bumped up and down in rhythm with his movements as if I were on horseback.

One of the women walked behind us, pushing her hands against my back to stop me from falling. Further behind, trotting along the path we were carving through the snow, the puppy followed, wagging his tail as if to emphatically underline his presence.

Snowflakes settled on our clothes and hair, covering us like a cold velvet sheet. The snowfall was so thick I had to use my last ounce of strength to shake my head to clear my eyes. I could feel my clothes starting to harden, and I was sure they would be frozen stiff soon. Maybe it was the fall or the fatigue, but I felt overcome by a sense of peace as the strange silence of the heavy snowfall became even denser.

A few minutes later, Antonis stopped to shift me onto his friend's back. It was hard enough to wade through the snow as it was, without carrying another person on your back.

Barely ten meters separated us from the steps leading to the door of the cabin, and the man carrying me seemed ready to collapse with exhaustion. Instantly, with the help of the two women, Antonis lifted me in his arms to carry me the rest of the way. He held me against his chest in a tight embrace. The others walked ahead, shoving aside the snow that now reached their waists to clear a small path.

One of the women rushed forward, hurriedly pushed the door open, and disappeared inside. A few seconds later, she shouted, "The landline isn't working!"

Inside the cabin, I felt the warmth of the fire burning at the hearth like a soothing wave. Antonis gently lowered me on a couch, and the two women asked the men to step into the other room before stripping off my clothes. The man who had dove into the frozen waters to rescue me left to change his clothes, too.

As the women raised me to a seating position to pull off my top, I caught Antonis looking at me before closing the door behind him. Still shivering uncontrollably, I tried to smile at him as a sign of my gratitude, but one of the women roughly tugged the top over my face, obscuring my vision. I tried to protest but the fabric was so wet and stiff, she almost choked me as she tried to pull it off.

Finally, the women removed all my wet clothes. One of them tried to shove my frozen limbs into a tracksuit bottom and a cardigan, while the other fetched a blanket to tug around me. I felt a prickling sensation on my forehead and saw bloodstains on the cloth they pressed against it. It must be a bad cut. My body slowly began to warm up again, gradually recovering from hypothermia.

"I'm Anna, and this is Giota," said the blonde woman, as she gently dabbed at my open wound with a clean towel.

"I'm Ariadne. Thank you so much for everything," I said through trembling lips.

The two men, in dry clothes, returned to the room and came to stand by the couch. "I'm Antonis," said the man who had rescued me. "This is Giorgos." They hovered over me to check my wound.

Just then, there was a scraping sound at the front door. Through the window, I saw the small dog scratching the wooden panel with his paws, yelping desperately as he tried to get inside.

"Can we let him in?" I pleaded.

"No, no way! I can't stand dogs inside a house!" Anna shouted, firmly putting an end to any thoughts of letting the dog in.

"Let's forget the dog for a moment," Giorgos said as I opened my mouth to protest. He gently probed my forehead around the wound with his finger. "Pretty nasty cut; you'll need stitches as soon as possible. You are also suffering from hypothermia, so we'll need to do something about that too... You barely escaped drowning, and I hope there aren't any other injuries."

A wave of nausea washed over me. The puppy will be sheltered from the heavy snowfall under the small porch, I thought.

Antonis picked up the phone, held it against his ear for a few seconds, then sighed and put it down. "The problem is we can't call anyone for help. The phone is dead."

"There's a large first aid kit in the bathroom. It's got bandages and medication," I said, pointing with a shaky hand.

This was not the first time someone had needed first aid up here, so we kept the first aid kit at the cabin as well-stocked as possible. Anna left the room to fetch it, and Giorgos put the back of his hand against my forehead, checking my temperature.

"Giota, could you warm up some water in the kettle, please? She'll need a warm compress on her stomach and her neck. I've heard it helps counter the hypothermia."

Without a word, Giota left the room just as Anna entered carrying the first aid kit. Giorgos opened it carefully and gave a small cry of satisfaction. He cleaned my wound with some gauze drenched in antiseptic, and I couldn't help but wince at the stinging pain.

"If you sit up a little, I'll bandage it up," he said. "It's bleeding a lot less now, but it would be good to cover it because I don't see us getting to a hospital any time soon."

Giota returned with a hot towel and handed it to Giorgos. He folded it carefully and placed it on my neck. Feeling the warmth I so desperately needed spread through my body, I sighed contentedly. "Are you a doctor?" I asked, sitting up as he'd asked me.

He gave me a look of surprise and refocused on the wound. "No, nothing like that. But I can take care of this cut, trust me. We'll bandage it tightly until you can get to a doctor."

A drop of blood trickled down my face in place of an answer. I was well aware that I had been lucky in my misfortune. My rescue had been a miracle, and I was now in the hands of a person who could look after my injury. I gently touched Giorgos's hand, signaling that he should go ahead.

"This will hurt a little. You'll have to grin and bear it, okay?" Giorgos said.

I looked at both men, and nodded. For the first time, I noticed how expressive Antonis's eyes were. I must have stared without meaning to, and he returned the glance with some surprise. His expression made it clear that he was trying to give me courage.

They kept a steady stream of conversation going while they tended to my injury, Giorgos handling the wrapping of the bandage while Anna acted as his assistant. I suspected they were trying to distract me from the pain in my forehead— and it worked, mostly. I was eager to learn more about my rescuers, and they were happy to share their story. Still in shock, I could not really feel pain. I patiently waited for them to finish, even though I was already starting to feel better and found out more about my unexpected companions.

Antonis and Anna were a married couple, as were Giorgos and Giota. They lived in Athens, and had driven up for the weekend. When I mentioned what I did for a living, besides occasionally helping out at my sister's café-restaurant, they seemed perplexed. It was not an unusual reaction—few people understood what it meant to help those seeking their purpose in life. Or perhaps, still dizzy, I had not explained adequately. All the same, it was rare for someone to understand what a wellbeing specialist did. They had heard about my sister's excellent cooking, though. They were planning to visit the restaurant for lunch the following day, but the weather had put a stop to everyone's plans.

"Thank you," I said, as soon as Giorgos was done tending to my forehead. "I wish I could find the words to express my gratitude... If it weren't for you, Antonis, I would have drowned in the lake."

Once again, Antonis and I exchanged a glance full of warmth. "All those first-aid seminars paid off," he said. "Even though we are to blame here."

I tilted my head at him. "How do you mean?"

"We called you to bring supplies, when we could have gone out ourselves. If we hadn't, you wouldn't have had to drive through a snowstorm. We came looking for a bit of adventure, and got more than anyone bargained for."

He cast a fleeting look at his wife, as if blaming her for what had happened.

Then, suddenly, the room was plunged into darkness. The storm must have knocked out the power. Luckily, the fireplace was still going, and we lit a few candles, hoping it would not be long before the electricity was restored.

"Just what we need," Anna said sharply. "This is what happens when you leave the city." She turned to look outside the window with an angry scowl.

Strangely, the dog had fallen silent in the past few minutes. Even though it had caused my accident, I still worried about what had become of it. It was only trying to shelter from the bad weather, after all. It was either lost, or someone had abandoned it in the wilderness.

My village, Avgerinos, was not too far away. Still, any attempt to go out in this weather without the necessary equipment could prove fatal, so we agreed to wait until the morning. My family might become concerned with my absence, although they were used to me disappearing for hours, and the cell phone signal was poor to non-existent around the village. At least I had spoken to my father and my sister before setting off, so they knew where I was headed.

Giota warmed up some water over a small gas stove and made tea for everyone. We shared some biscuits and chocolate they had brought with them, as the supplies I had been bringing were now at the bottom of the lake, along with the Jeep and some of my personal belongings. The tea beckoned to me, but Giorgos advised me not to drink anything hot yet as my body had not fully recovered.

The warm compresses had helped me regain some of my strength. I finally began to stop shaking and felt more in control of my movements. As I was feeling a bit better, I tried to stand up, but my legs would not hold me.

"Lie down," Antonis encouraged me, as I sank back down to the couch. "Your body needs to recover."

My lungs were still burning because of all the water I had inhaled. Giorgos read the instructions on a box of antibiotics he found in the first aid kit. He advised me to take a pill, but I gently declined, telling him I would wait until help arrived the following morning. To be honest, I never took any medication unless it was absolutely necessary. Giorgos seemed surprised at my refusal but did not insist, and soon left the room with Giota to go to bed.

Antonis and Anna remained in the great room with me. They sat at the dining table and spoke softly, but in such a small place, nothing could remain private. Evidently, there was some tension between them. Whatever was going on between them, however, I owed them my life, and I did not want to be indiscreet. Particularly towards the man who had not hesitated to dive into the frozen waters for my sake.

After a few minutes, Antonis and Anna rose from the table. Anna collected one of the candles to light her way up the stairs, and Antonis said to me, "We are all tired, and as you seem to be doing better, I think we should go to bed. It's much warmer here than upstairs. I hope you'll be fine on the couch."

"I'm fine. I'm sure I'll fall asleep straight away; I'm exhausted," I replied with a smile.

"If you need anything, just give us a shout," he said.

I asked him to blow out all the candles before leaving the room. Antonis obliged and looked at me again before following his wife up the stairs. The cabin was small, and the bedrooms upstairs had no doors so that the heat could travel up more quickly.

Everything suddenly became very still and quiet. I shifted on the couch to face the fireplace, the only source of light in the room. I pricked my ears, trying to listen for the dog, but all I could hear were the creaking floorboards upstairs.

My heart ached for the dog. In this weather, the poor animal could freeze. I tried again to rise from the couch, so I could open the door and let the dog in now that Anna had gone upstairs, but my legs simply hurt too much. The only thing that stopped me calling out to Antonis, pleading with him to allow the dog inside, was when I saw the snowfall beginning to ease. Soon, only a sprinkling of snowflakes danced in the wind. It seemed the storm had blown its course.

Under different circumstances, I would be tucked in an armchair at home with a cup of hot chocolate, enjoying the pristine white landscape through the tall windows. Now, exhausted, I closed my eyes and gave a little prayer that the puppy had found shelter...

I sprang up suddenly with a start. Something warm and moist was pressed against my hand, which was hanging off the edge of the couch. Instinctively, I pulled my hand away, only to realize it was just the tongue of the puppy, who had come to lie down beside me as I slept. In the dim glow of the fireplace, I made out the figure of someone sitting in an armchair by the fire.

"He kept scratching the door," Antonis whispered. "I let him in; otherwise, he would have woken everybody up. I didn't even get a chance to pick him up; he ran straight towards you. This little guy seems to really like you. I'm sorry if I startled you."

I gestured that I was okay. I was more than okay; I was happy. The puppy was panting excitedly. Thankfully, he was not growling, or he would have woken the others. I lifted him onto the couch, and he instantly snuggled between my legs, whimpering softly like a baby.

"I was worried he'd left," I said, stroking the dog's soft fur.

The trembling flames of the dying fire cast shadows on Antonis's face, altering his features. "Apparently, he can't bear to be parted from you," he said with a smile.

He reached down and carefully added a log to the embers, which caught fire instantly. I could spend hours looking at the flames, lost in their dance as I allowed my thoughts to order themselves. Soon it would be daylight, and help would be on its way.

The puppy protested when I stopped stroking it for a few seconds and nudged my hand with his snout. I preferred keeping the part the helpless creature had played in my accident to myself. Besides, it was thanks to his barking that the others had been able to locate me.

"Don't you want to get some more sleep?" I asked Antonis, and glanced at the staircase leading to the rooms upstairs.

"I'm okay. Unless, of course, you want to..."

"No, I'm not sleepy. Besides, I would be getting up soon anyway. And I'm already feeling so much better. Are you always such an early riser?"

He slid off the armchair and down onto the thick carpet, crossing his legs. "No, I was just worried about you. Wondered whether you might need the kiss of life again."

There was a twinkle in his eye as he said it, and we both laughed. Then we fell into an awkward silence.

"Antonis, I owe you my life..." I said, trying to break the awkward spell.

"You don't owe me anything, Ariadne," Antonis said firmly. "I used to volunteer with a rescue team, and this was the chance to apply everything I'd learned. I must admit I wasn't prepared for such cold waters, and I'm still not feeling warm enough."

He'd gotten carried away as he spoke, talking in a normal voice. When the floorboards upstairs creaked, he winced and immediately lowered his voice. "I read somewhere once that saving the life of one person is like saving the whole world."

"Is that how you feel?" I asked him, as I stroked the belly of the puppy who seemed to be slowly falling asleep.

"I feel good, that's for sure. Although I'm sure I'll catch a cold tomorrow. I'm already starting to feel feverish," Antonis said, pushing his hair back.

"Let me have a look," I said, and stretched out my hand.

He crawled toward me with a smile until my hand touched his forehead. We stayed still for a few seconds, our eyes locked in a long gaze. He slowly closed his wide, expressive eyes, as if soothed by the touch of my palm. I gently pulled my hand away, and only then did he open his eyes again.

"I don't know if I've got a fever, but your touch is very comforting," Antonis whispered and slowly moved away until his back was resting against the armchair.

"No, I don't think you do..."

As if wanting to change the subject, he sprang to his feet and walked over to the window. "The whether seems to be improving. The forecast was calling for sleet yesterday, and nothing more; that's why we decided to come up here. I've never seen them get the forecast so wrong. When the phone line's back on, I'll find out what happened, but this is very strange..."

"I don't remember anything like this before," I said. "My father told me that one winter, many years ago, the whole village was buried under snow for days. Of course, back then people didn't depend on electricity and all the modern amenities. They just made sure they stocked up on enough wood and food in the summer to see them through the following winter."

"Yes, everything is changing so fast nowadays. They're predicting dramatic climate change. We are experiencing the early stages of that change, which has already begun, and I hope will not rapidly deteriorate," Antonis said with a sigh.

The confidence in his words reminded me of something he'd mentioned last night. "You said you're a physicist, right?"

"Yes. I work on a European Union program studying climate change in the Mediterranean. Mostly how it is going to affect coastal areas."

I had spent the last few years living close to nature and, being involved in local production, I had seen enough to become convinced that the climate was indeed rapidly changing. Greece might not be experiencing intense repercussions yet, but one look at what was happening around the globe was enough to see that something was wrong.

"You said you have another job besides the restaurant, right?"

"The restaurant and everything that goes with it is mostly run by my sister and my father. I just help out whenever they need an extra hand. My house, though, is not far from here, along with the space I set up for my practice."

He looked intrigued but said nothing, waiting for me to go on. I smiled, because explaining what I did was always awkward for me, since most people had trouble grasping what I was talking about.

I sat up carefully, trying not to disturb the puppy's peaceful slumber. I was no longer shaking or feeling cold. I looked at Antonis and smiled again. "I've kind of already mentioned it, but maybe it got lost in all the talk. I'm a wellbeing specialist, and I employ my own therapy technique. To put it simply, I help people who feel lost find their way by using the power of nature and love. That's the reason I set up Evora."

"Very interesting," he said and pulled himself nearer.

In a low whisper, like two conspirators hiding form the others, we huddled and carried on our conversation.

"I'd like to hear more, but I imagine you must be tired..."

"I feel better. My head hurts a little, but I can talk." I gently moved the dog to the cushion beside me and stood up. I stretched slowly, feeling blood reach my limbs at last. "I have a degree in psychology. However, I have been practicing alternative therapies that are based on contact with nature for many years," I said, careful to keep my voice down. "Basically, I try to show people how to reconnect with nature. At the same time, we work towards changing bad eating habits, as well as a lack of physical exercise. Did you know that in Japan, there is a whole movement based on spending time in a forest? They call it 'forest-bathing.'"

"Meaning?"

"It's a new trend. It encourages people to live or spend more time in the countryside—or in green spaces, at least. Research shows that those who do so enjoy a better quality of life and boost their immune systems. The most significant benefits, however, are to our mental health. Contact with nature reduces stress levels, which cause a multitude of ills."

"If my feelings whenever I'm surrounded by nature are anything to go by, I'd say you're right," Antonis said with a smile. He slapped his knee with glee, struck by a sudden thought. "Of course! We heard about you at the village cafe. Someone thought we were looking for the restaurant and mentioned you and Evora, but we thought it was just the name of a hotel..."

"Oh, it's much more than a hotel," I smiled. "It's my slice of heaven and, I hope, a slice of heaven for everyone who has stayed there so far."

"Can I tell you something that's going to sound like a total cliché? It's how I've been feeling nonetheless..." He paused, looking for the right words. He took a deep breath and slowly exhaled. "When I gave you the kiss of life, I felt like I had done it before. I mean, I feel as if I've known you for a long time..."

I smiled, because I had heard this before, and often. I attributed it to the way I approached people. But in the case of Antonis, I was aware that I was talking to my savior. I kept stretching as I walked to the window and looked outside.

"I don't know if we've met before," I said quietly. "But I imagine that's not what you mean. I can tell you with absolute certainty that we have never kissed before…"

I turned back to look at him, and Antonis laughed and nodded. "I think I would remember," he said shyly.

There was a charming courtesy in the way he expressed himself. His words, the way he moved, all indicated a man who was careful about how he spoke and carried himself. I liked people who were in control of their body, their voice, so as not to disturb those around them. I hated it when people tried to impose themselves on others, talking loudly and making brusque movements.

"From now on, you and I will be connected," I told him. "A bond has been established between us that will exist, even if we never meet again. You will always be the person who saved me, Antonis, by sharing your breath with me. I have never come so close to death before. Now, I feel as if I have been reborn. I doubt anyone else would have dared dive into those frozen waters."

"Thank you, but why would we not meet again?"

"Oh, simply because at some point our paths will part and may never cross again."

"Isn't that up to us?" he asked, and came to stand beside me, following my gaze to the darkness outside.

"Not always," I replied, and reflexively looked up towards the bedrooms where everyone still slept.

"Why is it so hard to make our dreams come true?" Antonis bore the expression of a small child, and that made him even more likable.

"Because most of the time we set goals that we cannot achieve, and then we become disappointed. If we realized that the greatest beauty can be found in the simplest things, we would all have a better life."

We both kept our faces turned towards the window, our breaths misting the glass pane. Antonis lifted his finger and began to draw in the condensation. "Are you happy?" he finally asked.

"Happy... Happiness is a trap for those who pursue it obsessively, and a great gift for those who have encountered it."

"How about you? Have you met it?"

"I think so. You never know what tomorrow will bring and how things might change, but I feel that I have found what I was always searching for. For me, everything changed the day I realized I had to stop desperately seeking happiness and success. It takes a lot of work on ourselves to counteract all the rules society has ingrained in us."

He gave a sigh of agreement. It felt strange yet good to be with him. I knew we were not doing anything wrong, or inappropriate, but a little voice inside me was warning me not to get carried away. It was so easy to like Antonis. But he was a married man, and that meant there were certain boundaries I had to maintain.

As if reading my thoughts, he asked, "Do you live here... by yourself?"

"I guess you're asking if I'm in a relationship?" He nodded, ever so slightly. I smiled.

"I'm single. But I don't feel 'by myself' or lonely..."

A strong gust of wind shook the window, and we both turned back to look outside. I really wanted to change the subject, because I could sense that we should not become any more intimate than the circumstances allowed. I made a clumsy effort. "Well, as you are researching climate change, what do the experts have to say about what's happening around the world? The wildfires in Australia, the Amazon, even Siberia?"

Antonis seemed to understand my wish to talk about other things and gave me a smile tinged with some disappointment. He pushed his fingers through his hair, roughing it up. "At present, it's hard to predict the future impact of the fires; not only the ones you mentioned, but millions of others that broke out last year. In my opinion, they will further precipitate change. Like a drop that overflows a very, very full glass, if you like."

Despite the unpleasantness of what we were discussing, I felt myself grow calmer in his presence. "So you think all the terrible predictions will come true?"

"They already are. In the past hundred years, half the rainforests have disappeared. Humanity just refuses to own up to it. Sea levels rise every year. As we speak, they are about seven centimeters higher than they were twenty-four years ago. In a single century, sea levels have risen by twenty centimeters, more or less. What's worse is that this is not a gradual change. It is sudden and caused by human intervention. Things just keep getting worse."

I was not fully informed about all this, but not because I didn't care. I'd just been living in seclusion these past few years, and current affairs did not feature prominently in my daily routine.

"Unfortunately, none of us are doing their part for the environment." He huffed in frustration.

I nodded, agreeing.

"We think nature owes us, and we don't understand that our very existence is its gift. Nature is constantly showing us in the simplest way that nothing can be taken for granted, that she has the final say in everything. And when she does have the final say, it will be too late for mankind. We'll pass into dust and memory, but the flowers will keep flowering without us. The trees will spread their roots deep and their branches high. The environment breathes easier when we do not dominate it."

I remembered just then something I had learned recently. "There is an old African folk tale that goes like this: A forest catches fire, and almost all the animals start running away, trying to save themselves. All except a hummingbird, which flies towards the flame carrying a drop of water in its beak. The other animals start crying out, 'What are you doing? Have you lost your mind? You can't put out a fire with a single drop of water!' 'I know,' says the hummingbird. 'I'm doing my bit.'"

"That's beautiful!" Antonis exclaimed, and instantly lowered his voice so as not to wake the others. "If every one of us tried to set an example and walk the talk, everyone else would follow."

"Exactly," I sighed.

"I envy you," he said.

I felt a broad smile forming on my lips before I could contain it. "Envy what? You barely know me, so how could you envy me?"

"Ariadne, when I was trying to resuscitate you, I was convinced you were going to make it. I envy the strength that radiates from you, even when you are silent. Every cell in your body vibrates with serenity, and..." He paused, searching for the right words. "That makes you incredibly attractive."

Silence fell around us as our eyes locked. The logs burning in the fireplace snapped and crackled, and I could smell the resin from the fir logs stacked beside it. His attention was flattering, but could not continue, no matter how attractive he looked in the firelight, or how tempting it was to throw good sense aside. Flirting with a married man went against every principle I held dear. Even if the man in question had saved my life. My defenses were sturdy, and I had no intention of letting my guard down. Of course, it was always possible that what I perceived as flirting was simply an expression of interest on his part and nothing more. I was nonetheless surprised at how quickly we felt at ease as if we had known each other for a long time.

Again, I tried to turn the conversation towards safer ground. "Will we see more natural disasters in the future?" I asked.

"No more talk of calamities," he said with a smile. "I'd rather hear about all the wonderful things you do."

I smiled back at him. He was looking at me like a young boy desperately wanting to hear how the story ends.

"As I said before, I work with people seeking a different path in life."

"How do they find you?"

His question startled me, and he rushed to explain. "I mean, how do they end up coming to you for help? How do they reach you?"

"Love is the guide..." I whispered, my index against my lips as if sharing a secret that must be kept.

He smiled conspiratorially and cupped his hands around his mouth. "Tell me..."

We looked more like children planning mischief than adults having a serious conversation.

"There is an online therapeutic community that tries to help those who need it. Everything there revolves around the importance of love. Anyone interested can contact a therapist there. Then, from a certain point onwards, recommendations play a big part, especially word of mouth. It's not as hippy as it sounds, although most people think so, when you start talking about love. They are normal, everyday people, just like you and me. A little lost, perhaps, but who has not felt off-course in this day and age...? They come here as students, shall we say."

"Is love so important then, in what you do?"

"Of course. Without love, our world would not last a single day... However, the only way someone can learn how to love is by overcoming their narcissism," I said, tracing a heart on the misted glass with my finger.

"I'm trying to understand the connection between love and being at one with nature, as you said before."

"If you don't love the place where you live and the air that you breathe, you cannot love anything else. Our first desire, ever since we're babies, is to stay connected to the trees, the soil, animals, plants. They are our entire world at that stage in our life. If you were to release children into nature, they would just become one with it. They would roll in the mud, try to taste everything they could get their hands on. But as we grow older, we become removed from that primitive condition and lose our connection with the natural world. That's why we feel the need to fight the despair which we eventually sink into."

"So a person who lives in the city and does not have any real contact with the countryside cannot love?" Antonis pondered.

"I didn't say they can't. It's just that, if you maintain your bond with nature, you can love more easily. You can love without experiencing isolation so intensely. You know, that feeling of loneliness you get even when you are in the company of many people..."

"The most important thing, though, is to want to change the way you live, right?"

"Precisely. All of us can escape difficult situations and dead-end relationships if we try to be brave and make the right decision."

He bowed his head as if something had disappointed him, and sighed. "How can one define love, though?"

"Love cannot be described. It can only be expressed through our actions, Antonis."

"Such as?"

I looked at him, and the image of his face when I opened my eyes by the lake flashed through my mind. I would never forget that moment. "Such as what you did a few hours ago, when you plunged into the frozen waters to save me without even knowing who was drowning, risking your own life."

He gave me a restrained smile. "I acted instinctively, just as anyone else would have done."

"Not just anyone. The need to save the person in danger prevailed inside you. Survival instincts could have prevailed in someone else, and they would have stood by, helplessly watching the waters close over the car. It all depends on the values one has cultivated."

"What you say makes sense..."

"Your action was the ultimate manifestation of selfless love, the kind of love that nothing can sully. A kind of love that is unfortunately rare nowadays."

Slowly, he edged closer to me. The back of his hand imperceptibly brushed against my fingers. At first, I thought it was unintentional and pulled back, but he reached out again. This time, neither one of us dared move, unwilling to break this fleeting contact. I felt the warmth emanating from him even more than his fingers against mine.

Alarm bells went off inside me. Under the guise of crossing my arms, I moved my hand, trying to hide my awkwardness at the same time. We kept our faces turned to the window as if the broadest vista was stretching as far as the eye could see. In fact, we could see very little, as the landscape was buried in snow. I could not tell whether the heartbeat pounding in my ears was mine or his. I became aware that I had been holding my breath, afraid to break our silent yet intense communication.

I felt his eyes on me and turned slowly around. We still did not exchange a single word. We just gazed into each other's eyes, as if there was so much we wanted to say but did not dare. As if we had not been talking all this time, and now we had to come up with something to break the silence... But what?

I let my hands fall by my sides. I felt the warmth of Antonis' body again, and shivered when he gently brushed my arm. I made to pull back, but he held me there. This time I reacted instantly and did not let him get any further. Trying hard not to respond to his touch, I gently removed his hand from my arm. I struggled to rationalize my feelings, and attributed the intimacy I sensed between us to the gratitude I felt towards him for saving my life.

The distant cry of a wolf startled me, making me jump and grip Antonis's hand. Thinking that I was responding to his touch, he moved even closer. For the first time, I felt my defenses begin to crumble. However, I instantly remembered that his wife was upstairs. I pulled firmly away from him and walked over to the pile of logs by the fire.

I stoked the flames and thought about how we had become closer in the space of a few minutes. I felt flooded with guilt for letting things get even this far. I had never done anything like this before, and now I felt ashamed.

My hands shook so badly that the log slipped and fell against the grate, bits of charred wood exploding everywhere. Antonis dashed to my side and started picking them up before they set the carpet on fire. We ignored our singed fingers as we gathered the burning splinters and flung them back into the flames.

The small dog growled before we heard the footsteps coming down the stairs.

"What happened? Is everything all right? I heard a loud noise..." Anna's worried voice broke the silence.

"Everything's fine," I said calmly, straightening up. "Just an accident. I tried to add some wood to the fire, but my hands still refuse to obey me."

I hated lying, and I just had. I was in perfect command of my movements; it was my inner turmoil that had made me drop the log. The smoke was stinging my eyes, and I cracked the window open to let in some fresh air.

"Did you sleep well?" Antonis asked Anna as he went to stand beside her.

"Yes, fine. How's the weather?" Anna asked, rather abruptly, and turned to look outside the window, where dawn was just breaking. That was when she spotted the dog.

"What's it doing here?" Anna shouted, almost hysterically. The puppy, sensing her intentions, bared his teeth with a growl.

"I let him inside, and he will stay here until I go," I answered determinedly. I shut the window before Antonis, who was looking at me dumbstruck, could move.

My reaction was evidently not what Anna had expected. She turned towards her husband and said, "We need to find a way to get out of here. I've had enough with this adventure!"

"If no help reaches us by late morning, Giorgos and I will walk to the village," Antonis said. "I don't think it will snow again; the skies look clear."

The sound of people moving reached us from upstairs. The other couple was up. Giota came down first and bid us all good morning. Then she approached me, looked at my forehead, and asked me to move to a brighter spot. "The bleeding appears to have stopped, but it was a deep cut. You should get stitches soon, and possibly medication to avoid an infection."

I took her hand in mine. "Thank you for everything, Giota. I'll get it looked at as soon as I can."

Just then, the lights flickered to life—the electricity was back. My thoughts were still in turmoil from the moment of intimacy I had shared with Antonis. Needing a distraction, I announced I was going to make some tea in the kitchen.

"I'll help you," Giota said.

Giorgos came down the stairs as we walked over to the kitchen. Yawning, he gave me a wave and said, "Thank goodness, you seem much better."

"I feel better," I told him.

While the water boiled, Giota and I chatted about a plastic surgeon who was a friend of hers and could apparently erase all traces of even the most unsightly scars. I knew she was urging me to go see him, since the cut on my forehead would surely scar, and I feigned interest, but I had no intention of following up. I thought I could live with a small reminder of everything that had happened. I was firmly against plastic surgery unless it was for a serious, medical reason. I believed that attachment to beauty was a social construct that erased all the individualities that made every one of us unique. Nevertheless, everyone is free to do as they wish.

I snuck a look at the other three and, seeing Anna speaking to someone on her cell phone, I realized the phone lines must have been restored sometime overnight. I asked if I could borrow Giota's cellphone to call my father, as my phone was at the bottom of the lake. She dashed off upstairs to bring it, and Antonis and I exchanged a guilty glance as if we had done something wrong.

Awkwardly, I turned to look outside the window, and jumped with joy. Partially hidden by the fir trees, a deer was gazing at the cabin. You could just about distinguish its head and massive antlers among the snow-covered branches. I had not seen a deer in such a long time that the sight of it made my heart swell with happiness. Nothing can compare to the beauty of an animal in its natural habitat, especially when it is unaware of your presence...

Sensing Giota's approach, I turned towards her and took the phone she proffered. At the same time, I pointed to the window, but when we both looked outside, the deer was gone. It was as if it had never even been there.

"What was it?" Giota asked.

I shook my head, disappointed. "I thought I saw a deer between the trees, but it must have ran away."

A loud mechanical sound broke the silence, a sound I knew well—it was my father's snowplow, carving a path through the snow toward us. I asked Giota to mind the water simmering on the stove and went to the front door, throwing a blanket over my shoulders. The puppy followed close behind. As soon as we stepped outside, he started barking in the direction of the snowplow, which had yet to appear through the trees. A strange sense of melancholy came over me, like that feeling you get when you are watching a great movie that you don't want to end.

Everyone dashed to the porch and waved their arms in the air, as if trying to attract the snowplow's attention. Antonis came and stood so near me, I could once again feel the warmth of his hand against mine. Anna stood at the end of the porch, talking loudly on the phone, telling whoever was on the other line what had happened.

"Don't ever stop loving..." I whispered, without turning to look at Antonis.

He stretched out his hand to say goodbye, and I did the same. Our palms met, and the contact sent shivers through my whole body.

It was an uncomfortable yet sublimely beautiful feeling. I imagined that's how a cat burglar must feel when they pull off an art heist. That's how I had been feeling, ever since Anna had walked downstairs and found us together in front of the fireplace.

I pulled my hand away. Without another word, Antonis went to his wife, who had been calling him and holding out the phone towards him. I waved to my father as his big snowplow trundled up the path toward us. I had so much to tell him, but I was already dreading what I imagined his reaction would be to the news of my accident.

A firetruck was coming up the road the snowplow had cleared. I turned back to look at Antonis, and we exchanged another furtive glance. I would never forget how beautiful his eyes were, how expressive. Then, I picked up the puppy in my arms and waited for my father to pull up outside the porch. I was sure he could not even begin to imagine everything that had happened since the last time we'd spoken...

As the snowplow pulled away, I looked back just in time to see Antonis waving goodbye. The others were loading their luggage in the car, ready to depart now that the road had been cleared. Our eyes locked in a gaze that was only broken when I lost sight of the cabin. I leaned against the window and allowed my eyes to roam over the countryside spreading far and wide. The early rays of the sun lit the snow-covered ground, and a sense of peace and wonder spread across the land...

Kostas Krommydas

Some months later

I was always an early riser. Even today, on August 15th. The day of the Dominion of the Virgin Mary was a public holiday, but I was not one to split time into working and non-working days. Every day was unique and had to be experienced in the way that befitted it.

Even when I was not working, I liked to start my days early with a walk in the woods, always accompanied by my beloved Voras. The tiny puppy who had been the cause of my fall into the artificial lake had grown into a massive, snowy-white dog. I had been overjoyed to learn that he was a pure-bred shepherd dog and never ceased to be amazed at how he'd come into my life.

I had wanted my own dog since I was a child, and fate had ensured our paths crossed, albeit in a dramatic manner. I named him Voras after the north wind. He loved to climb up rocks and stand still as the wind whistled around him, alert as if trying to catch the secrets carried by the gusts. He only did that when the north winds blew, never at other times. Immobile as a statue, the wind rustling his thick coat, he looked magnificent. His size made some people wary, but Voras was a sociable dog, running towards everyone because he wanted to play. The only thing he could not abide was foxes, notably when they snuck into the restaurant looking for food. That made my sister and my father love him all the more.

Voras and I had enjoyed our daily foray into the woods and were making our way back to the house, my Evora. I needed to hurry up so I could get to the village square before the end of the church service. We entered the garden, and Voras made straight for the shade of the large chestnut tree by the porch to rest beside the armchair beneath it. We would spend countless hours there, side by side, me reading and him stretched out at my feet in companionable silence. I was sure he felt my father, my sister Eva, and I were his pack.

Voras also accompanied me at work, as everyone loved him and enjoyed his company. In fact, two months ago, he had assisted one of my clients more than I had. Before she left us, my client had adopted one of the village strays. Voras helped her experience the happiness that only an animal can give, asking for nothing more than to be loved.

Many of the villagers still did not understand how the building I had constructed next to my house could possibly be a workspace. Everyone who visited it called it "God's balcony" because of the stunning views.

I looked around the property contentedly. At long last, everything was as I wanted it. My father had greatly helped me make some changes during the spring. The guesthouse had been the most significant project. I had constructed it as an alternative for those clients who did not wish to stay at the village hotel. My guesthouse was now finally functional, ready to welcome my first visitor. After all, staying here was an integral part of the therapeutic work process. I loved living so near to my workspace. Just the fact that you could pause for a second and enjoy the magnificent view was energizing.

I heard the final church bell ring and swiftly stepped inside the house. I removed my climbing boots and went straight to the bathroom to take a quick shower. Passing by the photo of my mother, I touched the frame as always, a quick greeting, and then moved on. Thirteen years might have passed since we lost her, but I still sensed her presence here. She had been the one who taught me to love nature, and that had been her greatest gift to me.

When I entered the bathroom, I looked in the mirror. I absentmindedly stroked the small scar on my forehead, a memento of my misadventure at the lake. I would not be visiting the plastic surgeon Giota had recommended. I wanted the scar to remind me of that experience and how close to death I had come that day.

As the cool water trickled down my body, my thoughts turned to Antonis. We had kept in contact through social media. He would post beautiful photos from all the places he visited, and on the rare occasions I posted something, he would either comment or message me. The truth is that I never encouraged him; indeed, during our last interaction, I had been rather abrupt with him. Even this online contact felt different and special. Still, I was determined not to allow it to grow into something else.

The guilt I felt over that evening at the cabin was still intense, even if nothing untoward had happened. We had had no contact for some time now, not even a single message. Two months ago, someone had sent me a dozen rose bushes, and I instantly thought of Antonis. I planted them along the edge of the garden, in a line separating the guesthouse from my home. It was a distinction that only existed in my mind. Everyone else called both buildings by the same name. Evora...

Some days ago, I had held my final session, intending to rest until the end of the month. Interest in my method had surged after my winter adventure. As talk of my accident spread like wildfire, more and more people expressed an interest in coming to Evora. In fact, after a small article on Evora appeared on a travel website, the interest was so great that I had to turn some people down as I was fully booked.

Explaining to some people that I was not a doctor and that my approach would not benefit those who needed conventional medical attention had been hard. Then, there were the men who actually thought I offered massage services. Misinterpreting the content of my website, they believed that the short residential program I offered included sexual services. I was not surprised, as some people see no distinction between love and carnal pleasure.

As the water cooled down my skin, I reflected on the day ahead and tried to put my thoughts in order. Then, I was in a hurry once again and had to get ready to go.

Evora

I rarely used my new car. Voras and I preferred a shortcut through the fields and the forest, which led to the café-restaurant and the village. Along the way, I often stopped to pick cherry plums, wild berries, and any other wild-growing fruit in season. Cherry plum liqueur was particularly popular here. We would soon be harvesting the fruit for my sister to make the drink. Eva was an expert in local cuisine, and everything was produced cooperatively. Most of the products were based on my beloved mother's recipes, which she had passed on to us.

On days when I was not in a hurry, I would scoop up the fruit and stop by a spring. There, I would rinse them under the cold water and then savor the flavors of the wild fruit. From springtime onwards, I rarely kept fruit in my fridge. I liked to gather them myself from the fruit trees that were plentiful in this area, and I encouraged all of my clients to do the same from the very first day of their stay. We would take this walk together, talking and picking fruit. To my great surprise, I had discovered that this was the first time most of them were tasting fruit that they had handpicked from a tree themselves...

I picked up the pace and reached the outskirts of the village with Voras at my heels. I instantly noticed the disproportionate number of cars that filled the streets. On any other day, I would have felt angry at the sight of so many people driving rather than walking, but today I did not want to get upset. Luckily, my father would usually cover such distances on foot, setting an excellent example as president of our small community. That was also one of the reasons he was in such good health for his age.

Today, after the church service, my father and I would be discussing the water issue that had arisen. When I asked him why it had to be on a religious feast day, he told me that some people whose land bordered the water source would be in the village to attend church. He did not want to miss the chance to ask for their help. My family and some others had solved the water shortage problem by drilling our own wells. Still, most people relied on the central water network.

I finally reached the square and sat against the church bell tower, a childhood habit. The village houses and surrounding hills stretched out before my eyes. When I was a child, I would sometimes ring the actual bell, making the villagers dash outside their homes in alarm, fearing something terrible had happened. I was sometimes scolded, but I could tell that grown-ups remembered their own childhood mischiefs – a church bell is irresistible to any child, and they knew it well.

Voras flopped down beside me, puffing. Avgerinos, our village, was brimming with life. I felt glad for it as I took in the lively square before me. On days like this, people would visit from the surrounding areas, especially the town of Edessa.

Today was a special day for us all, as our church was dedicated to the Virgin Mary. Children were running across the square, making it look like a schoolyard at the beginning of recess. Some street vendors had set up their stalls and spread their wares, mostly toys, but also some household items. The queue by the candied apple and candy floss carts stretched all the way to the road. I remembered how enthralled I had been by it all as a child.

From the speakers mounted on the exterior walls of the church came the sounds of mass coming to an end. Our priest, a slightly tone-deaf elderly man, was one of the sweetest people I had ever met. I was always ready to assist him with whatever he needed. The large village square was packed with villagers and visitors in their Sunday best. Every year on this day, almost everyone would return to our beloved Avgerinos to spend time with family and to look after their property. At heart, however, they came seeking a respite from work so that they could return to their everyday lives reinvigorated.

When the priest intoned his final words, everyone spilled outside the church holding the chunks of bread that accompanied the holy sacrament. Greetings, hugs, and kisses filled the air. Many women named after the Virgin Mary were celebrating their name-day on this day. After a brief quiet spell, the sound of folk music replaced the sound of chants, a forerunner to the panegyri. This traditional outdoor feast would take place that evening.

I looked at the trucks lined along the other side of the square, piled up with plastic tables and chairs patiently waiting to take their place in the square when people dispersed for lunch. Suddenly, the music stopped, and someone tapped the microphone to check that it was switched on.

"One, one-two?" a voice said, and another voice was heard assuring the speaker that the microphone was working. I smiled, because the man testing the microphone was none other than my father.

"Good morning. Chronia Polla, everyone! In a few minutes, as president of this community, I will be at the restaurant to discuss a severe issue that has arisen concerning the water supply. Everyone is welcome to attend. We'll see you all tonight, at the panegyri."

The screeching sound of the mic being switched off pierced the square. Some people grumbled that they had chosen a holiday to hold a meeting. Not a month had passed since the abundant water source that fed the village reservoir had run dry. The community elders claimed that it had never happened before. Those prone to superstition took it as a bad omen.

People slowly began to disperse. Cooking smells drifted across the square from open doorways and tickled my nose, a tantalizing hint of the delicacies being prepared at homes and in the tavernas. Everything sparkled under the bright sun. The forest-covered hillsides surrounding the village, mainly spruce, chestnut, and beech trees, were still a vibrant green. I could only make out some yellowing leaves here and there, as if some plants were in a hurry for autumn to come and turn the landscape into a multicolored painting. The change of seasons in this part of the world, even from month to month, was breathtaking. Seasons were still distinct here, and you could enjoy all the transitions from one season to the next. That had been one of the reasons that had drawn me back home.

My father, walking up the cobblestone street, paused every few steps to talk to those greeting him. Seeing the community president, everyone had a question for him. He spotted me and motioned for me to join him so he could give me a lift to the café-restaurant, which stood outside the village. But I pointed to Voras, who had just stood up. We would rather walk. It was, after all, a beautiful day.

Voras and I took a quick loop around the square to greet my friends and then, following the woodland trails, we walked over to the restaurant. I glanced back before heading up the steps to the building and noticed the small convoy of vehicles making its way up the mountainside. Seeing that they were not too far away, I decided to wait for them to arrive.

The chestnut trees on either side of the winding road cast their thick shade and kept temperatures pleasantly cool. It looked like it was going to be a good crop year, and everyone was looking forward to the October harvest. Chestnuts were the primary source of income for many families in our village. We also had an orchard of chestnut trees, and their nut was one of my favorite foods. Our region was generally famed for its produce.

A few minutes later, everyone had arrived. My father stepped out of the car first. He came to stand at the foot of the stairs to welcome everyone. Having greeted all the arrivals one by one, we headed up to the café-restaurant where my sister Eva was waiting.

I knew the place well, but still looked around with pleasure. Everything was pretty and orderly. Eva and my father spent hours tending to the beautiful garden. We had chosen the location for its spectacular views, which stretched all the way across the flatlands to Lake Vegoritida. Drowning in the thick foliage of the surrounding trees, the café-restaurant was heavenly. We had worked hard on the restaurant, and our work had paid off. It had become a local pole of attraction for those who wanted to enjoy Eva's cooking and delicious homemade desserts and relax for a couple of hours.

People were still milling around the parking lot, so we huddled in a corner to quietly discuss the drought blighting our community. My father looked over the rooftops towards the peak of the neighboring hill where my home stood. He turned back and gave me a quick wink. I loved it when he did that. It felt like we were sharing a secret known only to us. I, too, turned towards my Evora. It felt fantastic to take in the panoramic view of the small waterfall gushing down into the canyon. We stood there for a moment, enjoying this heaven on earth that we had all chipped in to make a reality.

Evora

Among other things, today was the day I would be helping out at the restaurant as a waitress, as they were expecting a higher number of diners than usual. Coming into contact with all the customers was a unique experience in itself because it allowed me to encounter all sorts of people and behaviors. Exchanging wishes and handshakes with everyone attending the meeting, I joined some people at a table to listen to what would be discussed. Eva waved hello from afar and hugged Voras, who almost knocked her over in his joy.

Then, I carefully attended to what was being said. I understood that a landslide had cut off the mouth of the spring, and now new boreholes would need to be drilled to locate the water anew. My father, however, suggested we seek alternative sources of water to lead into the reservoir.

Another topic that preoccupied them was the renovation of the gym and the children's playground. It was irresponsible to spend so much time on other things, they claimed, but not give children the chance to exercise and play safely. As things were, they ran the risk of injury due to slipshod equipment and the state of the building. Everyone agreed to ask the municipality for the funds necessary for those works.

The festive atmosphere of the day and the local tsipouro served by Eva fostered a pleasant atmosphere among those gathered. In the end, everyone agreed that my father should take up these matters with the local authorities.

Then the first diners began to arrive, and it was time for me to get to work.

"Ariadne, you set the tables in front of the chapel..." my sister called out with a smile, and then rushed off to the entrance to greet people.

Work on days like today was tiring, but I needed to interact with people every now and then, as most of the time I avoided too much contact so that I could switch off. It was a good chance for my fellow locals to understand that I was an ordinary person, too, not a strange "mountain hermit," as some called me. Nina Simone's voice accompanied by the strains of My Baby Just Cares for Me lifted my spirits, and I began to set the large round tables with a smile...

The sun was beginning to set, and the guests seemed reluctant to leave. They had finished their main courses long ago but now lingered over dessert, enjoying Eva's delicious sweets. This was the season when the local delicacies she stocked often sold out. Most would head straight from the restaurant to the panegyri at the square come nightfall. For the time being, the mood had turned truly festive, people swaying and singing along to the tunes selected by my father. He had become an exceptional DJ over the years.

I reconnected with people I had not seen for long, some of them youthful crushes. I had worn my heart on my sleeve as a young girl. Early on, I became convinced that people could fall in love many times with the same intensity. I felt a sweet melancholy whenever I met friends with whom I had shared some of the happiest and most carefree years of my life. It was strange to no longer detect that child-like quality in them that I had thought would last forever. Observing some of the boys I had fallen in love with, I would notice that time had not been kind to them. What upset me most, though, were the lifestyle choices they were making.

I had not been in a relationship for some time now, not because I did not want to, but because I had not met the right person. I was not interested in anything superficial or conventional, without genuine communication, respect, and freedom. The only times I relaxed these standards was when I went travelling. My affairs were brief, always without any further commitment, and I was fully conscious that something could be both beautiful and last the short amount of time that befitted it.

All I wanted to do that evening after the panegyri was sit in my garden with a glass of wine and then go to sleep. The following morning I was planning to hike to the peak of Elatia, the highest local mountain, with some old friends. We went hiking every year, scaling a different peak each time, or enjoying the shady forests surrounding one of the springs. Drinking water where it sprung forth through a crack in the rocks high up on a mountain was a uniquely revitalizing experience.

"Ariadne!" Eva exclaimed, breaking me from my musings. "Could you please go take the order from the table by the cistern? I'm exhausted, and there's so much to do..."

"Of course, but I don't know what dishes are left. What am I supposed to tell them?" I asked.

"You'll think of something," she said, and then hurried away.

This seemed like a bad idea, as I usually had nothing to do with taking orders, but if Eva needed me to do this then I would just have to figure it out. I set down my tray, grabbed a couple of menus, and made my way to the table, which stood in the restaurant's most secluded spot, beside an old cistern. I often sat there when we were not busy because it was so out of the way.

Seated at the table with his back turned to me, a man with short hair was gazing at the setting sun. What struck me most was that Voras was sitting by his side, also watching the sunset. He had a habit of sitting by the tables of strangers, but usually it was to beg for food and pets; the peaceful picture that met me surprised me.

There was an empty chair across from the man, which I assumed meant he was waiting on company. I hesitated to approach, not sure if I was supposed to wait for his companion to arrive or not, but then I remembered how insistently Eva had urged me to take the order. I walked up to the table, set down the menus, and stroked my beloved dog's head.

"Good evening," I said. "It looks like you're waiting on someone, so I'll let you the menus and come back in a few minutes to take your..."

He turned towards me, and I froze.

"Hello," Antonis said in a near whisper, looking at me with his big, beautiful eyes.

It took a few seconds for his presence to sink in. Antonis was the last person I had expected to see. And despite whatever tension lingered between us, this was still the man that had saved my life. As soon as he stood up, I fell into his arms and embraced him like a long-lost friend.

"How did you get here?" I asked, keeping him in my arms.

"I was in the neighborhood, and I thought I'd drop in to see you," he answered, clearly taken aback by my enthusiasm. Perhaps he hadn't been sure how I would react to his presence.

I pointed to his chair, indicating he should sit down, and then took the chair across from him. "You did the right thing! You can't imagine how happy I am to see you. You look so different with short hair. It suits your face, frames it nicely." I looked around, and saw no sign of Anna. "Are you here by yourself?"

He gave me an intense look. "Yes."

I spotted Eva out of the corner of my eye, watching the two of us at the table. When Antonis leaned back in his chair, she must have caught a glimpse of his face, because her jaw dropped. I had shown her some photos he had posted, and she had taken an instant liking to him. She motioned for me to stay where I was, understanding that this reunion took precedence.

"Don't tell me this strapping dog is the puppy from that night?" he said, scratching Voras behind his ear. The big dog made a happy noise and wiggled his rear end closer to Antonis so the scratches would continue.

"One and the same," I confirmed. "I adopted him."

"Good on you. He looks great, and I think he'll be grateful for the rest of his life."

"Same way I'm grateful to you?" I asked playfully.

He just smiled, saying nothing.

I was tempted to ask why Anna wasn't here, but that seemed too forward, so instead I said, "Are you staying, or just passing through?"

I had barely finished my question when my father arrived in a flurry to greet Antonis. He, like my sister, had heard all about my savior and his daring rescue—after the incident, he'd sent Antonis a large basket with various co-op products to thank him for saving my life. Now, he seemed overjoyed to meet him.

Antonis, who did not understand who the exuberant man was, was initially taken aback. But then my father introduced himself, and Antonis's face relaxed. I watched them chat, my father insisting that Antonis stay overnight as our guest at the newly completed guesthouse.

Antonis looked at me awkwardly, probably trying to guess how I felt about it. I don't think my feelings were difficult to detect. I was so excited by his unexpected arrival, and wished he could stay longer. With a nod, I showed him that it was up to him.

For some time now, something inside me had been telling me that we would meet again. Maybe because I fervently wished it. The bond that had arisen between us was powerful, and nothing could change that. For a long time, I had felt guilty that he had overcome my defenses to the extent that he had, that night in the cabin. But now, there was no chance of me getting carried away, not even for a moment, as I had back then.

While he talked with my father, I stroked Voras, who seemed to share my joy at seeing Antonis again. It had been Antonis, after all, who had brought him in from the cold. I wouldn't be surprised if Antonis was Voras's favorite person—after me, of course.

After some time, my father finally left and we were alone once again.

"Please excuse my dad, but he really likes you. You can understand why."

I touched his hands tenderly. He seemed puzzled, and gazed down as my fingers brushed his. Before he could respond, I gently pulled my hands away. I knew I shouldn't be touching him, but something extraordinary happened every time I did. I had only felt such an intense bond with very few people before. When we'd said goodbye on that wintry day, I'd felt an electric jolt surge through me.

His voice interrupted my reminiscences. "Of course I understand, Ariadne, but I don't want to impose. I popped in to say hello before heading to Kastoria, where some friends are expecting me."

"If you need to go, do so. But honestly, we would all be happy if you stayed. However, I do understand that your wife might be expecting you, so..."

"Anna and I aren't together anymore," he said in an expressionless voice, and lowered his gaze.

"Oh, I'm sorry to hear that," I awkwardly stammered.

"Don't be. It's better for both of us. It was some time ago, all water under the bridge now."

To be honest, the news did not shock me. There had been no tenderness between them, that night at the cabin, and Anna's callous attitude toward leaving a puppy out in a storm still irked me. I had never been able to figure out how someone so selfless could be with a woman like her.

Seeing Antonis' reluctance to discuss the matter, I did not insist. "Well, if you have no other obligations, then, stay! There is the panegyri tonight; you'll really like that. You will also be my first guest at the guesthouse. They only finished working on it a few days ago. Come, you'll tell me what you think of it. Help me fix any imperfections."

He made to speak, but I stopped him. "And tomorrow you can come on the hike with us, if you like." I turned towards the mountain and pointed out Elatia. "That peak, with a couple of friends from the village."

Antonis laughed. "That's quite the schedule! It all sounds great, but I don't want to be an inconvenience. That's my only worry."

"Antonis, you heard what my dad said: you are a part of this family now."

"Like a big brother?" he teased.

"Something like that," I managed to reply. Our eyes locked, and I tried to stare into this extraordinary man's soul and understand his feelings toward me, whatever they might be.

My father changed the music just then. A jazz melody filled the air, ideally accompanying the moment. Across the horizon, the sun was slowly sinking, tinting the lake with the pink and purple shades of dusk. Antonis turned away from me with an exclamation of wonder as he took in the dazzling sunset. I would never tire of watching sunsets, but it's always a different experience when you can share such beauty with someone you care about.

After the silence had stretched on a bit too long, I decided to lighten the mood. "I can't believe I've been sitting here all this time without offering you anything! Have you eaten? Would you like a drink?"

"Thanks, I've had something to eat," Antonis said. "But I wouldn't say no to a glass of wine, if you were willing to join me."

"I would be happy to."

I left him at the table and went back inside, greeting those who were leaving along the way. I would be seeing most of them at the panegyri in a short while. I did my best to hide my joy, my happiness that not only was Antonis staying, but that he was now single. I felt ashamed of myself, and fought against my innermost thoughts—the kind of thoughts that no amount of self-control can keep in check.

By the time I returned with the two glasses of wine, Antonis had stood up and gone to the edge of the fence with Voras. There they stood, gazing at the sunset colors. I felt a chill course down my spine. This was something I always did. It was like seeing myself looking into the red horizon.

He did not sense my approach, but my dog betrayed my presence. Antonis instantly turned towards me and took one of the glasses.

"I did not get a chance to see anything during my winter visit. It's stunning," he said, and moved to clink his glass with mine.

"Maybe now you can understand why I choose to live here."

"I understood that during our very first conversation," he replied, and raised his glass.

"To love," I said, and noticed that my toast seemed to affect him.

"To love," he slowly repeated with a smile.

Down in the valley, the lights came on at the village square. The soundcheck echoed up the hillside, disrupting the peaceful moment. Everything has its own beauty, nonetheless.

"Ariadne, I need to tell you something," he said, looking grave.

Terrible scenarios flashed through my mind, and for a moment I felt worried.

"Yes, of course."

"I'm not a festive kind of guy."

My puzzlement must have shown on my face. Antonis laughed heartily at my confused expression and explained. "I think it's better if I don't come to the panegyri. Please don't miss it on my account, but I would rather stay here and enjoy the peaceful surroundings, enjoy being in nature. I need it, given the circumstances."

I understood him perfectly. I felt obliged to at least put in an appearance, but if it were entirely up to me, I would have chosen to spend the whole evening with him. I was already in holiday mode anyway, and I, too, needed to escape from the demands of everyday life.

"You should do what you feel like, Antonis. I must go, though. I'll drop you off at the guesthouse and let you settle in. The view is almost the same as here, only from higher up. I will be back in an hour—I don't feel like staying much longer than that." A small white lie. If it weren't for him, I would be staying at the panegyri at least until midnight. "And if you don't feel like it, there is no reason to push yourself to join the hike tomorrow, either."

"I'll come tomorrow," he said, and took a long gulp of wine. "But I don't want to be a burden. I could stay at the hotel in the village."

I raised my hand sternly. "You will stay at the guest house, and that's that! You're the perfect candidate to inaugurate it."

"Is that so? Why?"

"Because it would never have been completed if a certain someone had not dived into the frozen waters of the lake to save its owner. As a matter of fact, its construction finished just a few days ago."

"I can't refuse with you giving me that look. I can't risk you throwing me to the wolves in this wilderness!"

We both laughed, but my laughter was somewhat subdued. I had just remembered an encounter I had with a wolf many years ago. He had come into the garden and was roaming as if he were in his own back yard. The way he had looked at me had haunted my dreams for some time. Luckily, I was in the car at the time, and the wolf contented himself with baring his teeth and slowly walking away. From that day on, I was much more careful in the evenings. Fencing my plot of land, along with Voras's presence, had increased my sense of security.

Nonetheless, the fear I had felt was etched inside me. In the meantime, I had made sure to learn as much as I could about the behavior of these wild animals. Many wolves had found shelter in the nature reserve around here. Hunting was prohibited along with any kind of alteration to the forest, and offenders were severely punished.

Eva and my father joined us after a while. We spent some time talking about the sudden weather changes, until my father asked Antonis about his work.

"I decided to leave Athens for a while, and a job opening came up in the wider region of Macedonia. I thought I'd look into it, see if I can take over that post," Antonis explained.

"What kind of post is it?" I asked with interest.

"I don't know if you remember where I work."

I nodded. In fact, I remembered every word of that whispered conversation we had shared that night in the snowed-in cabin. "You're a physicist specializing in climate change."

"Exactly. Some studies are being carried out within the framework of the same European Union climate studies program, focusing on the mountains of Macedonia. Measurements relating to snowfall and rainfall across the Balkans."

So, not only Antonis was single, but he would also be working in the region! Perhaps he could even do part of his research here, in my mountains. That was unexpected. "Where will you live if you take the job?" I asked, with undisguised enthusiasm.

"I will probably be based in Thessaloniki and travel from there. We'll see," he replied, as if he did not want to say more about it.

It was getting late, and we had to head up to the guesthouse in his car so I could help him settle in. The others left to get ready for the panegyri, and we agreed to meet at the village square.

With Voras following the car, we set off. Over time, my dog had discovered all the region's shortcuts and preferred to run along rather than get in the car. He would reach the house before we did, if he didn't get distracted by any interesting smells along the way.

As we drove, I tried to show Antonis where the lake was that my Jeep had fallen into on that fateful day. The landscape had been covered by snow then, so it took him several moments to recognize the location as we approached the spot.

"Ah, yes, now I recognize it now," he said. "We wouldn't be here now if you hadn't fallen into the lake. Of course, I wish none of that had happened even if it meant we'd never met." He had an appealing, child-like quality as he looked flustered, trying to explain what he had meant.

"I believe that everything in life happens at the right time," I said, trying to save him from embarrassment. "A near tragedy led to our meeting. What we often perceive to be an unfortunate event could simply be the path that leads us to something beautiful we would not have experienced otherwise."

He turned to look at me, and momentarily lost control of the car.

"I don't think I could go through another car accident so soon," I teased, as he hastily straightened the wheel.

"I'm sorry," he apologized, and kept his eyes on the road.

"Don't worry about it. If we do have an accident, you're already here to save me."

"We could pretend that you're drowning, if you feel like a reenactment..."

We did not stop laughing as we joked and teased, maybe because deep down, we both desired the exact same thing.

"Pull over here!" I exclaimed, a little further up the road.

He stopped at the edge of the road, and I jumped out. I walked up to a cherry plum tree, pulled down a branch, and picked as many fruits as could fit in my palm. I stepped back into the car and, without even asking him, popped one in his mouth. He looked surprised at first, but chewed as he started driving again.

"Last cherry plums of the year," I said as I bit into one.

"They're delicious," Antonis said, with a sigh. I noticed he kept casting fleeting glances outside the window as if looking for something.

"What's the matter?" I asked.

He pointed at his mouth, and I realized he had no idea what to do with the stone. I burst into laughter again.

"Watch me," I said. I rolled down the window, spat out the stone in my palm, and flung it outside. Antonis hesitated. "Next year, a new tree might be growing there. Don't even think about it."

He followed suit as we drove to the house until all the cherry plums had been eaten.

"So many new plum trees will grow here next year!" he joked as he flung the last stone outside the window.

"We'll name them all Antonis to honor your contribution," I replied, and we burst into a new round of laughter.

We arrived at my home a few minutes later. Voras, who had taken a shortcut, was waiting for us by the gate. "You're late!" his expression said. I showed Antonis where to park the car, and we stepped onto the cobblestones. The stone walls of the house, as well as the guest house beside it, were softly lit up by hidden lights. I had become accustomed to the sounds of the waterfall, but standing next to Antonis was like hearing the gushing waters for the first time. An exclamation of admiration escaped Antonis, who took a deep breath, like the breath I had taken when he'd brought me back to life.

"That's how I imagine heaven to be at night," he said, and his admiring glance drifted from the buildings towards the horizon.

"I think you'll also find it heavenly tomorrow morning."

He picked up his suitcase and followed me, observing the house.

"How beautiful it must be to have your coffee and enjoy the view from up here all year round. Either outside, or indoors by those tall windows."

"Let me give you a tour of the house before I show you to the guesthouse."

"Won't you run late for the festival? You can show me the house tomorrow. The sooner you go, the sooner you'll be back, right?" Antonis added with disarming forthrightness before I had a chance to reply. What could I even say to that?

"Right," was all I could come up with, before walking off towards the guesthouse.

I opened the door and turned on the lights. "I need to bring sheets, towels, and pillows from the house. I didn't know I would be welcoming someone so soon. In all other ways, it's clean and ready, as you can see."

He was standing by the door, open-mouthed, taking in the open plan ground floor and the staircase that led to the bedroom in the small attic. My father's idea to place a modern suspended fireplace made of metal in the sitting area had been excellent. Surrounded by the couches, it made the room feel cozy and heated the space uniformly. My sister Eva had called it the "oyster," to our great amusement. It did look like an open oyster suspended in mid-air.

"Don't bother with the sheets now," Antonis urged. "Go to the panegyri and meet with your friends and family; we can sort all this out later."

I hesitated for a moment, but I could tell it was what he wanted.

"Okay, if you don't mind. Please make yourself at home, play some music, have a drink. If you get hungry, you can come into the main house—there's food in the fridge, and I'll bring more food back, too. I mostly keep cheese, fruit, and vegetables here. It's all local."

"Trust me, I'll be fine. Please don't bring anything back." He sighed, and moved towards the windows.

"Don't worry about it; in fact, I'll probably grab a bite when I get back too because down at the panegyri, nearly every dish is meat-based. I'm not really a fan of meat."

"I understand," he said, and kept examining the space.

I tidied up a little and made sure the kitchen window was closed. A ferret had snuck through that window the other day, and it had taken me ages to get it back outside.

"Really excellent work. My compliments to whoever constructed it," Antonis said, and turned towards the large wooden bookcase, which covered the entire wall of the sitting room from floor to ceiling. "I could stay here reading forever," he added, as he gently stroked the spines of the books.

I could understand how he felt. I had wanted to make this space as snug as possible, a cocoon that would allow everyone to gain the utmost enjoyment from their stay.

"My compliments to the architect, truly!" he exclaimed admiringly.

"My father supervised the works, having been a craftsman himself, but the local stonemasons are truly exceptional."

As soon as we stepped outside, I switched on the remaining lights on the side of the guesthouse.

"By the way, what beautiful rose bushes," he said in a teasing voice.

"Yes, an admirer sent them." I spoke the words like a diva, making him laugh.

He reached out and brushed my hair away from the scar on my forehead. "It hardly shows," he said, tracing it gently.

"It shows just enough, so I never forget," I said.

"Did you go to the hospital to get it stitched up, in the end?"

"No, I didn't need to."

We looked at one another for a moment, with silly, awkward grins on our faces.

"Well, go!" he said, shooing me away.

"Yes, sir!" I answered with a laugh, and ran to fetch my car keys.

If I hadn't been worried about running late, I would have gone on foot like always. Now, however, I did not want to be gone for long. Before leaving the house, I put on my favorite music from my travels.

"Wonderful," Antonis commented, when the first strains resonated from the speakers outside.

"It's a fairly large collection of songs I heard and loved in various places I've traveled to. Mostly Africa and the East."

"I like that kind of music too," he said with a smile.

Antonis escorted me to my car, where we looked at one another for a moment, without saying a word.

"Well, then. See you in a bit."

"Thank you, Ariadne," he said, and held my hand before I could step inside the car.

"What for?" I asked, mainly to hide my embarrassment.

"Everything. Especially the trust you are showing in me."

"I should be the one thanking you for the rest of my life, so don't even mention it."

I sat behind the wheel, cast one last look at Antonis, and then slowly drove down to the village. Through the open car windows, I welcomed the evening chill, which sent shivers of anticipation through my body.

Evora

ANTONIS watched Ariadne's car until it was nearly invisible among the trees. He looked up at the starry sky and took a deep breath. A much-needed sense of tranquility descended all around him. Voras yawned noisily beside him and stretched happily. It was a sight brimming with tenderness, such a large dog acting like a puppy.

They played together for a few moments, and then Antonis stood up and slowly walked towards Ariadne's house. He opened the door and stepped inside, where he realized that the same architectural philosophy as the guest house reigned in here as well. The main house was slightly more spacious: a large ground floor with an open plan kitchen and sitting area, with comfortable couches facing the fireplace on the opposite wall. A wooden staircase led to the level above, which was split into two bedrooms. The bookcase here occupied the space beneath the stairs, smaller than the bookcase in the guesthouse.

He paused for a moment to look at the photo of Ariadne's mother, because the resemblance between them was striking. The woman was sitting in a garden, her apron filled with wild herbs and vegetables. She was looking into the lens with a bright smile. A wave of sadness washed over him when he realized she was probably no longer alive.

Voras, trained not to enter the house without permission, was sitting on his hind legs on the porch outside the front door, patiently waiting. Antonis noticed a pile of clean sheets and towels on a chair, and guessed they were intended for the guest house.

Passing through most of the rooms, he then entered the main bedroom, which was nested inside the roof of the house. Everything exuded coziness, although the decoration was sparse. The texture of the stone on the walls combined with the shadows cast by strategically placed sunken lights made any further decoration unnecessary.

He then returned to the kitchen and opened the fridge, which looked more like a vegetable patch. He picked up a bottle of white wine and saw wine glasses on a shelf. A mischievous grin lit up his face as he began rifling through the cupboards, enthusiastically searching for something, swaying to the unknown strains of music filling the house all the while.

Down at the village square, everyone was having a ball. I had not seen most of my friends since last year's festival and could not let the opportunity to spend time with them pass me by. We picked up right where we'd left off, as if a day instead of an entire year had passed.

Strong bonds of love born of shared childhoods preserved this familiarity over many years. We were all following our own individual paths in life, but Avgerinos remained our base, our source of strength. Despite this, I kept my stay as brief as possible. My thoughts kept returning to Antonis.

Using the following morning's hike as an excuse to turn in early, I discreetly took my leave. A part of me hoped that Antonis had not gone to bed, and I told myself that it was unlikely, as the beds at the guesthouse had not even been made.

I was nearly at the gate to my house when I realized there was something different about the garden lights. I slowly pulled up the driveway and, for the first time, Voras was not there to greet me. Puzzled, I brought the car to a stop.

The front door was wide open as if someone was expecting me, and most of the garden lights had been turned off. I stepped outside the car and, as I walked towards the house, I slowly realized what was going on. The garden was lit by the flickering flames of dozens of candles. In fact, a whole line of candles had been carefully placed on the cobblestones to form a small corridor leading to the front garden.

First, I head Voras's bark, and then I saw the table under the large chestnut tree. Antonis had just stood up, clearly expecting me. He had laid out a white tablecloth and set the dishes and cutlery as if he was hosting a formal dinner. A large bowl of salad was set at the center of the table. Dumbfounded, I just gaped at the scene before me. I had never seen my garden so beautifully decorated before. Voras ran towards me as if he wanted to walk me down the last few steps.

"I'm speechless, Antonis. This is so beautiful."

"I tried to prepare a special dinner with whatever was around. To thank you. If I had known I would be staying over, I would have brought something, too. In any case, I think I managed to rustle up something decent. If you're hungry, that is."

"It looks delicious."

He gallantly held out my chair and waited for me to sit down. Then, he removed a bottle from the wine bucket and filled our glasses. He moved to his chair across the table and raised his glass. "To love, then!"

I smiled, repeated his toast, and then we both took a long sip. I had never experienced anything like this before. It was like everything had been prepared by a very capable professional. The only thing Antonis had not managed to control was the loud music from the panegyri. That was probably the reason he had turned our music off.

Antonis sprang up and returned to the house. Voras gave me a conspiratorial bark. I wagged my finger at him, telling him off sweetly. A few minutes later, Antonis made his way back to the table, cheerfully carrying two large platters. Another surprise. He placed them on the table, like a child proudly displaying the mischief he had been up to. One tray held a variety of sliced vegetables, mixed with local cheeses and Eva's rusks. The other platter was piled high with sliced fruit. Both dishes had been so beautifully laid out they resembled works of art.

"It didn't take long to figure out what kind of food you like, so I made us a quick snack with whatever was available," he said humbly.

"That's the understatement of the year, Antonis! I can tell you not only know your way around food, but decorating, too!" I said, pointing to the lanterns hanging from the chestnut tree branches.

"You give me too much credit! I just like to improvise. I found these beautiful lanterns and candles and let my imagination run wild. How was the panegyri?" he asked, quickly changing the subject.

"Very nice. It's a great opportunity for people who have not seen each other in a long time to meet. Love overflows on days like this, and that's always beautiful."

I tried some of the salad, and it proved to be very tasty. I could instantly tell that it had been dressed in a sauce made with the aromatic herbs I grew in my garden. "I want the recipe," I said as I kept eating.

"I'll gladly pass it on, provided I can remember it. The ingredients are all around you," Antonis said with a sweeping gesture.

I drank another sip of my wine, impressed by the unexpected welcome he had prepared for me.

"My mother used to say that the tastiest dish in the world could be made with a little flour, olive oil, and freshly picked wild greens."

He looked up from his plate, his eyes questioning me.

"Those are the ingredients of my favorite pie, hortopita. Shortcrust pastry filled with wild greens. I could live on just that."

"Your mother..."

He hesitated for a moment, and I instantly finished the thought for him. "She passed away a long time ago. However, I feel like she never left."

"Both my parents are still alive, but I think I can understand how you feel." His voice was filled with tenderness. "You look a lot like her," he added, and I understood he'd seen the photo by the front door.

"I like to think I resemble her as a person, too, not just physically."

"Unfortunately, I never met her. But everything I've seen so far shows she must have been a good mother."

I smiled, flattered. Antonis refilled my glass.

"I think she came into the world to make it a better place. The way she lived, her actions, most of which were never widely known, showed a generosity of spirit I have rarely encountered in others."

"I hope you got the chance to tell her that."

"I was away for many years, studying, but yes, I did tell her. I've come to terms with the idea of death. I know that all that matters is what you do while you are still alive; the imprint you leave behind when you are gone."

I was beginning to relax, and I felt that the man sitting across the table from me was someone I could open up to. I was used to listening rather than talking about everything that preoccupied me, so it was a welcome change to air my thoughts aloud for once.

A small pause in the music echoing from the square gave me the opening to carry on. "My mother knew all the families in need, both in Avgerinos and the surrounding villages. She never gave charity, but encouraged them to sell something so she could buy it up to three times its real value. She wanted to help people without wounding their pride. So she bought things she did not need, often at great expense. She told me once, 'It's better to wrap up charity in a bit of dignity before you offer it.' That's what she did. She wrapped her donations in love and dignity."

"At the end of the day, a wealthy person is not one who owns a lot, but someone who gives a lot."

I nodded in agreement, while I savored some of the wild berries he had added to the salad. "What you just said reminds me of a book you should read at some point. It's called The Art of Loving. I could lend it to you, if you like."

"Yes, please. So, learning how to love is also a matter of training?"

"Of course. Mostly, it's the work you do on yourself daily, so long as you know which direction to follow. My mother opened the way for me. The only meaning our life has is the one we choose to give it. The reality is that we are all alone, and the way to escape loneliness is by helping someone in need. I remember my mother always said that when love is shared, it does not diminish; it multiplies."

"I can understand where your need to share so much love stems from now. It's because it's an art you've mastered," he whispered. In the brief silence, his words carried more weight.

Then he touched my hand. For a split second, I felt the same kind of awkwardness as on that winter's night when we first met, but I quickly overcame it and responded. A few moments later, though, I pulled my hand back and carried on tasting and enjoying the dinner he had prepared.

"By the way, what are those numbers on the tree trunk?" he asked, looking at the small plaque on the chestnut tree.

"It's our altitude. Evora, 1,129 meters above sea level."

"I hadn't realized we're so high up," Antonis said, laughing. "And you are happy here..."

"Are you asking a question, or making a statement?"

"Both!" he replied, and smiled.

"Although happiness is a notion that stresses people, yes, I would say that I am happy."

"You seem made for this place. As if you are at one with all that surrounds you."

I smiled, because that was precisely how I felt. "All these years high up on a mountain, I got to know myself, mostly. You want to know what else I learned?"

"Tell me. I really want to find out," Antonis encouraged and leaned forward.

"As I grow older, I become more aware of how great it feels to do things on your own. I don't mean that I have abandoned my friends or human contact. I'm just surprised by the fact that many people despise or are afraid of being alone. Yet solitude can be salutary when it is a choice."

He sighed deeply as if he agreed with me.

"A person's inability to be alone can be their ruin," I continued. "Very few can stand their own company for a long time. The moment most people find themselves alone, they scurry to turn on the TV or surf the internet. I think that if a government were to ban both, people would go crazy, terrified by the silence. People used to be more in touch with themselves in the past. Nowadays, that is unattainable. In a sense, we are already experiencing our decline, since modern man is incapable of handling solitude."

"The truth of the matter is that we live in a world which views people who enjoy solitude as weird and antisocial," Antonis said, completing what I was trying to say.

"But going to a concert or anywhere else on your own does not make you weird or crazy. On the contrary, it shows that you want to enjoy all that life has to offer. It also shows that even if you have not found anyone to accompany you, you refuse to miss out on enjoying something that you love. I learned to listen to my heart without caring about what anyone else thinks. It's liberating to be able to make the most of every opportunity that comes your way."

"If only you knew how many things I missed out on because no one was willing to join me," he sighed.

"Many people cannot and do not want to step outside their comfort zones and experience new things. Discovering new things that bring you joy is fascinating. And it is so important to understand that loving what you do is the most invigorating thing in the world."

"I read somewhere that a happy person is someone who creates beautiful memories."

"And never forgets what they read!" I teased to lighten the mood. It worked, and Antonis laughed long and hard.

A few moments later, his face became serious again. "Tell me, what else have you learned?"

There was a thirsty look in his eyes, which urged me to share what I felt. Not the clichés, but those thoughts and feelings you rarely reveal to someone else. I took a deep breath and carried on. "I learned, for example, that rain coming in from the east can reach this spot in eight minutes. I can tell where hail has fallen and if there is snow on the peak of Mount Kaimaktsalan. On a perfect summer day last year, I forced everyone to come inside the restaurant because an east wind had risen. I was shouting, 'Get inside right now, the weather is turning! Hurry!'"

"And? Did they listen?"

"My father was staring at me like I'd lost my mind. I told him, 'I don't know if it will happen now, but last time the wind blew in from the east, the sky turned bright orange, and a violent storm broke out soon after.' The same thing happened that day, too. So violent and sudden, the winds whistling like demons. It's only ever happened three times since I came to live here. Imagine, no one had ever noticed the pattern before. But you could see people were afraid. There is a sense of awe when you are confronted by nature, as you must surely know."

"Sounds like you're ready to start a new career as a meteorologist," he joked, and I smiled.

"Well, I would not want to put everyone out of their job," I joked back.

How nice it was to sit together, talking and laughing. I loved people who had a sense of humor, and Antonis was undoubtedly such a person.

"What else have you seen?" he asked, covering the back of my hand with his palm.

My blood began to course faster through my veins, but I found talking to him very pleasant. It felt as if I were addressing the most attentive audience in the world.

"I have seen the sky turn red like fresh blood. There have been days when Evora has stood above the clouds while the village was shrouded in mist. On such days, I learned that everything is a matter of position and perspective. You can say that you live in a fog, or you can get up and climb a little higher. I understood that you can do anything you like, but you can never rush a flower into blossoming. Because spring will always come in its own time. I also learned that no matter how beautiful the colors of autumn, they are always followed by fall and decay. That is also something you cannot stop.

"Some people hate winter, but if you observe carefully, you will notice that there is something in winter that leads to purification. You see a forest naked, stripped bare of leaves, grass, animals, absolutely empty. If we allowed nature to teach us, we would see that there is nothing wrong with letting our 'leaves' drop. We would see ourselves clearly, uncovered, relieved of everything but the essential. Winter gives you the time to examine who you are and where you are headed, so that you can dress in the youngest leaves and most beautiful blossoms in spring. And then, the cycle starts all over again." I paused, and then added, "I hope I'm making sense and not rambling on."

"You are making perfect sense, Ariadne," he answered, stroking my hand tenderly all the while. "But how do you handle loneliness?" he added, as I took a sip of wine.

The crickets accompanied our conversation like an orchestra. At the same time, the music came back on at the square, and the synchronicity was funny.

"I have met many lonely people who were either in a relationship or married," I said, when our laughter died out. "Many of the people who come here seeking my help are experiencing something similar, unfortunately. As far as I am concerned, I don't feel lonely at all. Especially since I moved to Avgerinos permanently. I don't miss the noise of the city. On the contrary, the prospect of living a stifling life in the cement boxes of apartment blocks stresses me out. Most apartment blocks look like communes where many people are called to co-exist under the illusion of some kind of neighborhood. Over years of talking with people seeking help, I have become convinced that there is no worse form of loneliness than that which a person experiences while surrounded by other people."

"How can you detect something like that?" he asked, and leaned back in his chair.

"Antonis, our words and conduct may not reveal our true feelings, but our eyes do not lie. The bitterness born of the numbness a long-dead relationship carries overflows."

I could see that my words had affected him. Maybe because he too belonged in that category. Obviously, he had his own feelings concerning his recent breakup.

"Do they actually speak to you about it, or do you sense it in some way?"

"Initially, it's something I pick up on, a gut feeling, but then they open up. The people who come to me and commune with the beauty of nature... It's like they become reprogrammed. They become students, and I just guide them. At that point, they let down their guard, which they had kept up when they first arrived. The moment I see their loneliness, though, my mind conjures up beautiful moments they might have experienced. I picture them like in a movie: celebrating with their loved ones, exchanging vows of eternal devotion at their weddings, having children, going on holiday. Then, suddenly, I return to the gloomy image of their loneliness. These wonderful manufactured memories are lost in the mist as if I never thought them."

His gaze had become lost in my face, and I thought that I had tired him out or rubbed salt in his wounds. "Are you okay? Am I boring you?"

"No, on the contrary! You have a magical way of speaking, both as a knowledgeable professional and a girl next door whose plain talk can make you understand anything."

I felt my cheeks start to burn.

"Go on, please," he urged me, as my gaze drifted across the horizon.

Under normal circumstances, I would have asked him to join me for a walk to the waterfall. But everything was so pretty, even with the background music from the panegyri and the smell of grilled meat wafting all the way up here.

"The first person I counseled was a woman I met at the restaurant. When she found out what I did for a living, she asked to meet me in private. At the meeting, she sat across from me and showed me the white mark around her finger, the only sign that she had worn a wedding ring for many years. It didn't take her long to confess that she had been lonely in her marriage for many years. At the age of sixty-five, however, she decided to announce, first to her children who were grown-ups by then, and then her husband, that she couldn't take it anymore. For thirty years, she fooled herself that things could change. Until the day arrived when she fell head over heels for another man. Then, she was reborn. 'I enjoy his company,' she told me over and over, and her face would light up just at the thought of this person. She kept pointing to the white mark on her finger, and said something I will remember for the rest of my life: 'Now, when I look at this mark, I remember how lonely I felt for years. Finally, I have discovered what life without loneliness can be. I now know how it feels to not be suffocated by the company of a person who seems silent to you even when they speak...'"

"So this woman found her way in the end, on her own, right? So why did she come to you?" Antonis asked, puzzled.

I smiled at the innocence that shone through his eyes. "People don't just want to talk about everything that has hurt them. They like to talk about what they have achieved, too. They want to show that they can be strong if need be.

That they don't give up. Talking to someone about your achievements can be liberating..."

"Do you think people compromise?"

I took a deep breath and looked around me, to commit to memory the moment we were sharing. It was nearly midnight, and I was sitting under the chestnut tree with the man who had saved my life, talking about relationships and solitude.

"The only reason we avoid solitude, and would even rather be with someone toxic than be alone, is fear. The moment the front door closes and two people are left by themselves, confronted with their silences, nothing can remain a secret. Whether they are together by desire or by habit becomes apparent at that moment."

Antonis had turned his whole body towards me and was observing me. Everything I had refused to acknowledge all evening now loomed before me. The way he was looking at me had me mesmerized. He was undisputedly a handsome man, but something inside me warned me not to indulge in such thoughts. The fact that I often followed my instincts now hindered my attempt to lay some boundaries.

"But doesn't this reasoning mean a relationship is impossible?" he whispered, bringing me back to our conversation.

"Not at all. However, when you're desperate for a partner and end up settling for someone you are incompatible with, you will almost certainly end up spending what is left of your dreams and desires in an empty embrace. Some may say that it is impossible to sustain the intensity of the early days of a relationship for its entire duration. That's true. If falling in love does not grow into respect, caring, and true love over time, then it will end. In that case, the most insignificant issue can become the death blow of whatever might have existed in the early days. Of course, there are many instances where people spend their whole lives in mediocrity and the rules imposed by marriage, or society itself."

I had hit my stride, and for as long as I saw him hanging onto my every word, I would not stop. "On the other hand, many couples break up to banish their loneliness and silence their demons. They look for someone to make their heart feel complete, without even knowing what it is they're looking for. The hope of a better life is undermined by the impossibility that they will actually meet a knight in shining armor, or a princess leaning over the castle ramparts as she awaits her savior. So, instead of going after their dreams, they stay as they are in similar unhappiness caused by thoughtless choices."

I pulled myself to a stop. In my enthusiasm, I had forgotten that Antonis was one of the people I had been describing. He looked troubled, and I felt terrible.

"What can someone do to be happy in a relationship? Not just at the beginning, but later, when years have gone by?" Antonis asked, with a catch in his voice.

"A relationship needs to be constantly attended to if it is to stay alive. Love and caring go together. A person loves what they have striven for. What they have worked to achieve. Both parties in the relationship must not rest on their laurels, taking their other half for granted. Every single day they must fight for the person whose eyes once held the world for them. They need to respect and admire their partner. Otherwise, the beautiful memories will slowly fade away, leaving misery and bitterness in their place. And, of course, we must never lose our connection with nature and everything that we can learn from it."

He sighed, clearly troubled. I pulled closer and stretched my hand on the table, towards him. Slowly, he brought his hands nearer, and our fingers met again.

"It may be arduous, Antonis, but the beauty of everyday life becomes more valuable when we share it with someone… Especially small, insignificant moments, such as this one we are now sharing," I whispered, feeling a little tipsy. "A relationship should be the fulfillment of your heart, your soul, your mind, your very existence. True love does exist, Antonis. Remember that, every time, every day, when you wake up and before you go to bed…"

"But I've never had a partner like that," he said, and in those few words I felt his overwhelming need to change his life. "How did you do it?"

"Do what?" I knew what he was asking, but I preferred not to show it.

"Figure me out so quickly?"

"It's my job," I answered, with a mischievous wink.

Voras distracted us for a moment as he stretched noisily. He instantly lay down again, appearing to enjoy the moment, too.

"Enough about me," I said. "Now, you tell me about yourself. You've made some significant changes in your life recently. That takes courage, you know."

"Making the actual decision to separate and change jobs was the work of a moment when it came down to it. I felt that the respect needed to keep any relationship alive was gone."

"You can tell me how it happened, if you like…"

"A few months ago, I was stuck in traffic, as usual. To pass the time, I was watching the drivers of the other cars. Their faces glum, irritated, the stress and lack of time weighing them down even more than the packed highway. Suddenly, an ambulance tried to push its way through the endless line of cars, its siren blazing. I hope it's nothing serious, I thought. I pulled to the side to let it pass, as the emergency lane was occupied by those drivers who simply didn't care. Just then, it happened: time stood still for me. A man, just like me, had begun his day in an ordinary manner. But on that day, life had had other plans in store for him. At a time like this, everyone thinks it could have been them in the ambulance. But it is a fleeting kind of thought. Usually, it comes and goes like a spell to chase away our fear of what fate may have in store for us. Life is a game of Russian roulette. Every day a number is picked, regardless of our luck the previous day or the future bets we were counting on. Life steps on the path that we thought would lead to our future and instantly transforms it into the past, a past that has come to a standstill and which you can neither change nor reverse nor relive."

He paused, and took a sip of wine. His words were beautiful. I followed suit and raised my glass, too. In the dim light, his eyes looked moist, as if he had been moved by his own confession. "At that moment, then, it became crystal clear to me that life is a gift. Every breath is a gift, every morning we wake up is a gift, every moment we spend with our loved ones... I had told myself this many times before, and forgotten it just as many. Just like everyone else, I, too, had become oblivious to my hopes and wishes, trapped in cycles and toeing lines imposed by others. Plans that forever remained dreams, as they did not fit in with the obligations that shaped my everyday life and relationships. Most of us feel trapped in a vicious circle of insignificant situations that we deem all-important. So, I decided to change, because I understood that real life is found in the moments that slip away and never come back. All that remains of those moments is what fills the void inside us."

"Nobody said changing your life was easy..." I claimed, but he was now unstoppable.

"No, I'm not saying it's easy to ignore difficulties and everything that spoils your mood. What I am saying is that when we realize that every minute we are given in this life is a gift, we owe it to ourselves and to those we love to live it to the fullest, as intensely as possible."

He stopped for a moment, as if reminiscing, and I held my breath like a child waiting to hear how the fairytale ends.

Finally, Antonis sighed and carried on. "I don't know how long I sat there in the car—maybe a few minutes, maybe an hour—but the traffic had come to a standstill and I was already running late. However, I didn't care, because this would be one of the days when getting to wake up in the morning mattered. One of those days when I had opened my eyes and greeted what was to come without caring about trivialities. It was a life-changing moment for me..."

I loved listening to him. He had done what everyone who felt oppressed, who lived a life foreign to them, ought to do. Moreover, many of the things he had said were the same things I discussed with my students.

"You would make an excellent guide," I told him as he drained his glass.

"I'd need to find my own way first," he replied, his voice filled with meaning.

"I think you are on the right path."

The bottle was empty, but neither of us made a move to retrieve another. In a few hours, after all, we would have to wake up for our hike.

As we fell silent for a moment, Voras moaned and stretched in his sleep. I pet his big head tenderly. To break the silence, I told Antonis that Voras had been partly responsible for my car accident in the winter. Voras was now part of the family, who adored him, and part of Evora.

"Why Evora?" Antonis asked, after a small pause.

"I had planned to call just the guest house Evora, at the start, but as you can see now, everything around you is part of Evora. I imagine you don't know what the word means, right?"

"I must confess I have never heard the word before. I've been wondering what it means for some time."

I stood up, and spoke solemnly. "Evora is the wind, the breeze, the cool weather, a peaceful place, a shady spot such as this one, under a chestnut tree at midday. Evora means 'the perfect hour' the right moment in the day..."

"So, being in the right place at the right time, just as we now are..." he said with a mischievous grin.

I ignored his teasing and carried on. "There's a local saying: Let evora come into your heart. That is how you find peace, tranquility. You admire the majesty and power of nature as well as man's need to be close to it, to be restored, and feel fulfilled by it. A small word, evora, yet it encompasses our whole world. That is how we were raised..."

He was looking at me with admiration.

Evora

"There is also a town in Portugal called Evora, by the way. I have never been, but I've seen photos, and it looks gorgeous. I plan to visit that Evora someday."

"Will you take me with you?" His question surprised me, but I did not get a chance to reply. "You have a wonderful voice, Ariadne. I get transported just listening to you..."

"I like that you told me." For the first time, I detected fatigue in his eyes. "If you struggle to wake up tomorrow at dawn, you can stay here and do as you please until I come back."

"I would love to come, if it's no bother," he said. I gave him a look that said I hoped he would join us.

"Then it might be best if we call it a night," I said. "It's past midnight, and we need to be ready at six. It's best to start climbing before the sun reaches its peak."

He gave me a military salute. "Yes, ma'am! I will be on time, ma'am!"

Our loud laughter woke Voras, who jumped up, barking. He ran to the fence and yapped at the forest.

"I think we gave him a start," I said, and called him to come back. Voras ignored me and kept up his fight with the darkness. "Let's clear the table. If we leave it this way, we'll be raided by weasels during the night." I started collecting the dishes.

Antonis gently gripped my wrist. "Yes, but you must allow me to do it. This evening and everything that goes with it is my responsibility..."

I did not manage to disguise my surprise. Not many men who would have done what Antonis had done for me tonight. I did not want to spoil it for him, so I handed over the dishes I was holding.

"Thank you. I'll go make the bed in the guesthouse and..."

"It's all been set up. You don't need to do anything," Antonis called out, as he stepped inside the house.

I hesitated. What did he mean? "But, I need to make your bed..." I said, as he returned to finish clearing the table.

He came closer until our bodies were nearly touching. "Don't you think a man is capable of making a bed and hanging a couple of towels in a bathroom?" he whispered in my ear.

The sudden proximity of his body was disorientating. I felt his breath brush my lips, and was overwhelmed by the desire to kiss him. Something inside me, though, held me back.

Suddenly, Voras fell quiet, and I turned towards him to hide my embarrassment. As if he had sensed the tension between us, Voras was looking at us, waiting to see what would happen next.

"Well, I think it's time for bed, or we won't be able to wake up tomorrow..." I said, taking the only remaining glass and moving inside the house. I could feel Antonis's smile following me all the way to the kitchen.

We placed everything in the sink, and I expressly forbid him to do the washing up. Then I offered to walk him to the guesthouse.

The music from the square had temporarily stopped, and only the sounds of nature filled the air.

"Thank you, Antonis, for tonight... Everything was wonderful..."

"Yes, it was lovely..." he agreed, and touched my hand as we walked across the grass.

"I hope you don't mind the music from the square. It usually goes on until the small hours," I said, and stopped at the entrance to the guesthouse.

"I think it will be fine. If it gets too noisy, I might ring your doorbell. What kind of neighbors would we be otherwise?" he said, the mischievous grin once again lighting up his features.

"Only ring if you run out of sugar..." I teased him back.

He hovered by the front door of the guesthouse, not going inside. He seemed to be waiting for something.

"Do you want me to wake you up when I get up tomorrow morning?" I asked.

"Yes, although I'll also set my alarm..." he said, and took my hand in his. "Normally it is boys who escort girls home at night..."

"Normally, yes, but a lot of what's been happening falls outside the norm, so don't worry about it."

Although I had spent most of the evening in a state of bliss, and desperately wanted to go to bed with him, I had to resist. If anything mattered at this point, it was the anticipation. Before he could say anything else, I moved closer and kissed his cheek, very close to his lips. "Good night..." I said, pulling my hand away, and turned back towards the house.

I moved a few meters away and glanced over my shoulder. Antonis was still looking at me with a smile. Voras, like a spy, drifted between us, feigning indifference but, in reality, seeking our attention. I waved goodbye, before stepping inside the house and closing the door behind me. I leaned against it with a sigh. I could barely resist succumbing to his charm. A charm so rare, so discreet...

I washed all the dishes and checked that all the candles had been put out. Then I lay down in my attic bedroom, after taking a quick look outside the window to check on the guesthouse. No lights were on, a sign that Antonis, too, had gone to bed. Feeling slightly dizzy, I closed my eyes and recalled his beautiful smile...

Evora

IT WOULD SOON BE DAYLIGHT, and absolute stillness reigned outside. The panegyri had ended a short while ago. Silence had descended on the village at last.

Voras, who liked to sleep outside, was lying down on his small mattress beside Ariadne's front door. He was almost holding his breath as he tried to determine what was the sound that had woken him.

With a low, menacing growl, he approached the fence and began patrolling Evora, the fur on his back and around his neck bristling. He stopped and gazed far into the predawn, towards the opposite mountain. Faintly, like an echo from afar, the howl of a wild animal split the silence.

Hearing the cry, the calm and kindly dog turned into a ferocious animal and snarled menacingly, revealing his long white fangs. His eyes shone in the dark as if he were ready to attack.

A few minutes later, silence returned, and Voras started to calm down. He did not retreat, however. Like a vigilant sentry, he held his post a few minutes longer, and only then did he return to his mattress by the front door. Without lying back down, he sat on his hind legs, alert to the slightest sound coming from the forest.

I opened my eyes, and the soft light told me it would soon be daytime. I rarely drew the curtains in the attic because I liked being woken by the early rays of the sun. I turned my alarm off before it had a chance to ring, and rolled over for a little snooze.

The blackbirds outside were already composing their melodic songs. I knew I had to get some things ready for the hike, but I was enjoying the sweet coziness of the early morning hour. I hugged the other pillow and wondered what it would be like to wake in his arms. I thought back to the beautiful moments we had shared the previous evening, and realized I had not felt this way in a long time.

Enough with the snuggling in bed; I had to get ready. I got up slowly, and after stretching languidly, I picked up the glass on my bedside table and took a few sips of water. Then I walked downstairs to begin preparations.

I opened the front door to feed Voras, but my faithful companion ignored me. Ears pricked, he kept his eyes trained on the forest. I had never seen him show no interest in his food before. With my encouragement, he half-heartedly approached and started to eat, stealing glances in the same direction all the while.

Just then, the light in the guesthouse came on, a sign that Antonis was awake. Avgerinos's predawn was the only thing I could make out in the sky. Everything promised clear blue skies ahead, a beautiful day even though we desperately needed rain. It had not rained in months. Soon, the autumn rains would come, however, and the parched earth's thirst would be assuaged.

"Good morning, neighbor!" I heard him calling from the front door.

"Good morning! How did you sleep, kindly neighbor?"

"Like a baby," he said as he stretched.

"I'm making tea and a bite to eat. We're due to meet the others in an hour by the spring above the cabin. It's a thirty-minute walk. Would you like some coffee, sir?"

"Tea is just fine. I'll be over in a few minutes," he replied with a laugh.

We held each other's gaze for a moment, and I stepped back inside the house first. I quickly loaded some food into a backpack and remembered to add a rope and a knife to our supplies. We would find water on the way, so a small flask would suffice.

"Good morning again, fair lady of the manor," Antonis said with a playful smile as he stepped into the kitchen.

I dashed towards him to greet him with a kiss on the cheek. As if he had been waiting for this opportunity, he hugged me and wrapped his arms around my waist. I instantly responded and hugged him back, feeling our bodies join harmoniously, fitting perfectly like two adjoining puzzle pieces.

We were locked in the embrace for a few seconds, until Antonis took a step back. "We don't have much time."

I motioned at him to sit at the kitchen table, where warm slices of bread smothered in the fruit of the forest jam made by Eva stood on a large platter. His expression and appreciative sounds as he wolfed down his breakfast showed me how much he was enjoying it. "Both the bread and the jam are great," he mumbled, and wiped his lips with his thumb.

It was a gesture that made me go weak at the knees when done unconsciously, without pretension.

"I'll pass on the compliments to Eva..."

"Tell me about this hike. I hope I'm suitably dressed. I have these sports shoes and took an extra t-shirt in case it gets really sweaty."

"You're fine. Don't worry, it's not a difficult hike. It's uphill, but not rough terrain. It's more of a path, which will take us to Elatia. We're taking the easy route, it's just longer. The only difficult stretch is halfway up the slope, when we'll need to cross a small gorge. Everything else just requires enough stamina for a long walk...."

"I work out regularly, so I think I can manage that."

"If you get into difficulties, I'll give you a piggyback ride like you gave me in the winter."

Antonis almost choked with laughter. He drank some more of his tea, still smiling.

"I'm ready," he eventually announced. "We can set off whenever you like. What do I need to bring with me?"

"I packed a backpack with the basics. So, only what you think you might need."

"I'll bring my phone, because I'm sure there will be many amazing landscapes to photograph. I hope you don't mind..."

"Not at all. Please do, and be sure to send the photos to me. I'll leave my phone here; I need to download the photos already on it to clear some memory."

I rarely took my phone with me on my hikes, and only when I wanted to photograph something. I had come to the conclusion that excessive use of electronics can disrupt your equilibrium. It was tragic to see people so dependent on their phones. I understood that for many people, it was part of their life, even their work, but the excessive use was harmful. For many, reality began and ended with social media, and all their activity was exclusively contained there.

"I have an app that automatically sorts all my photos and videos," Antonis said. "It makes it easier to keep what I want, and delete what I don't. I'll show you how to use it, so you don't end up with memory space issues."

"Yes, you must show me..." I said. "Although your phone looks much more high tech than mine. I bought the simplest model possible, after my old phone sunk in that lake last winter."

"Well, I admit I love high tech. This phone switches on when it recognizes my face; my retinas, actually," he said, turning the bright screen of his phone towards me.

Just then, I wanted to tell him that I, too, switch on and glow when I see his face, but I held back. Besides, it was getting late, and we had to hurry.

Before I could get up and clear the table, Antonis had already placed all the dishes in the sink. We then stepped outside, where Voras was waiting for us, wagging his tail.

"Are we taking him with us?" Antonis asked, and I shook my head. I knew he wanted to tag along, but today it would be best if he did not. "We'll be going deep into the forest, and I don't trust him not to start chasing after wild animals. Then we'll spend the whole day looking for him."

Antonis bit his lip as he stared at Voras, who was giving him his best puppy dog eyes. "I feel bad leaving him behind..."

I laughed. "He'll just go to the restaurant. And if he doesn't go on his own, I'm sure my father will start whistling for him. They love having him there, and of course Voras loves being there—attention and food, what more could a dog want?"

As we left the garden, Voras made to follow us, but I spoke to him sternly and motioned that he should stay. He obeyed, sullenly returning to his bed. It was one of those moments where if Voras could speak, he would tell me he did not like me very much.

"I see you can boss around the males in your life quite happily," Antonis teased me. I pretended to kick him, but he saw the move coming and jumped aside with a laugh. "I'll sue you for assault!" he cried out, and hugged me with one arm as we walked up the path.

Dawn was approaching. The colors of the sky became all the more intense as the sun prepared to rise behind the mountaintop. Antonis, carrying the backpack, followed me along the small street that led to the trail, which we would follow all the way to the cabin and then the spring. The morning breeze cooled our steps.

"It was so different in the winter," he said, as he bent down to avoid some low-hanging branches. "I barely recognize it now."

"The seasonal plant growth here reshapes the whole region. It's an astonishing transformation."

"I haven't hiked in a long time."

"You'll make up for it today," I promised.

"I won't be able to walk by the end of this hike, will I?" Antonis said ruefully. "You're trying to make my feet fall off."

"You caught me," I said, and we both laughed.

As we continued along the road, Antonis said, "Ariadne, when was the last time it rained?"

"I would say over two months ago. Not a single drop since. Winter, we had more than the usual amount of snow and rain, as you remember, but we haven't seen a drop of water in a long while."

"It shows." He gestured at the canopy of trees above us. "I can see a lot of leaves are starting to turn yellow..."

"In these parts, we call autumn the 'second spring'. In the early days of September, the leaves start to change color, but when the first rain comes, they turn green again before the temperature finally drops. Then, we enter winter proper, and the leaves fall with the first strong gusts of wind..."

"That's impressive. I've never heard that before," Antonis said, and looked towards the cabin that was becoming visible in the distance.

"What is impressive is watching the colors change from one day to the next. Unfortunately, the drought this year has somewhat spoiled the usual process..."

"If you only knew how much things will change in the coming years..."

I felt a sense of dread. Antonis had spoken as a scientist, and his words were based on research, not conjecture. I stopped walking and waited for him to catch up. "I have been hearing and reading a lot about climate change, and the truth is that I'm not really clear on what is happening," I said as reached me.

Antonis took a deep breath. "The last five years have been the warmest in human record. In itself, that is a massive change in the way nature behaves." He nodded at me to keep walking, and added, "I imagine your question really is to what extent has human intervention contributed to this situation."

"Well, evidently, human activity affects the environment, but yes. What I would like to know is whether these changes were bound to happen at some point anyway, or whether we accelerated them or, even worse, caused them."

"At a world conference in Brazil, scientists presented a model which demonstrates the speed at which everything changes. Ten thousand years ago, the ice age ended, an event which changed the way people lived as they migrated to more temperate regions."

"Could that happen again?"

"Just the fact that it has already happened once means it can absolutely happen again. Except this time humanity is the cause of the change, and we are heating up our planet instead of cooling it down." At this point, he stopped walking and looked up at the wooden cabin at the end of the road. "This is where it all started... Remember?"

"Every single second of it, Antonis."

Shivers ran down my spine as I sensed a presence behind us. I turned around abruptly and spotted Voras, ears downturned. As soon as he saw my frown, he made to turn back.

"Aw, poor doggy. Let him join us and have a fun outing," Antonis urged.

It wasn't the wisest idea, but he seemed so keen on it that I threw caution to the wind. Calling Voras over, I cupped his head with my hands. "You won't go running off into the woods, eh? You'll stay with us."

As soon as he understood that he was allowed to tag along, Voras started wagging his tail so joyfully that he raised a cloud of dust. His reaction made us laugh. Then I looked at the slope and moved in that direction, urging Antonis to follow me.

"You're about to taste the most amazing fruit..." I said when I reached a Cornelian cherry tree, the weight of the bright red fruit dragging its strong boughs towards the ground. It was easy to reach, and after I picked some cherries, I offered them to him.

"I haven't had cherries in years," Antonis admitted. "Unless you count the candied ones they put in cocktails."

I smiled. "My father and I planted this tree twenty years ago. It's a little out of the way, so few people come across it. We come here every year and pick the fruit."

His face twisted when he started chewing.

"Let them fill your mouth," I instructed with a laugh, because I knew some found the taste too sour. "They don't taste like traditional cherries you'd buy at a store, but they're very nutritious, and they really do grow on you."

We ate a few more, and Antonis's pinched expression gradually relaxed. "Hmm... You're right, you do get used to the flavor after a while. I like them. Of course, I feel like I've just been electrocuted, but they are delicious. See, I'm throwing the seeds on the ground here so that more Cornelian cherry trees can grow," he said, grimacing at the sourness.

I laughed, because I could understand the sensation. "They're still a little unripe. In ten days they will be sweeter. When we get back, I'll give you a glass of the liqueur Eva makes from them. I meant to last night, but I must have forgotten ... And I'll ask my father to give you a shepherd's staff made from Cornelian cherry tree wood; it's one of the most robust woods around here..."

"A staff?" Antonis said skeptically. "I wouldn't know what to do with one."

I looked him up and down with pretend seriousness. "You know, with a staff and a thick mustache, you would make the perfect shepherd."

He threw a berry at me as he burst out laughing, and I ducked just in time. "If you braided your hair and pinned it around your head, you would look like a milkmaid," he retorted.

I gripped my hair in two bunches and twisted them around my head, making him laugh again. Then I remembered we were supposed to be meeting my friends soon, so I gently pushed Antonis to keep walking toward the cabin.

We soon reached the little cabin. The cars parked outside indicated that it was occupied, so we walked around it and entered the narrow path behind it that led into the woods. It wasn't wide enough for us to walk side by side, so I put Antonis ahead of me and Voras behind me as we made our way to the spring.

"It's so pretty here!" Antonis exclaimed, as we passed a small waterfall. He took a deep breath, a blissful expression on his face.

I thought about telling him that the water had been more plentiful in previous years, and what he was seeing now was barely a trickle, but instead I left him to enjoy the beauty around him with all his senses. Voras descended the slope and drank thirstily from the creek.

I whistled to Antonis, who was startled to be summoned in this manner. "I'm going to have a drink at the creek... Are you coming?"

He laughed as he followed me down the slope to the water. "Just when I was getting thirsty…" he said, offering me his hand to help me down.

In the mood to wind him up, I ignored the gesture and, with a leap, I landed next to the running water.

"At one with the wild…" he commented, as he descended much more carefully than I had.

He stepped beside me, and we walked a little further down the creek, where the water flowed more gently.

"Come," I said, and indicated the ground beside me.

"Are we going to have a competition about who can drink the most?" Antonis asked in a funny voice.

"I'll see you and raise you…" I replied, and laughed loudly as I bent down and sank half my face in the bubbling creek.

I raised my head and wiped the drops dripping from my lips as he looked at me with large eyes.

"Aren't you going to drink?" I prompted.

"I want you to drink again…" Antonis replied softly.

The cool water was so refreshing that I did not hesitate. I repeated the motion, but when I lifted my head, Antonis held my wrist before I could wipe the drops away. He inched closer, and I instantly understood he wanted to kiss me. This time I did not intend to resist; I had desired his kiss from the moment I met him.

I closed my eyes and eagerly anticipated the feel of his lips against mine. I felt his mouth brush against my chin and taste he fresh droplets. My whole body shivered as he drank the water on my face like a bird collecting the dewdrops on leaves with its beak. As his lips made their way down my neck, I experienced a full-body shiver, from head to toe. We looked into each other's eyes, and suddenly our woodland hike was the last thing on my mind.

"What do you say, shall we go on?" he whispered softly, and I knew he wasn't talking about the hike. My heart pounded in my chest. The birdsong in the woods resounded in my ears, louder than ever. I felt as if all my senses had been sharpened.

He had been tormenting me with fleeting touches and burning looks ever since he'd arrived. And although I desperately wanted to grab him and kiss him, the temptation to torment him for once was too strong to pass up.

Purpose misunderstanding his meaning, I pulled away from him with a mischievous twinkle in my eyes. "You're right," I said. "We should go on. They'll be waiting for us."

Antonis watched me with hungry eyes as I stood. "We wouldn't want to disappoint them."

"No, we wouldn't," I agreed cheekily. "Are you going to drink before we go?"

"Turns out, I don't mind staying thirsty for a while," he replied.

Evora

The end of the path led us to a wide opening like a plateau, which we called a 'springboard' because, from this point onwards, the way to the top was quite a steep climb.

Antonis stopped and laughed when he read the wooden sign erected by the members of the hiking club.

In your excursion through the woods, please behave like animals. Animals never leave their rubbish behind.

"Very clever," I heard him say as he followed me.

"You can't imagine the kind of things people throw away in the forest," I said, and pointed to a plastic water bottle peeking out among the dry grass.

"Unfortunately, I can," he said, and moved to pick it up.

"We'll pick up any trash we see on the way back," I told him. "I brought a garbage bag just for that purpose."

I could never understand the mindset of the people who littered with no qualms, not just in the forest but anywhere else. It was like they believed the rubbish would just magically disappear. I told people off whenever I saw them littering.

Among a row of bushes and beneath a large rock, the water from the spring emerged. From a distance, I saw the two friends who were waiting for us. Another couple had been due to join us, too, but they had partied late into the night and overslept. Their text message to me this morning had been garbled but coherent—I was amazed they had been able to send a message at all, given the amount of alcohol they had consumed.

I introduced Yiannis and his wife Myrto to Antonis, who was charming as ever as he shook their hands and commented on how beautiful the hike had been so far. We decided to take a ten-minute break to catch our breath, as they too had only just arrived. When Antonis bent down to have a drink, he gave me a look full of meaning, as if he wanted a repeat of what had gone on before. I, taking care not to be seen by the others, shook my finger 'no'.

What I liked most about being around Antonis was the carefreeness and child-like wonder that seemed to surge between us. We were both nearing forty, but that did not mean anything. I don't ever remember losing my zest for life. Over the years, I had become more composed when I worked, but in my personal life, I gave free rein to the little girl inside me, allowing her to play and laugh to her heart's content. Being with Antonis allowed me to feel young, free as the leaves dancing on the breeze.

Once the sun's rays had warmed our faces, we stood up and set out on the hike to the mountain peak. It would take us nearly two hours to reach the top. We would be making another stop at Chameno, the 'Lost Spring,' which was twenty minutes away from the peak.

"Why do you call it the Lost Spring?" Antonis asked as we climbed.

Yiannis, who had explored the whole region and knew all the details, explained. "The Lost Spring is one of the oldest springs around here. There used to be a small cave nearby, just a few meters deep, where the snow would last till late in the summer. The locals would come to fetch ice whenever someone fell ill and they had to lower his fever. During the Nazi occupation in the Second World War, the morphology of the ground changed as a landslide blocked the cave's mouth forever.

"Nevertheless, the water found a way out through the stones all by itself. It's called the Lost Spring because it's tough to reach it unless you know the area well. Those who failed to find it said it had disappeared, become lost forever, hence the name. When we get there today, all tired and sweaty, be careful not to drink too suddenly. The water is so icy it might upset your stomach."

"But we won't worry about that until we get there," Myrto said, giving her husband a gentle push. "On we go, dear. You can tell them as many stories as you want while we climb."

We stepped into the forest, under the thick firs, with Voras at our heels.

"There's a spot further up the trail where the fir trees are so tall and dense it's always twilight," Yiannis said. "I remember a story about this forest, I think it was my father who told me..."

As he launched into his tale, Antonis approached me. "He'll be telling us gnomes stories soon enough," he whispered.

"Nah, you're the only gnome around," I teased him.

We burst into such loud laughter that the other two stopped and gave us a puzzled look. I waved my hand to indicate it was nothing, but as we kept walking, I whispered to Antonis, "I do wish all gnomes were like you, though..."

"Ah, that's because you're starting to rub off on me," he replied, and chivalrously stepped aside to let me walk ahead because the path was becoming narrower.

The deeper we moved into the woods, the darker it got, the branches and lush tree canopy blocking the sun. The silence that reigned was seductive and scary all at once. When I was a young girl, my mother would tell me stories about the fairies and the gnomes who would snatch you and make you their eternal slave if you lost your way. Although I was no longer a child, a shard of fear had remained inside me, and as we walked on, I looked around with a mixed feeling of awe, pleasure, and anxiety.

We were in what was probably the darkest part of the forest, and I struggled to make out the details of the shapes around us. My friends ahead stopped, and we followed suit. Only the sound of our breathing could be heard. The temperature had dropped by around ten degrees. The humidity helped mushrooms sprout where the tree trunks met the ground. Some mushrooms were supposedly a delicious treat, while others were poisonous. I had never managed to tell them apart, so I left mushroom foraging to my parents. However, I was always enchanted by how danger lurked so near beauty. I loved feeling like an animal whose instincts are forever on the alert.

Antonis briefly veered off the path. He was trying to reach a purple flower that had grown atop a small mound of soil.

I walked up to him and gently pulled his hand back. "Don't cut it," I said softly.

"I wanted to give it to you," he said, looking deep into my eyes.

"I know. Thank you. However, it's beautiful just as it is. Imagine the strength it took for this flower to grow in this spot, where the sun's rays rarely reach the ground. If you cut it, it will wilt in a few minutes."

He lowered his eyes, and I felt a pang of guilt for scolding him. Antonis was only going to offer me a flower, and I had made such a fuss. I hoped he was not angry, but the smile that formed on his lips chased my remorse away. "You are absolutely right," he agreed, and urged us to keep climbing.

Seeing that Yiannis and Myrto were walking with their backs turned to us, I moved closer and kissed Antonis on the cheek. "Thank you... You don't need to give me another gift, ever," I whispered, reminding him that his gift had been saving my life. It was hard for me to imagine a more precious gift than that.

We fell silent for quite a while because the climb had become more arduous, and no one felt much like talking. Soon, we began to see the sun's rays lighting patches of ground and tree trunks in small bright bundles. A haze of evaporating moisture made the scene look otherworldly. Antonis walked ahead, eagerly photographing all the beautiful images that sprung before us.

"I want a photo with you," he said, and I immediately went up to him. He stretched out his arm in front of us, trying to capture the magic of the different colors behind us. As soon as he took the photo, he put his phone back in his pocket, and we carried on. "Our first photo together," he said.

I patted Voras, who had come near us, and then followed Antonis with a smile. Soon, we were out of the dark woods, and birdsong livened up the air around us. It was like another dawn on the same day.

As we neared the gorge, we began to struggle a little. The chasm was not too deep, but the path was very narrow. Antonis kept looking around and snapping pictures, clearly enjoying our hike. Just the fact that he had come to see me as soon as he was single meant a lot. What Antonis's behavior told me was that he did not pass through Avgerinos just to say hello to the woman he had saved from certain death. Something had been there, between us, from the moment we'd met. Something that was starting to grow into something beautiful. Now, we were both single, and no moral dilemmas could come between us...

"Are you coming?" he called, interrupting my daydreaming.

"Yes. I'll just put Voras between us so we can cross the gorge."

As soon as he heard his name, my beloved dog gave a happy yelp and came to step in front of me. Yiannis and Myrto were already walking ahead, and we followed them.

"Everything here seems unsullied by human presence," Antonis said, looking at the unhewn rocks.

"As I told you, it's a protected nature reserve. You're not even allowed to snap a twig in the forest."

"Yes, I gathered that," he replied, and laughed because he understood I was referring to the flower incident earlier.

Luckily, the gorge's slopes were lined with trees, and you could steady yourself against the trunks. However, we still had to be extremely careful. One false step could send you hurtling towards the rocks, which lurked further down the slope, sharp as knives. Antonis managed very well, and it did not take us long to make the crossing.

The trees began to grow more sparse, and only a few firs dotted the land around us now. The warmth of the sun followed the coolness of the forest. It was like someone had suddenly turned the heating on, and we all sighed contentedly. What was odd here was that the grass and the vegetation in general were dry, even where the ground was not rocky.

We climbed for a few more minutes until Yiannis, who had found shelter from the sun under a giant fir, called out, "Shall we take a break here, and then head to the Lost Spring?"

Rest sounded like a wonderful idea, and soon we were all taking a break in the shade beside him. The last to arrive, panting, was Voras. He collapsed onto the dry grass, his tongue hanging out.

"I guess he's regretting coming along," Antonis said, laughing. But I was confident that my faithful friend was enjoying his walk with us more than anything in the world.

Myrto then handed each of us a piece of fruitcake she had made. "Last bit of shade," she said, and took a large bite. "We'll cool down at the Lost Spring, and then reach the peak at Elatia nearby."

"Great," Antonis said, then groaned with pleasure when he bit into the cake.

"It's a shame we didn't see any wildlife," Yiannis sighed, his eyes scanning the horizon.

"Making so much noise and having Voras with us, it's not likely," I replied.

We sat there for a few minutes, chatting. When they heard that Antonis was thinking of moving to the region for work, my friends were envious. "We live in Athens, and come to Avgerinos whenever we get the chance. It helps us recharge our batteries," Yiannis explained. "You're lucky to get the chance to work here."

"I'll be making my decision soon," Antonis replied, stealing a glance in my direction.

Sticking to our plan, we continued our hike under the now searing sun. We were following Myrto, who was the only one who knew the exact location of the spring. The morphology of the ground varied significantly here, and we had to be particularly careful as we wove our way through the large, sharp rocks. The only one who seriously struggled was Voras, who did not like walking on rocky terrain.

Antonis was sweating a lot and, at some point, stopped to change his t-shirt. I caught myself stealing a look as he wiped down his sweaty body. Controlling my instincts was difficult.

After a relatively long climb, Myrto finally announced that she had found the Lost Spring. We were all very thirsty, and just the thought of the cold water ahead put a spring in my step. I picked up speed, sweeping Antonis along.

When we arrived, I was puzzled to find that neither Myrto nor Yiannis had bent down to have a drink. "What's the matter?" I asked, concerned. Myrto pointed to a small opening between two large rocks that had turned green with humidity.

"That's strange," Myrto muttered, as she examined the rocks and the surrounding area carefully. "The spring is literally lost," she concluded bitterly.

"It can't be," Yiannis said, perplexed, his arms spread wide. "This time last year the water was gushing like a torrent. What happened? This has never happened before."

"If I may interrupt," Antonis said. "Could it be the same reason that the spring which feeds the reservoir has run dry? A landslide or an earthquake?"

"I don't know what's happened. The elders say that the spring has been here since the end of the War and never runs dry, whatever the season," Yiannis replied.

I did not know what to say, and just listened to them carefully. The truth is that we had not brought enough water with us, thinking we would be refilling our flasks here. With Yiannis's encouragement, we fanned out, seeking some other source of water to quench our thirst, but our efforts proved futile. Voras greedily licked the moisture left on the stone from which enough water to satisfy an entire herd of sheep had once run.

"It looks like it stopped running some time ago," Antonis said. "It could spring forth again soon. This faint trickle is a sign that it has not completely dried up."

Our disappointment was evident, as was our concern. The only sure thing was that the aquifer had changed abruptly in our region. We stayed there for a while, gathering all kinds of trash that lay scattered around, intending to take it with us on the way back. Through gritted teeth, Yiannis cursed everyone who littered. I was sure that if he ever caught someone in the act, they would not get off lightly. We all agreed to complete our mission and reach the imperious peak that was waiting for us. At least that would give us some joy. We shared the water prudently, saving a full flask for an emergency.

The last stretch was steep and hard. Our willpower, however, was great, so before long we had reached the highest point of the mountain. A stone construction resembling an altar was a sign that we were now standing on the peak. The wind was so strong that you could lose your balance if you were not careful.

"Florina and Ptolemaida are in that direction, and Veroia a little further away," Yiannis said, pointing towards the little towns.

The view from up here was majestic. Myrto propped her cell phone against a stone so we could all pose for a picture. Antonis also gave her his phone. She asked us to huddle in a spot and, at the right moment, dashed to enter the frame, having previously pressed the timer on both phones. Only Voras was absent from the photo. He had gone to the other side and was looking down at the valley.

We stood still, smiling, and waiting for the shutter sound. I felt Antonis's hand stroke my lower back, and a chill ran down my spine. We instantly stepped apart, exchanging a glance laden with meaning.

"There are a lot of mountain goats up here," Myrto said.

"And bears," Yiannis added, with a laugh.

Antonis gave me an anxious look, but I shook my head reassuringly to signal that meeting a bear here was near impossible. Their exceptional sense of smell and hearing enabled them to avoid undesirable encounters. Besides, it was a well-known fact that they kept away from humans. Only once had a bear destroyed some beehives. What the bears in the area usually did was crush the cherry plum trees around the village. It used to anger Eva because it stopped her from gathering enough fruit to make her delicious jams. Indeed, our mountains were full of wild animals, but they rarely ran into humans, especially in the summer.

After celebrating our achievement, we took a short walk around and then decided that it was time to eat the goodies we had brought with us. We would have to start making our way back shortly, especially now that we did not have much water. We spread the food on the rocks and started eating hungrily.

"How time flies," Yiannis mused.

"It flies, and we change with it," Myrto said with a sigh.

"Time changes our exterior. The people we meet change our interior," I said, looking at Antonis.

Myrto noticed the look we exchanged, and gave a dry cough before splitting the last slice of pie between Antonis and me. I had known Myrto since we were children, and I loved her very much. From the way she was looking at Antonis and me, I suspected she fathomed what was going on between us.

"So, Yiannis, what's it like being a teacher?" Antonis asked, as we nibbled on what remained of the food.

I was glad he was making an effort to get to know my friends better. I had sensed that he loved people in general, and I was pleased that he sought to communicate with them.

"It is tough and beautiful at the same time. Teaching children about the world, and not just reading and writing, is a great responsibility," Yiannis replied.

"Reading is such a pleasure, though," I said as I took a small sip of water.

"Do people read much nowadays?" Myrto, a renowned bookworm, wondered.

"There have been two moments in the modern history of mankind that changed everything concerning reading and writing," Antonis replied, and we all looked at him attentively.

Although the sun was burning, a cool breeze provided some relief as we savored our conquest of the peak, eating and chatting together.

"The first moment was when houses in ancient Pompeii were fitted with windows," Antonis said, gulping down his last bite. "Suddenly, daylight entered rooms that until then had been dark, being sealed off. Especially during winter, when they could not even open the door. That's when mankind took its first important step as far as writing goes."

I had not heard that story before, and I impatiently encouraged him to go on.

"The second step came with the discovery of artificial lighting. That's when writing flourished, along with the increased desire for reading. Imagine people's homes suddenly filled with the light of electric bulbs, in an instant. Their time, particularly the evening hours, became more interesting, as they could now lose themselves in a book. Keep in mind that back then there were no televisions, no phones, no social networks. From that point onwards, the landscape of reading in general changed, as there was a publishing revolution, if you can call it that..."

"To reach the present day, when most people live in the dark despite having acquired ample light... mostly cast by the screens of their smartphones," Yiannis said, with some bitterness.

I thought back to a conversation we had had about children becoming addicted to tablets and phones from a very young age. I always thought that every era provides you with the right tools to make your life easier. The real issue is how to use those tools, so they do not become a source of addiction and isolation from the rest of the world.

The screech of a bird interrupted our conversation, and we all raised our eyes to the sky. Two falcons were playing.

"Peregrine falcons," I said, a species I could easily recognize.

"How do you know so much?" Antonis asked with a smile.

"I have learned to observe. I make the most of my stay here by learning about animals and learning from animals..."

"What did these falcons teach you, then?" he asked playfully.

I liked being teased by him, and smiled. "I learned that it is the fastest bird when it dives down. A few years ago, they almost became extinct due to the excessive use of pesticides. Also, when they mate, they build their nests on remote rocks to evade predators and sometimes occupy the nests of other birds..."

"Meaning?"

"They chase the previous owners away."

"Now, that's not fair, is it?" he said, raising his eyes to the sky.

"Life and nature have their own sense of what is fair and what is unfair. There is only one fixed point of reference that can make us all better beings."

"Love," he completed my sentence, surprising me.

"Yes. Love can conquer all..."

Myrto had started to pack up the remnants of our meal, and I hurried to help her. Besides, it was time to start heading down. The ringtone of Yiannis's phone split the scenic tranquility that surrounded us. It was my sister, worrying about Voras, as I had told them I would not be taking him on the hike. She also asked me if Antonis would be staying over tonight, too, but I did not know. I had not even thought to ask him. I only knew what I wished for, not what he was planning to do. I tactfully communicated to her that I did not know, then ended the call and returned the phone to Yiannis along with my thanks.

We stayed at the peak a few minutes more to enjoy the view. Up at this height, we felt like little gods. A sea of mountains spread all around us, and I watched Antonis's eyes thirstily drink in all the beauty surrounding us. I gave him some time to take more photos, and then we all agreed to begin our descent.

We arrived at the Lost Spring reasonably quickly. It was silly, but somehow we all hoped that we would find water running through the rocks, that the source had not really turned dry. We were of course disappointed. We filled a bin bag with the rubbish and continued downwards. The three of them had started a conversation on climate change. I was walking ahead, following Voras, who seemed parched with thirst and in a hurry to return. When I reached the first trees of the forest, I stopped and waited for them. The temperature instantly dropped and, at long last, I felt my body cool down. We moved to cross the gorge and the dark woods once again.

A cold northerly breeze fluttered through the leaves, and I felt a chill surge from the top of my head to my toes. Voras, who loved this wind, jumped up as if he wanted to enjoy it to the fullest. Then he clambered up a large stone, where the wind was at its strongest. It was impressive how much he loved the northern wind, as if he secretly communed with it.

I bent down among the rocks and snapped off a twig of wild oregano to rub between my palms. Then, I brought my open palm close to Antonis's face so he could smell it. He sighed with pleasure. I picked two more twigs, taking care not to snap them too close to the roots, and put them in my pocket. "Herbs for our dinner."

Antonis shot me a troubled glance as we entered the gorge. "I was thinking of taking off when we get back. My friends are still waiting for me to join them."

"If you're not careful, you'll be taking off down the gorge! Pay attention, it's very slippery," I advised him, noticing how carelessly he was walking, not even looking at where he placed his feet.

"Yes, ma'am," he replied with a smile.

"And you can of course leave if you like, but please know that the guesthouse is yours for as long as you need. You should follow your heart, though," I said, trying to disguise my own feelings.

"If I follow my heart, I will stay here forever," he whispered. I stopped in my tracks, trying to understand whether he was joking. Once again, our eyes locked in a silent challenge.

I turned away to follow the others, but, after taking a couple of steps, I turned back towards Antonis again.

"Then stay…"

"I'm sorry, I didn't hear you," he said, even though I was sure that my voice had carried over the noisy rustle of the trees.

I turned away. "Then stay…" I whispered.

"Can you look at me when you say it?" he insisted, gently grasping my arm and turning me toward him.

My cheeks flushed at our proximity, and I stared deep into his eyes as I planned to repeat myself a third time. Then, Myrto screamed.

Startled, I whirled around to see what had happened to cause my friend such alarm. At the same time, Voras started to bark ferociously. Faintly, I heard the sound of pounding hooves approaching. I grabbed Voras before he could go tearing off after the source of the noise.

A large deer burst through the dry branches and galloped down the path toward us, oblivious to our presence. It had a wild look in its eyes, and I knew instinctively that the beast was terrified. The path here was narrow, and it would have no room to veer away before it reached us.

"Step aside!" I screamed, as Yiannis spread his arms wide to stop it. I immediately noticed some shapes following the deer like shadows. I was not sure whether it was a trick of the light as the sun's rays flitted between the trees, but something inside me was telling me that what would follow would not be good. The terrified animal, spooked by Yiannis, stopped for a moment and looked at us. It was a beautiful and rare red deer, its wide antlers almost meeting over its head like an imperial crown.

A howl split the air, making all of us jump. There was no mistaking the sound. The deer was being chased by wolves, and we had been caught up in the hunt.

As growls filled the air, the deer panicked and turned towards the gorge. The abrupt turn made its hooves slip on a pile of dry branches, and it clumsily tumbled towards the sharp rocks until it noisily smashed against them. I pressed my hands against my mouth, horrified at seeing the poor animal in such pain.

Then the first wolf menacingly appeared on the path, and I froze. Its fur was pitch black, making its sharp fangs appear even more prominent. Antonis, who had grabbed Voras's collar from me, was skidding on the trail as he made a superhuman effort to stop the brave dog from lunging at the wolf. Yiannis picked up a large stick and raised it over his head, trying to frighten the wolf. Myrto followed suit, throwing rock after rock in the wolf's direction.

But the wolf was not alone. Behind him, another two animals loomed. To our right, through the foliage, I could make out at least one more wolf walking towards the higher ground to circumvent us and come at our backs.

"They're circling us!" I cried out, pointing at the wolves slipping through the trees.

"Come nearer, we need to be close together!" Myrto screamed.

Trying to calm down Voras, I helped Antonis pull him with us towards the others. We instinctively formed a protective cross, so that all our flanks were covered. I looked at Antonis, who was sweating but did not seem afraid. On the contrary, he was shouting to scare the wolves away, but to no avail. The wolves were neither making a move to attack us, nor to turn away. We were locked in a sort of primal stalemate, each waiting for the other to make a move.

Another wolf had crossed to the other side through a small passage, trying to get near the wounded prey. From where it stood, it would have to take a jump, and the great height was evidently acting as a deterrent.

"They're after the deer, not us," I realized.

"Let's move away," Yiannis whispered. "Walk slowly!"

Hearing the wounded animal's harrowing cries, I looked around me once more. The wolves could only approach the deer from the spot we were standing on. That would happen the moment we walked past them. The deer, wounded and helpless as it was, would be easy prey, and the wolves would instantly devour its flesh. The cries of pain reaching my ears broke my heart.

"Wait!" I cried out, to stop them from moving too far away.

I rushed towards Antonis and quickly removed the knife and rope I had packed from the backpack on his back.

"Hold it tight, so I can go down the slope," I told Yiannis. Everyone cried out in protest. I was adamant I was going down, so Yiannis wedged his foot against a tree as a counterweight and helped me climb down the gorge, which was luckily not too steep at this spot.

I looked up at Antonis for a second and felt his anxiety, as he still had not understood what I was planning to do. At least he understood enough to keep a firm grip on Voras, who would have plunged in after me without any concern for his safety.

The wolves were now very close, and the longer they were kept away from the deer, the angrier they seemed to get. At least they could not reach the spot where I was.

In a few seconds, I set foot on the bottom of the ravine and bent over the exhausted creature that was gasping for breath. Its right leg was shattered. Blood flowed freely from its wounds, tinting the stones and the creek. Now that the wolves could smell fresh blood, I knew they would not stay away much longer. Even if the deer tried to get up, it would be futile.

I spoke to it gently to calm it down, despite the tumult around us caused by Voras barking with all his might. He was so wild, he looked no different from the wolves.

The deer, frightened by my presence, tried to move, but it was impossible. I gently stretched out my hand and touched its belly. Its heart was about to break with the agony and terror. The others higher up the slope were crying out, but everything around me had faded away. I was shaken by this animal, which now felt its end was near. I spoke to the deer a tender stream of words, and managed to make it slowly lay its head on the ground. I removed the knife from my belt and gripped it as tightly as I could. Everything had to happen with surgical precision, and quickly.

I stroked its neck one last time, struggling to keep my composure. For a moment, I raised my eyes and saw the others looking at me anxiously. They had understood what would follow.

Suddenly, I felt as if the world had frozen over and all the sounds had died out. I felt that even the wolves now stood numb before the sacrifice about to take place. The only thing I could hear was the beating of the wounded deer's heart, and the water that flowed through the rocks.

I slowly brought my knife to its neck and, mustering all my courage, slit its carotid artery. A crimson jet sprang up in the air. Reflexively, the deer tried to stand up, but it instantly abandoned the effort. It was too wounded, too exhausted. Maybe it wanted everything to be over as quickly as possible, too.

I moved closer and spoke soothingly, stroking its belly. My vision was blurred, tears stinging my eyes. I stayed there comforting it until it drew its last breath, so it could have a peaceful death, safe from the rage of the prowling predators awaiting to tear its flesh.

The wild howl of one of the wolves brought me back to the present with a start. I realized I must hurry. I turned back and, tears streaming down my face, I sought the piece of rope. Soon, I had climbed up the slope and rejoined the others.

As we carefully moved down the path, the wolves backed away, melting into the foliage like otherworldly beings. Once we were out of their way, the pack sprung forth and rushed down the ravine to reach the dead deer. Just before we lost sight of them, I saw the wolf from the path turn towards us, baring his sharp teeth. Was he thanking me for making the kill easier? I felt no fear as we looked at each other. I knew that such were the laws of nature, and they were not about to change today.

Antonis pulled me away urgently. It was clear we had to move on. I followed him, and a short while later, still very alert, we crossed the gorge and entered the dark forest.

As soon as she got cell reception, Myrto called my father and informed him about the wolves' attack. By the time we reached the cabin, a small group of villagers were already waiting for us. News of the incident had traveled fast.

I was in shock and spoke very little, so it fell to the others to inform them about what happened. On the last stretch of our hike, Yiannis had advised me not to mention what I had done. Not out of fear, but because there was no reason for the whole village to talk about how I had killed a deer so that the wolves would not eat it alive. Yiannis insisted all the more because the deer was a protected species. He didn't want us to get drawn into a protracted and meaningless legal battle to prove that I had killed the deer to ease its suffering.

I agreed with him, and we decided to keep it a secret.

We narrated the incident exactly as it had happened, omitting only my brief intervention. We did not mention it to my father or Eva, but I intended to reveal everything to them once I'd calmed down. They had noticed the blood on my clothes, and understood that something else must have happened, too.

That type of red deer was nearly extinct, and everyone wondered how one had ended up in our region. Wolves had attacked herds and other wild animals in the past, but rarely at this time of year and never in the presence of humans.

Myrto's grandfather, who was present, mentioned that just after the end of the war, the wolves had savaged a German in the woods, who had been a prisoner in the village and tried to run away. My father discreetly gestured to me that it was just a tall tale. I, on the other hand, could not put the image of the deer stopping to look at us before crashing down the ravine out of my mind. If we had not stood in its path, it might have escaped. The fact that the wolves did not leave but stayed on the spot showed they were desperately hungry. If we had prevented them from reaching their meal, they would have certainly attacked us.

The questions and chattering of the villagers became too much, and I suggested to Antonis that we return to Evora. Voras was limping, and I needed to nurse his feet. I made my excuses and asked my father to give us a lift because I was exhausted.

When we arrived, I kissed my father goodbye and told him we'd talk about everything the following day when I felt better. I waited for him to pull away, and then turned towards Antonis and Voras, who was still unable to step on his right front leg properly. It was nearly dusk, and I felt greatly relieved to be back at Evora.

"I'm going to tend to his foot," I said, moving past Antonis. But, once again, he held me back and brought me around to face him.

"I want you to know that I admire you even more after what happened today. I could never have done what you did to relieve the deer's suffering and spare it from the agony of the wolves' teeth. It was an act of great courage."

"Antonis, I don't know where I found the strength to do that. I've never done this before."

"That's good. If it was a habit, I'd be getting worried," Antonis said, and stifled a smile. I burst into loud laughter despite myself. Besides, I really needed to feel better. "Do you need some time alone?"

"No, Antonis, I enjoy having you here."

"So, I should not be afraid?" he said, bringing his hand to his neck.

He was making every effort to make me smile, and he succeeded.

"I'm fine. You go get some rest. I'll have a bath and then make us something to eat. Do you like pasta?"

"So much, you'd think I was Italian! Mamma mia!" he exclaimed, adding a series of random words in an Italian accent.

I really was enjoying having him around. I kept trying to hide my mixed emotions, hoping that I would feel better soon. I made to move, but stopped. "You've got to admit, every time we meet, it's an unprecedented adventure."

He laughed. "I've no complaints on that front. Although I would not mind this being the last one. Of this kind, I mean. Bad things coming in threes, and all that," he said after some thought.

We agreed to meet shortly. I called Voras, who followed me with some difficulty. A quick examination had shown me that it was not a severe injury. Still, I wanted to clear the grazes with antiseptic and check that there were no other injuries elsewhere.

Luckily it was only superficial scratches and a splinter in his foot. I tended to them and left him lying on his little mattress. Then I looked in the cupboards to see what I could prepare for dinner. Through the window, I saw Antonis cross the bottom of the garden in the direction of the waterfall. I was surprised, but imagined he probably wanted to enjoy the view. I thought about taking a shower and going out to meet him, but I hesitated, trying to understand whether I should follow him or not.

I turned my attention to the kitchen and laid out all the ingredients I would need for cooking. I looked again outside the window, but Antonis was out of sight. My desire overwhelmed my reasoning, and without wasting another moment, I started walking to the waterfall, which stood a few dozen meters beyond the back garden. I walked carefully, like a wild animal stalking its prey. To me, Antonis was a man who fell outside the usual stereotypes. An endangered species, I would say, and I was so drawn to him that I was now wandering around looking for him.

I slipped through the shrub border, listening to the water splash onto the rocks from a great height and then gush further down the slope. A small spotlight was hidden among the trees to discreetly light the place at night.

When I saw Antonis standing naked beneath the tumbling water, I froze. The sensible part of me said to walk away, to respect his privacy. But I was seized by the yearning to make him mine. I inched closer, tiptoeing from tree to tree. I was seized by the yearning to make him mine. I felt like a predator that was waiting for the perfect moment to pounce on its prey.

I was mesmerized by the way he cleansed his body from the day's sweat and dust, oblivious to my presence in the twilight. He did not detect me as he relished the water, placing his hands above his head in an attempt to break the force of the waterfall. The water bounced off his palms, enveloping him in a liquid cloud.

I finally reached him, and the waterdrops began to splash my clothes as I stepped into the water. I hurriedly removed them and flung them aside, taking more steps towards him. Now we stood next to each other, and Antonis, with his back turned to me, was still ignorant of my presence. Or was he?

I reached out and touched his shoulder. He jumped in fright, like the deer had when I'd approached it in the ravine. Then he lowered his eyes to my hands, as if searching for the knife that had ended the beast's life earlier.

So, my actions had really affected him. I pulled him towards me as I backed away. He calmly followed me. Here, the force of the water was weaker, allowing our bodies to move closer still. He waited for my next move, although I was afraid to act in case I scared him off. But no. As if he had been expecting me, he stretched out his hand and gently touched my body, sending a frisson all the way through to my core.

Our defenses collapsed as we embraced like two broken pieces flawlessly joining at last. I instantly felt his warmth flood through me, and felt a newfound sense of relief. I felt him quiver, and I quivered with him. I pulled him further away from the water as my hands traveled all over his body. My lips surrendered to his soft mouth, and I let myself go, closing my eyes. I knew that my choice left no

way back. But I was ready. Readier than ever...

Stretched across the bed in the guesthouse, we touched each other, releasing every feeling that had been born inside us when we'd first met. It was late, and tranquility reigned. The room was softly lit by a scattering of lanterns. A jazz melody dominated by the sound of the piano slowly drifted up from downstairs. All the magic that had started at the waterfall was being completed here.

"Evora," he whispered in my ear, and I smiled.

"Evora," I repeated hoarsely, agreeing that this was the ideal moment to be in a tight embrace.

I rested my head against his chest, which rose and fell to the rhythm of his breaths. I listened to every inhalation, every exhalation, every beat of his heart that coordinated with mine. His fingers, tangled in my hair, were sweeping me away. I had forgotten the harsh incident during the hike. Surrendering to his arms, I was savoring our Evora—our moment.

"Ariadne, I've been thinking..."

I turned to look at him.

"What you did in the forest was an expression of the love inside you, a love that makes no distinctions, that is indiscriminate. Disregarding personal risk, you climbed down the gorge to ease the pain of this animal, risking your own life…"

"I don't usually meddle in the laws of nature, but I simply couldn't allow that poor creature to feel the pain of being ripped apart. Besides, it's not as if I deprived the wolves of their meal." I traced my hand along his chest. "Did you not feel the same, when you pulled me from the lake? That you had no choice but to act as you did?"

"I did, but I'm not sure I would have gone into that water if it had been a drowning deer, not a drowning person. You loved that deer enough to risk your life for it. I can't say I'd do the same."

"Everything I know about you tells me you probably would. You're just not aware of it right now. Love is a power that galvanizes people and tears down the walls that separate us from our primitive instincts. It pushes us to overcome our boundaries, to not limit ourselves to our egos, and the things we need. It is wrong to pigeonhole love. Either you love, and that is your rule of thumb, or you do not love."

He was gaping at me.

"What's the matter? Was it something I said?" I asked.

"I've told you this before. The way you become transformed when you talk about things relating to your work is impressive. From one moment to the next, you become the ultimate professional, answering every single question— both the ones I voice aloud, and the secret ones inside my heart."

"At your service. Any other questions?" I said, stroking his neck.

"I've always wondered how two people can tell whether they truly love one another."

I raised my head and propped myself up against his chest.

"The desirable outcome when it comes to love is for two people to become one, while successfully remaining two separate entities entirely. If they can manage this simple thing, then yes, they truly love one another. But, as I already said before, you can't just love the man or woman you are with."

"What do you mean?"

"Love means loving everything that exists and surrounds you," I replied, tracing his lips with my fingers once more.

"What about envy and jealousy?" he asked, raising himself on his elbows.

"Envy and jealousy, just like vanity and greed, are passions. Love, on the other hand, is a virtue that you cultivate without anyone forcing you to do so."

"I have to tell you that after I met you, I looked up some books on love..."

"That's great!" I exclaimed with pleasure.

"I remember something I read that really stayed with me."

I held my breath, hanging on his every word.

"A wealthy person is not one who owns a lot, but someone who gives a lot."

"I couldn't have said it better. That sentence is so significant because it applies to more than material belongings. It applies to feelings, too."

He took my hand and brought it to his mouth, solemnly kissing every finger.

"I, too, have a favorite saying that I often share with the people who come to stay here," I said.

"I would love to hear it."

"Love is a force that generates love. If your love does not cause the same feeling in the other person, then it is incompetent, it is a failure."

He looked at me for a few seconds without saying a word. Then he said, "Can I tell you something, Ariadne?"

"Yes, of course." I replied, unsuspecting.

"There is something that has been troubling me for some time, and I don't think I can keep it to myself any longer."

His tone worried me. What could have happened to change his mood so suddenly?

"Antonis, you're scaring me. What's the matter? Tell me."

He sighed, and my anxiety skyrocketed.

"I'm starving."

I think our laughter must have echoed all the way across the valley. I sat up on the bed and wacked him with my pillow. He had given me a fright, but he was absolutely right. The ingredients were still lined up on the counter, waiting for someone to cook them.

"Me too," I said, as my stomach rumbled.

"You promised me dinner. You're letting me starve, and I'm hungry like a..."

As if he had been about to utter a taboo word, I covered his mouth with my palm as I got a flashback of the wolves.

"Come, let's go cook!" he cried out enthusiastically, trying to lighten the suddenly somber mood.

We dressed hurriedly and soon were at my house, stepping past Voras, who barely moved from his spot.

"My poor dog, he's so tired," I said, and gave him a fleeting caress.

"Had you ever seen him so fierce before?" Antonis asked once we were inside.

"No, first time. I didn't think he had such instincts. It's what we were just saying about love. He would not have thought twice about taking on the whole pack to protect us."

"Especially you, because he loves you," he said, pointing at me with the packet of pasta.

"You will open a bottle of wine for us and go sit on the couch. Tonight, I'm the cook."

I grabbed the pasta from his hand and pushed him towards the fridge. Without taking a step back, he pulled me towards him. "I like you, you know," he whispered and, without touching me, brought his mouth close to my throat, turning his breath into the most torturous caress.

"I've been getting a few hints," I managed to say, and pulled back because if I responded, we would never get around to eating that evening.

While I filled the pot with water, he opened a bottle of wine. Then he came to me and handed me a glass.

"To Evora..."

"To love, which is the same thing," I added, before taking a long gulp.

He imitated me and leaned against the counter, attentive.

"My father has this favorite saying, and I named this place after it."

"Meaning?" he asked, puzzled.

"When he wants to say 'all in good time,' he says 'all in evora,' meaning that everything must come to pass when the time is right."

Antonis raised his glass with a laugh. "The time is evora for you to kiss me, then. Evora!"

I loved his sense of humor. I skipped across the kitchen towards him and planted a kiss on his lips. I felt complete. Both at the waterfall and afterward, I had experienced very unique and extreme emotions. My body was still under the influence of those breathtaking sensations. It's easy for two bodies to meet and share a momentary thrill. However, it is extremely difficult for them to merge in a true union, and not just share a few intense moments during lovemaking. I knew first hand that sex without love was nothing but a temporary bridging of the void that exists between two human beings. I was curious to see where our meeting would lead us...

I picked up the knife I had been chopping vegetables with, and then froze, my hand suspended in mid-air. I'd suddenly remembered that I had left the other knife beside the deer.

"What's the matter?" he asked, but I didn't want to spoil the mood of our evening. I tried to suppress the gloomy emotions rising to the surface at the memory of everything that had happened.

"Nothing! I was just trying to remember the recipe," I excused myself. It wasn't a complete lie.

"So, what are you cooking for us?"

I smiled, and looked at the ingredients spread out before me. I put the pot of water on the stove and brought out a frying pan. "Being pressed for time, today I will be making a simple dish. First, I will boil this beautiful linguini, a gift of a friend from Tuscany. Then, I will chop up my vegetables. Most of them come from our vegetable patch."

"Kindly provide a detailed description of all the steps," Antonis said. His joy at teasing me lit up his eyes.

"First, I will chop and sauté the onions in a drop of olive oil. Then, I will add the wild mushrooms my father picked."

"Oh no..." he said, as he grabbed his neck and made a choking sound.

I flung the stem of a bell pepper at him, and he ducked.

"Do you think my father wants to poison me?" I asked. He was giggling like a schoolboy.

I chopped and sautéed as I continued narrating my cooking technique. "After the mushrooms, I will add zucchini and peppers, finely chopped. I will let them simmer for about ten minutes, then turn the heat off. I must keep stirring them throughout so they don't stick to the pan. When the pasta is ready, I will add the parsley. Just before I serve the dish, I will sprinkle some freshly ground pepper, et voila! I avoid using salt, so you will have to add some if you wish. I will garnish everything with some of the wild oregano we picked in the woods. Finally, we will accompany our meal with local goat cheese, coarsely grated, if you like."

"Sounds delicious," Antonis said, and pushed himself off the counter to put some music on.

"As I said, it's a simple recipe. Next time, I'll cook something special."

I regretted the words the moment they left my mouth. They betrayed my desire to be with Antonis. His reply instantly dispelled my doubts. "Next time, I'll cook. If I'm invited again, that is."

Our eyes locked, and we fell into an awkward silence. We were probably thinking the same thing. While I set the table, Antonis examined my bookcase. He then stood gazing at the darkening horizon though the tall windows. He looked so at ease in the room, as if he had been living here for years. My eyes blurred and began to water.

"Onions are so moving, aren't they?" he asked, as I wiped my eyes and laughed at the same time.

"Tragic, isn't it?"

"You should use a very sharp knife; it releases less of the irritant that makes your eyes water," he said, and sighed. "I must leave in the morning..."

I felt a small knot in my stomach and tried to ignore it. I wanted to ask him not to go, to stay here with me in the beautiful evora we had created together, but I held back.

"I have to meet the head of the team I'll be joining tomorrow at Giannitsa," Antonis said. "Then I need to get to Thessaloniki to make some arrangements, and then return to Athens for a few days before I move permanently north."

His words sent hope coursing through me. If he was moving permanently north, that meant he would be nearby, that we could see each other whenever we liked.

In a considerably better mood than I had been a minute ago, I said "Great!" as I piled steaming pasta onto the plates.

"It does smell great," he murmured as he returned to the kitchen.

"All set. Please take a seat, sir," I said, placing the plates on the table.

He leaned over my shoulder and exclaimed in admiration, before taking the seat across the table. I did not intend to say anything regarding his stay or his plans for the future, so we started eating, making small talk, laughing, and drinking wine. I was happy to see him clear his plate and return to the stove for a second helping.

He told me things about his life I did not know. His parents lived on the island of Thasos, where he had grown up. He had an older sister in Strasburg, France, where she and her husband ran a cute little bistro. Christmas in Strasburg was magical, he told me, and I couldn't help projecting us sitting at a bistro table together, warming our hands on a hot cup of chocolate, in that beautiful French town.

We finished dinner late, and soon enough it was time for bed. I wanted to ask Antonis to spend the night here, in my room, but I hesitated, as he stood up to go. Suddenly it was all awkwardly formal between us. We agreed to have coffee together the next morning before his departure, then stop by the restaurant so he could say goodbye to everyone.

I walked him to the front door, and he kissed me goodnight on the cheek, gently stroking my face. I felt that our night was ending too abruptly and wondered if I should do something else. He started to walk back to the guesthouse, but suddenly stopped. Voras had woken up, and stood staring at us.

"I think it would be great if we woke up together..." Antonis said, slowly walking back towards me.

"I think so, too," I agreed, without thinking twice about it.

He took my hand and asked with false solemnity, "Your place or mine?"

Voras jumped in fright as our loud laughter echoed in the empty garden. He started barking, thinking something had happened. I patted him to calm him down, then turned to Antonis. "Let's pick up where we left off... Your place, dear."

He pulled me near him, and we walked to the guesthouse, his arm around my shoulder. The sounds of the night accompanied us all the way until we finally fell asleep in each other's arms...

Evora

NEARLY THREE WEEKS HAD PASSED since the day Antonis left Evora. The first rains fell on my birthday, easing the thirst of the parched earth. Never before had the rainclouds been so late to arrive, and we were all relieved when the first drops fell.

A few days earlier, my last student -as I liked to call my clients—had departed, and I was expecting the next one in a few days. My greatest joy was the peace in their eyes as they took their leave. Most booked their next session even before they left, but I never accepted anyone before six months had passed. I advised them to use the interim to work on what we had practiced at Evora on their own. I wanted them to understand that this was not a resort. It was a parenthesis that would make their lives better from that point onwards if they applied everything we had discussed and employed at Evora once they left.

Every year on my birthday, I would review the previous twelve months and set my new goals for the coming year. For the first time, I wanted only one thing: to see Antonis again, and soon. Just the thought of him filled my heart with joy.

Once or twice, I caught myself becoming distracted by thoughts of Antonis as I spoke to my student about her relationships and way of life. Most of the people coming to

Evora were dealing with issues in their interactions with others, particularly with family or in other close ties, especially romantic relationships. Concerning romantic relationships, I had come to the conclusion that the leading cause behind modern-day difficulties was the wrong first impression people formed about their love interests. Unfortunately, we were living in the age of false impressions. Countless apps could improve our appearance in an unnatural manner. A case in point was the young woman who had left Evora the previous day. I had tried to convince her that the closer to reality the image we project, the higher the chances of meeting someone who would genuinely appreciate us. The prospective partner might not end up hurting us, because he or she would know from the start who we truly were. She had chosen to project something entirely different and, most importantly, had lost all touch with nature.

Nonetheless, after just one day at Evora, she was waiting outside my front door in the morning to go for a walk in the woods. Then we would sit in the shade of the grove by the waterfall and talk.

It was terrifying to observe the extent to which social media had changed our lives and how relationships had now come to be, especially among young people. However, no virtual reality could ever replace the real connection between two people who touch and feel one another. No photo or video could supplant actual live contact with nature.

Seated by the window now, I was doing just that: gazing at the garden outside, a cup of tea in my hand.

Antonis and I had agreed to talk later in the afternoon. Not a day passed by without a phone call, our conversations building upon the foundations of our newly formed relationship. We spent hours on the phone every evening. My family was starting to worry about me, seeing me dash back to my house after work to spend the evenings alone.

Today, on my birthday, I feverishly wished he was here. Unfortunately, an unexpected work trip abroad was keeping him away, but he was hoping to finally make it the following week.

Although it was early afternoon, the sky had grown dark as the clouds gathered and the rain grew stronger. Voras appeared outside the tall windows, wagging his tail happily. Ignoring the downpour, he stood in the middle of the garden, his snout pointed expectantly at the gate. I guessed my father and sister must have arrived, and I stood up to let them in. We would all be dining together to celebrate my birthday.

I opened the door and, to my surprise, I saw Yiannis and Myrto huddled under an umbrella. I could not believe they had come all this way for my birthday, and cried out with pleasure. Walking behind them were my father and Eva. I was so happy to see them again, but was puzzled by the strange look on their faces as they came inside. As if they were holding something back from me.

I had barely closed the door when I heard another knock. I was baffled—no one else was expected to join us. I opened the door and, for a brief second, registered that no one was there. Then my heart leaped into my throat. Antonis, hiding by the wall, had suddenly sprung up before me.

I squealed with joy, scuttled into his open arms, and squeezed him tight. I desperately wanted to kiss him, but I controlled myself in front of everyone. We were both drenched, and, without wasting another moment, we stepped inside.

I stood there, immobilized with surprise, looking at all these people I cared about here with me now. It was difficult to take it all in and not shriek with happiness. Antonis had got me this time, lying about coming next week. Now, my disappointment was replaced with joy at the surprise. They all wished me a happy birthday as we moved to the sitting room.

"This is such a surprise, I can't believe it!" I exclaimed, hugging everyone.

"Antonis told us he was going to surprise you, and we're always happy to drop everything to come to Avgerinos," Yiannis said, brushing raindrops off his shoulders.

"I'm so happy," I murmured, taking Antonis's face in my palms.

"I missed you. Happy birthday," he whispered in my ear, and gently kissed my lips.

He put a small envelope into my hands as he kissed me. I realized he didn't want any of the others to see it, so I carefully tucked it out of sight.

Evora

My sister and my father went back out to the car, and returned carrying pots of food and a cake. A loud clap of thunder shook the windows. Antonis looked outside where Voras, drenched to the bone, was pacing in the garden, carefree.

"He loves this weather. If he wants to come inside, he'll bark at me to let him in. You need to be fast to dry him before he gets a chance to shake..." I did not get to finish my sentence because Antonis had already let Voras in.

We looked at each other, and I was bursting with everything I wanted to tell him.

"Ariadne, come help us!" Eva, who had begun to set the table with Myrto, called out.

Everyone had guessed by now that there was something more than friendship between Antonis and me. Still, I had not said anything explicitly, not even to my sister. I could tell she wanted to ask a thousand questions.

I went to them, and Antonis walked with the other men over to the tall windows that lined the front of the house and gazed at the lightning forks that split the sky. I loved this weather. Any extreme expression of nature that was not catastrophic enchanted me.

We laid out platters loaded with the delicious food my sister had prepared, and soon everything was ready. Before we took our seats, they started singing Happy Birthday to me, and Myrto approached the dining table with the amazing chocolate cake Eva had baked. I blew out my candles, and another round of hugs, kisses, and well wishes followed.

"May you always be happy, and love with all your heart," Antonis said, giving me a fleeting kiss on the lips.

"You too," I wished him back.

We then took our seats, talking loudly and piling food on our plates from the platters laid out along the center of the table.

"What's this?" Antonis asked, looking perplexed at the small loaves of bread.

"My specialty," Eva replied.

The confusion did not leave his face.

"Eva bakes these round loaves in a wood oven, fresh every day. Then she slices the top off and carefully removes the crumb, creating a bowl from the crust."

Antonis nodded, although clearly he was still perplexed as to what he should do with the bread bowl.

"There's hot vegetable soup in the tureen," I explained. "We'll serve it inside the loaf and eat it before the crust gets soggy. Then, you can eat the bread if you want to, soaked with all the herb and vegetable flavors of the soup."

"Oh, wow. Whoever came up with this is a genius," Antonis said, as Eva ladled the soup into the bread bowls.

It was so lovely to have everyone here. I felt complete. We enjoyed Eva's soup and then moved on to the rest of the dishes, accompanying everything with wine. We only stopped eating to laugh at my father's jokes and gentle teasing of Yiannis, who had an educating story about everything, as always.

"What's been happening with the village's gym and playground, Mr. Thomas?" Myrto asked my father. "Are they ever going to fix them up?"

"I'm starting to get really angry about it," my father admitted. "The mayor reassured us that everything was underway, but nothing has happened so far."

"That's a shame. I've been told that when the weather is bad, the children have nowhere to exercise."

"If we don't see any serious steps being taken, I will be making our case more forcibly," my father said. He had to fight even for the basics, always overcoming obstacles. His expression softened as he turned to Antonis. "This is the first year that I can remember where it did not rain for almost four months. It's finally here now, but there are many nearby areas still desperately in need of rain. What do you scientists think about it, Antonis?"

"I wish it were that easy, to know what's going to happen next, Mr. Thomas," Antonis said thoughtfully. "Around the world, research and studies on water are constantly underway, as it's the primary source of life on our planet. In fact, I'm in your region to complete a study on whether we need to construct large dams in the Balkans—to produce energy, but mostly to act as water reservoirs in times of drought."

"Yes, I've heard something about that..." my father admitted.

Antonis gave me a look, and then continued. "The wider region here is lucky when you consider that a large part of the planet is entirely dry. Moreover, in other parts of the world, the water available has become unusable due to pollution."

"When I visited India for my studies," I interjected, "I saw regions where people have to walk ten miles to get to drinking water. Can you imagine having to go through that every day, just to survive?"

"Unfortunately, what is still plentiful to us is a scarce resource—even a luxury—for many people," Antonis said. "One-fifth of the Earth's population faces this problem. That number will snowball in the coming years because water is diminishing or becoming polluted. Many think that the next humanitarian crisis will break out because of a lack of water."

I loved to hear him talk. Every now and then, he would cast furtive glances, full of meaning, in my direction. I could not wait for the moment when it would be just the two of us.

What we were discussing was very interesting, nonetheless. At some point, while the others chatted, I stood up noiselessly to clear the table and serve the cake. Eva and Myrto pushed their chairs back to get up and help, but I gave them a stern look that said, "Don't even think about it."

"If we could store the rainfall of the wider area," Antonis was saying, "we would collect enough water to meet the needs of a large city for quite some time. But most of the rainwater is lost and ends up in rivers and the sea."

"What can we do about all this?" Myrto asked him.

He sighed. "As simple as something sounds, putting it into action is quite hard. What really matters is that every one of us reduces their carbon footprint by changing some of our everyday habits."

"Such as?"

"Our way of thinking, for a start. Also, ,simple things, like turning out lights we're not using, and using low energy lightbulbs. Additionally, we can easily reduce our overconsumption of meat, particularly beef."

Yiannis tapped his finger against his temple and looked at Myrto as if to tell her, "I told you so."

Antonis carried on. "It's fundamental that we develop new renewable energy sources—not only develop them, but actually use them, like you're doing with the solar panels on your roof."

"My father is trying to teach the people in the village to recycle. I've heard that Greece is way behind other countries," I said, as I brought slices of cake over to the table.

"That's true," he said. "Recycling would greatly help. In Greece, unfortunately, it's an unknown word for most people. Education needs to start early, both in schools and at home. The point is that recycling should be a habit, not a chore."

"I remember the day the teacher asked me to talk to the schoolchildren about the love they must show animals and nature. I realized then that they knew next to nothing about recycling," I said.

"Another thing that is important and detrimental to the environment is transport and travel," Antonis said after a small pause. "We all need to curtail our use of cars and airplanes to what is absolutely essential. You can't imagine the toll that even a domestic flight takes on the environment."

"We mostly walk everywhere here," my father proudly proclaimed, as he dug into his slice of cake.

Yiannis, troubled, was staring at his plate. He had not eaten a bite. "Let's assume that, in some magical way, people start applying everything you just said. Will the climate situation change?"

"Anyone who answers your question with certainty would be lying. We need to understand that climate variation is different from climate change, which is due to human activity. Carbon dioxide levels today are higher than at any point in the past 800,000 years. We need to do the best we can, especially for the next generations. The battle against climate change is a battle for the survival of humanity itself."

The mood had grown somber, and Antonis, taking notice, raised his glass, calling our attention. "I would like to say a couple of words as your guest."

I put my spoon down, trying to guess what he could possibly say next.

"We're all ears," my father said. He'd had a couple of glasses of wine, and was in a cheery mood.

"I would like to ask for your daughter's hand in marriage," he said.

The time it took for Antonis to add, "I'm joking," and for all of us to burst out laughing, felt like years to me.

When our laughter somewhat subsided, my father cried out, "If you can get her to give you her hand, son, I'll give you anything you want! For Ariadne, I'll even hand over a dowry!" More laughter and clinking of glasses followed his exclamation.

My father joked about a dowry because he knew my unfavorable views on marriage. I hated the model of an outwardly successful marriage that functions smoothly when both spouses conform to societal stereotypes. That kind of union could never be more than a simple collaboration, like a contract between two people who remain complete strangers for their entire lives. Mostly out of politeness rather than real love, they make each other feel better as much as possible, all the while seeking to escape the unbearable sense of loneliness encompassing them.

On the other hand, how many couples does one see who, steeped in intolerable boredom, believe that things will get better later on? For many people, marriage is not just a path to the completion of love, but the launch pad to a dull and boring life. The parties and the spectacular ceremonies give way to the pain of reality that is the result of loneliness.

"You young people should keep something in mind," my father said, when we'd all quietened down, pointing to Yiannis and Antonis. "A man marries due to a lack of experience, divorces due to a lack of patience, and remarries due to a lack of memory!"

We all laughed, although Eva and I had heard the joke many times before.

"You, Dad, fell head over heels for Mum, though!" Eva exclaimed, reminding all of us of the love our parents had shared.

A melancholy look came over my father. Antonis noticed it, and tapped his spoon against his glass, calling our attention. When we fell silent, he cleared his throat. "I would like to thank you for embracing me so warmly, and accepting me into such a tightknit group. I know that you feel a sense of obligation towards me after the incident at the lake.

However, I genuinely feel grateful that, thanks to my intervention, the world was not deprived of this wonderful human being, who is a great source of love."

I was lost for words. "Come, come now..." I finally managed to say, and raised my glass. "For my part, I would like to say that I love you all, and feel blessed to have you in my life."

My eyes met Antonis's before he continued: "I also want to say that you are all excellent cooks, and this soup and bread is unique! Truly delicious!"

"That reminds me!" I exclaimed. "Dad, tell us the story of the king and the tastiest loaf of bread. I always loved that one."

My father smiled, always happy to indulge his daughters, and then launched into the tale he'd been telling Eva and me since we were little girls.

"Once upon a time, a king asked all his subjects to bake bread, announcing that the person to bake the tastiest loaf would receive unimaginable wealth. All his subjects fired up their ovens. Soon, the whole kingdom was filled with the aroma of freshly baked dough as the ovens blazed, and everyone prepared loaf after loaf in the hope of becoming rich.

"The following day, a long queue formed outside the palace for the bread tasting to begin. The king tasted one loaf of bread after another, but every single one failed to pass the test. Disappointed, he declared himself unimpressed, despite all the skill of the land's bakers and the efforts of his other subjects.

"Desperate to find the elusive bread, the king left the palace and went from home to home, asking each person to give him a sample of the bread they'd baked, just in case he'd missed a loaf. But no matter how many doors he knocked on, no matter how many loaves he tried, none were what he was seeking.

"Eventually, he arrived at a farmer's hut. The farmer had not baked anything. The king asked him why, and the farmer smiled and said, 'Your majesty is certain to find my bread the tastiest, but must first do as I ask.'

"Exhausted from his futile quest, the king readily accepted, and returned the following day at dawn as instructed. The farmer gave him a hoe, and they walked out to the fields, where the king hoped the tastiest bread would be waiting for him. But the farmer told him he would have to be patient until lunchtime, when his wife would bring the bread to the field."

"I bet it's because she had to go to the hairdresser's first," Yiannis interrupted, with a big grin, and we all laughed.

My father gave us a few moments for the chuckling to die down, then resumed his tale. "The king asked the farmer what they should do while they waited for his wife, and the farmer showed him how to work the fields. Unused to such hard labor, the king began to complain; but every time he did, the farmer reminded him that he would only be able to eat the tastiest bread in the world if he did what the farmer asked of him. And so the king toiled.

"Drenched in sweat, his hands full of blisters, the king eventually sank to the ground, exhausted and unable to go on. 'I have not had a bite to eat all morning, and am as hungry as a bear! How can you stand it?' he complained.

"The farmer's wife appeared just then, carrying a bundle over her shoulder. She spread a tablecloth in the shade of a tree, carefully removed a warm loaf of bread from the bundle, and placed it in the middle of the cloth. The king grabbed a chunk of bread and greedily munched it, groaning with pleasure. 'I have never tasted bread like this before!' he said over and over, and promised to make them wealthier than they had ever dreamed possible.

"When he was full, he asked them for the recipe. What was the secret ingredient that made this loaf so tasty? The farmer laughed. 'Your majesty, it's the same bread everyone in the village bakes. You turned it into the tastiest bread in the world because you worked for it, and now you can enjoy it. We always gain more pleasure from the things we earn, rather than the things we are given.'"

We all nodded in agreement.

"Did he get the riches?" Yiannis called out again, and we burst out laughing.

My father knew him well, and was prepared. "That's immaterial. The farmer gave everyone a lesson that if you want to enjoy something, you have to work for it. Today, most people don't want to exert themselves. They expect everything to be handed to them on a plate."

He was so right. My father had told us this story many times before, but I enjoyed every retelling as if it were the first time.

"So the incident with the wolves has now been forgotten," Yiannis said.

The mood in the room sobered up instantly. "It became a conversation topic in the village for a while, but then everyone moved on," my father replied.

"I'll never forget the look the alpha male gave me just before we left," I said quietly, although I generally did not like to talk about it.

"The way things happened, maybe he thought you were helping them," Yiannis said. "The leader of the pack decides when the other members can feed on the prey. The last ones to eat are always the weakest members of the pack."

"So, you are saying they consider Ariadne as their leader now?" Antonis asked, looking at me intently.

It was true that the pack had seen me kill a deer and leave it for them. But there was no way the wolves could have sensed the motives behind my actions. "I don't think the wolves analyzed the situation anything to this extent. Their behavior that day was driven by hunger," I said.

Yiannis pointed at me and said, "Just remember that when you feed a wolf, he always comes back..."

I stared at him. It was a phrase that one of my Buddhist teachers in India often used, a metaphor for negative thinking. He meant that the more we feed the negative thought in our mind, the more they return and grow, like a wolf that wants to consume us. The mood was becoming too gloomy, and luckily Antonis picked up on it. "Well, the wolves won't be getting at us here," he declared. "Voras will protect us!" He pointed at my dog, who was licking the windows as if they were made of candy.

"He is also an excellent window-cleaner," Myrto added, and we all laughed at the funny quirks of my faithful companion.

It was enough to lighten the mood again. The subject turned to Eva and her line of traditional food products. A well-known grocery store in Athens had expressed interest in stocking it at their stores, and we were all delighted for her. All the while, the storm raged outside, making the dinner feel even more cozy and intimate. Of course, I could not wait to put my arms around Antonis in the absence of the others.

"Evora to go!" my father cried out, marking the end of this fantastic evening.

It was almost midnight, and Antonis and I walked them to the car. Alone, at last, I looked at him under the umbrella. "Shall I make up the bed in the guesthouse for you?" I asked. He laughed heartily. We had both drank a little too much.

"If you want to sleep there, by all means. I'm staying at the house," he answered, and it was my turn to guffaw.

He stroked the scar on my forehead and then kissed it tenderly. "That's the sign of our meeting," he said, as we walked back to the house hand in hand.

The rain did not stop falling for a single moment. I could still hear it pounding the roof as we fell asleep in each other's arms.

EARLY THE FOLLOWING MORNING, Antonis woke up and looked for Ariadne. He got out of bed and ambled to the window, pleased to discover the sky had cleared. He yawned, stretching his hands over his head, and called out her name. Receiving no reply, he walked downstairs.

All was quiet. Puzzled, he made his way to the kitchen. There was no sign of Voras either, so he guessed they must have gone for a walk. A note was waiting for him on the kitchen counter.

Good morning! Don't have breakfast. Come to the waterfall and then follow the signs. – A

Antonis smiled. Without wasting a moment, he attentively wrote something on a piece of paper. He reread it and then put it in his pocket.

Stepping out into the sunny garden, he made his way over to the waterfall. The rain had soaked everything, but the sky, a bright and clear blue, announced a beautiful day ahead.

He instantly sensed the drop in temperature as he arrived at the torrent of water falling from a great height. He looked around, seeking a sign of Ariadne, but there was none.

Taking a closer look, Antonis spotted a small blue ribbon tied around a branch. He walked to it and examined it more carefully, discovering one end of a thread which led to the narrow path beside the waterfall. His face lit up. He picked up the end of the thread and began to follow it. The dense growth forced him to bend down to pass under the canopy of thick branches.

In some places, the ground had been shaped by human hands to form steps. A few minutes later, Antonis came to a large opening in the trees. There, at the base of a massive rock, stood a cave with two mouths, almost like a tunnel. The thread stopped at the cave's entrance, showing him that he had arrived at his destination.

He stood in the center of the cave, ready to cross the few meters that would lead him to the other side. As he walked, the sudden transition from light to darkness hindered his progress, and he fumbled along until he neared the exit, where Voras welcomed him with a wag of his tale. A little further away, on a large tablecloth spread on the ground, stood a basket filled with food.

A sound from behind him drew his attention, and as he turned, he saw Ariadne skipping down the rocks toward him like a mountain goat.

"Good morning!" I cried out to Antonis as my feet touched the ground. I ran towards him. He stood, gaping, his gaze darting between me and the horizon. I gave him a quick peck on the lips and walked to the other end of the tablecloth.

"Welcome to Kathisma, the Armchair," I said, and gestured that he should sit down.

"This is a stunning location," he muttered, enchanted by the beauty surrounding us.

Nature itself had taken care to create this idyllic spot. We called it the Armchair because the ground had been shaped into a plateau that allowed you to sit down and enjoy the breathtaking view of the valley below.

"You have a name for everything up here, don't you?" he said, as I unpacked the basket and laid out everything I had prepared for our breakfast. "Honestly, do you ever run out of surprises?"

"The best surprises are the ones that are all around us, and we have not discovered yet. So yes, for as long as you are here, you can expect many."

Voras came up to me, waiting for his treat. He gobbled it down and went back to his post by the cave mouth. Suddenly, Antonis leaned towards me and gave me a tender kiss. "Thank you," he whispered without pulling away.

"Let's not start a thanking contest again, for you are sure to lose."

He laughed. "I think that whatever happens in this game, I'll come out the winner in the end."

"There is this African tradition: when someone saves your life, you are supposed to serve them for the rest of your life."

"Not a bad tradition at all..." he acknowledged, and gently ran his fingers through my hair.

"Well, don't hold your breath. Here in Avgerinos, it's the other way round," I said, and laughed. He playfully wrestled me to the ground and pulled himself over me.

"I could serve you for the rest of my life..." he said in an impish voice, mocking me. He suddenly turned serious, and began to kiss me.

Voras, evidently jealous, came to stand by my head and nudged Antonis with his muzzle, seeking our attention. We burst out laughing and sat up to finally enjoy our breakfast.

"I think I've told you this before. This is how I picture heaven..." Antonis said softly, indicating our surroundings with a sweep of his arm.

"Me too," I said, and squeezed his hand.

I felt something in his palm. He pushed a piece of paper into my hand and looked at me. "Read it when we get back home."

I lowered my eyes to the folded note in my palm, and smiled with child-like delight.

"Yes, sir!" I laughed and, despite being eaten up with curiosity, I carefully put it in my pocket next to the envelope he'd given me yesterday.

Opening both would be the first thing I did when we returned. In the distance, clouds began to gather and move in our direction, a sign of the restless motion of nature and time, which I wished I could pause right there and then...

Kostas Krommydas

7 months later

I OPENED MY EYES and slowly turned towards Antonis. He was peacefully asleep. Outside, dawn was beginning to break, and although we were well into spring, the evenings were cold. I carefully covered him with the blanket, and my gaze was lost in the view gradually emerging through the open windows of the attic. The morning mist restricted visibility but created a feeling of snugness at the same time. As soon as the spring sun burst into view, it would clear the fog and highlight the intense shades of green coloring the land.

The mockingbirds flitted restlessly here and there. It was nearly mating season, and their song was more poignant than ever. The last few months had been the best months of my life. Antonis spent half the week at Evora and the other half in Thessaloniki. Often, when my schedule would allow it, I would accompany him in his travels all over Macedonia. By now, we had toured almost the entire region.

The note he had given me at Armchair contained the most beautiful lines I had ever received. His words reflected everything I felt, too. The envelope he had given me as a birthday present enclosed two tickets to Portugal. Our trip included two days in the town of Evora. He knew how much I had wanted to visit it. There, we also discovered the meaning of the word in Portuguese: "of the yew trees." It was not too far from our meaning of Evora, with its references to the cool shade of trees, besides the definition of the perfect timing.

Portugal had enchanted me, and I had fallen in love with the town of Evora, the namesake of my slice of heaven. Picturesque, with a long history, it looked like it had stepped out of a fairy tale. The landscape there was beautiful and well-looked after, despite the wildfires that had struck the wider region, consuming a large part of its forests. Unfortunately, around the world, wildfires would break out every summer, destroying vast tracts of virgin forests. The scarred land would then be turned into farmland or, even worse, tourist resorts. We discovered that there, too, the drought was causing many problems. As part of his job, Antonis had spoken to the locals extensively about the climate changes of recent years.

We spent our time in Portugal visiting scenic villages in an electric car we'd rented. If I ever had to leave Greece, I would like to live in a place like Portugal. Antonis had adored it, as well as many of the people we met during our stay. I loved that he was so open and kind-hearted. The more I got to know him, the more I fell in love with him and surrendered to our bond, which grew more profound with each passing day.

He had put together a photo album of our trip, and I had felt embarrassed when I saw it. It was as if he had made a movie of mostly my moments, which he had managed to capture without me even being aware of it.

Every month, I tried to keep a week free from work and spend it with Antonis. Unfortunately, he was due to leave for an extended business trip to Brazil. Although I really wanted to accompany him, I had already booked a group session that was impossible to cancel. We had, however, agreed to spend August together sailing around the Greek islands. He loved wandering the seas and exploring locations that were only accessible by water.

We decided to spend the next two days at home, as it would be nearly two weeks before we could be together again. I was delighted to see him enjoy his stays at Evora—our "slice of heaven," as he called it. He liked gardening, and was good with his hands, allowing my father, who was busy with community matters, to catch his breath. Antonis helped him considerably with the recycling initiative, too. Gradually, everyone in the village began contributing to the proper disposal of waste, which was now taken elsewhere in special trucks and in an organized manner.

The winter this year had been milder, with little snow, but our fireplace had never stopped roaring. Gathering wood in the forest was an activity we both enjoyed. We used to double up with laughter every time Voras would pick up a twig to carry it back home, a useful member of our little pack. Even a few nights ago, during a chilly spell, we had sat beside the fire, enjoying the warmth and coziness of the bright flames.

The incident with the wolves, however, was never far from my thoughts. I often caught myself trying to discern whether the distant cries at night were the howls of dogs or other wild animals. Still, we never heard anyone mention coming across the pack, or any signs of attacks on a deer herd. It was as if the wolves had withdrawn to the depths of the thick forest after that incident.

Our favorite evenings besides those spent in one another's company were when our friends joined us, and Antonis cooked for us. A couple of times, he had helped out Eva at the restaurant, and the results of their collaboration had been exceptional. I had no idea what the future held for us, but the present was wonderful. We took care to live in the moment, savoring it thoroughly, and taking things one day at a time.

"Good morning," Antonis whispered hoarsely, half-opening his eyes.

"Good morning," I replied, and stroked his cheek.

"You're up first, again," he said, and stretched.

I snuggled up against him and gently kissed his neck. He instantly responded and put his arms around me to pull me on top of him. I didn't need to be persuaded. The desire between us was always simmering, ready to be set alight by the simplest gesture. Our bodies, entangled in constant motion, were the harbinger of a perfect start to the day. Another perfect day...

As we ate the breakfast Antonis had prepared, the mist began to lift, and the sun's rays slowly dried out the dew that had sprinkled everything. On spring mornings, I loved to walk barefoot on the grass outside and feel the moisture soak the soles of my feet.

Antonis had adopted my daily routine, and we nearly always began our day at dawn with a walk in the woods. There is no hour more creative than the early morning. Then we would come home and only start our work and chores at noon. It's a privilege to start your day early with an activity you enjoy. Today, however, we decided to be more laid back and enjoy a long breakfast at home. It's important to be disciplined and follow a schedule, but not become its slave.

"Eva wants us to go over for dinner. Her new boyfriend will be there, and she wants you to meet him," I said as I scrolled through my messages.

Antonis nodded, liking the idea. Then, still hungry, he decided to make another omelet with the eggs a friend had brought from the village the previous day. We had been eating heartily and talking about his trip to Brazil when my ringtone interrupted us. I picked up my phone and saw it was my father.

Before I could even say hello, I was assaulted by a torrent of words. It was impossible to understand what he was saying. I asked him to calm down and explain more slowly, and only then was I able to grasp what he was saying with such anger. I felt a knot form in my stomach as I listened. A shepherd had informed him that he had spotted some hunters in a pickup truck on one of the more secluded forest trails. Evidently, they were poachers going on a hunt. There had been similar incidents in the past, but I believed that the strict laws against hunting in the area had put a stop to it. The forests had been declared a nature reserve and a breeding place for protected wild species.

As soon as I understood the location where the poachers had been sighted, I told my father we would pick him up in a few minutes, and hung up. He had notified the forest rangers, but they would need some time to get here.

Antonis, listening to our conversation, looked on in despair, and urged me to go at once. His urgency did not leave me enough time to consider the possibility of waiting for the rangers and heading there with them. Without a word, I hurriedly got ready, although I had my doubts about whether we should arrive on the scene first. In the end, I did not voice my thoughts.

"I can't understand these people. As if it being a protected nature reserve is not enough, it's not even hunting season!" he fumed.

"Let's hope the shepherd was mistaken," I said as I pulled on my walking boots.

I locked up Voras inside the house to keep him from following us, and we set off.

A few minutes later, we were on our way to the village to pick up my father. We met him at the square, and he hurried into the car. He knew the area we were heading to well. It was about half an hour from the main road, but to get there faster, we decided to take a dirt road through the woods. It was more challenging terrain, but shorter. As we began to make our way up the slope across from the village, we discovered that the mist had not lifted here. The drop at one side of the road was steep, and we were forced to slow down.

My father advised us to be careful, as we had no idea what kind of people we were dealing with. Given the proximity of the border, there was a chance they could be drug traffickers. In that case, we would let the police do their job. We had been faced with similar unpleasant incidences in the past. On the other hand, the unscrupulous poachers were responsible for the fact that many species were in danger of becoming extinct, particularly birds. It was ironic that so many of them thought of themselves as environmentalists. Under the delusion that they were protecting the forest, they slaughtered anything that crossed their path. All they wanted was to show off their hunting prowess to others of their ilk, stuffing their fridges with prey that ended up in the garbage. They were so ruthless that they would even kill in nature reserves and during the reproduction season.

At some point, my father asked Antonis to slow down and turn into a narrow dirt track that barely fit the car. "They went this way," he said, pointing to the tire tracks and the crushed grass.

A little further down the track, we came across a pickup truck parked at the edge of the forest. The fog here was thinner, and we had better visibility. Wisps of mist curled through the branches, making the landscape seem dreamlike. We pulled over and carefully stepped out of the car, observing the parked vehicle. A portable dog kennel was in the truck bed, giving weight to the claims of the shepherd.

Here, the forest grew thick, oak trees and firs alternating as if a divine hand had planted them in a row. Ferns, vibrant green and bushy, covered nearly every inch of ground. The trodden ferns indicated the way the poachers had gone.

"Follow me," my father whispered. "I think I know where they're headed. This road leads to the Valley, where many animals find shelter. We'll take a shortcut to catch up with them."

Although we hesitated, we followed him, ears pricked for any sound that might betray their presence. We reached a spot where the path split in two, and my father examined the footprints on the ground. "They split up here. It looks like they know the area, so they're probably not strangers. I think we should split up, too. You two go one way, and I go the other. After a couple of kilometers, both paths end up in the Valley."

There was no way I was letting my father go on his own. He was getting old and I did not want him to confront the poachers on his own. Antonis sensed it and spoke before I could. "Thomas, sir, I think that it's best if Ariadne comes with you, and I take the other path."

My father hesitated for a moment but, seeing that Antonis would brook no argument, agreed.

"Don't veer from the path, Antonis. Turn right when you reach the end of the path, and we'll meet there. The terrain is easy. If you come across one of them, don't get into an argument; just call us, so they understand that you are not alone."

I don't know why, but at that moment, I regretted coming here without waiting for the rangers. My father did not seem to share my worry, and was already setting off. I moved closer to Antonis. "You don't have to go. I think it would have been best not to have come on our own. I'll tell my dad we should turn back and wait at their truck. The rangers will be here soon."

Antonis cupped my face, and pressed a soothing kiss to my forehead. "I know you're worried, but it will be fine. What matters is getting to the poachers before they make a kill. We could never forgive ourselves if we let that happen."

I glanced back at my father—he was almost gone from view. I reached up to Antonis and gave him a kiss. Then I turned to go, but he held me back. "Be careful..." he whispered. "I love you."

He dropped my hand and walked away without looking back. For a moment, I stood there, breathless, watching him walk away, unable to believe he'd said the words. We often talked of love, of how great it was to be able to love, but we had never said "I love you" to one another. And yet, all my teachings were based on how we should not only learn how to love, but express it, too. Antonis had not just found the courage to say the words, he'd said them as if he believed them.

I found my own courage, and prepared to run after Antonis and tell him that I loved him, too. But my father called me over to him, and then Antonis was out of sight, and the moment was over.

"That's a happy smile if I ever saw one!" my father said, as I reached his side, still replaying Antonis's confession in my mind. As soon as we met up at the other end of the path, I vowed I would pull him aside and speak the words back to him. I needed him to know how I felt, that it was the same as his feelings for me.

As we walked along the path, vigilantly on the lookout for any sign of the poachers, I became angry with myself for not chasing after Antonis when I had the chance. And I was growing increasingly uncertain about coming out here to search for the poachers instead of waiting for the rangers. But Antonis had been right—the rangers weren't here, and someone needed to stop them before an innocent animal was harmed.

We had walked for some time before my father called the head ranger again to explain where we were. He reassured us that two of his men were not far away. Finally, I was able to drop my guard and relax a little, knowing that backup was on the way.

After some time, we finally arrived at the Valley. I had not been here in years, and had forgotten the breathtaking splendor of this place. Enclosed by tall mountains, the Valley was about the size of a football pitch. A river cut through it, and tall grass stretched along its banks until they met the massive firs at the foothills of the surrounding peaks.

My father had told me that, a long time ago, the villagers used to farm here, but it was still notable how the forest had not reoccupied this patch of land. Other, infertile fields that we owned near the village had been overtaken by the forest in the space of a few years. Nature was snatching up what mankind had stolen, but had shown no interest in this spot.

The Valley was technically private property, but the rumor was that the multiple heirs with claims to the land were unable to agree on what to do with it. And so here it stayed, untouched, a little piece of heaven amidst the rugged wilderness.

The air was clear, and a sense of peace reigned over the Valley. Only birdsong could be heard. A cool breeze suddenly gusted down the mountain, making me shiver. A little further up stood a rocky outcropping, where the snow used to melt only at the end of June. Now, when I looked towards it, not a trace of white could be seen.

We had not stopped walking for a moment, and my father was panting heavily. Our eyes roamed over the flat land, trying to detect some movement. I looked at the slope across the valley and came to a sudden stop. I squinted as I carefully peered between the trees. I gestured to my father to turn in that direction. Right then, a dog trotted out of the woods and started barking the moment it noticed us.

My father shouted at the man. He seemed to hesitate and raised his gun as he turned towards us but lowered it as soon as he saw us. I felt a jolt of fear for a moment. Gesturing at us, the man asked us what we wanted. My father told him the rangers had been notified. He slung his gun over his shoulder and slowly walked towards us. When he was a few steps away, we recognized him. He was married to a local, and they visited the village in the summer.

"This is a protected area, and it's not hunting season," my father said sternly. "You shouldn't be here."

"I'm not hunting," the man said. "I'm out walking in the woods, and I took the gun for protection. They told me wolves had been sighted in the area. Does it look like I've killed anything?"

"Not yet. Where's your friend?" my father asked, while his hound paced closer and sniffed at us.

For a second, the man was at a loss for words. "What friend? I'm on my own," he said, but the lie was evident.

My father's phone rang again. It was the ranger, wanting to know where we were. My father turned towards the path. Before long, two rangers stepped out into the clearing. A wave of relief washed over me. They could now take over.

"Put your weapon down," one of the rangers called as they approached. "We're just here to talk."

Shakily, the man set his gun on the ground.

"Thank you," the ranger said, while his partner carefully retrieved the rifle. "Now, where is your partner? We saw two sets of footsteps, so we know you aren't alone."

The poacher said something, but his words were drowned out by the sudden crack of a gunshot ripping through the air.

Birds surged up in the air, abandoning the trees in terror. Horror gripped my heart. The sound was coming from the direction where Antonis should be. Without a moment's hesitation, I sprinted towards the sound. Neither the cries of my father nor the poacher's dog chasing me were enough to stop me. Like a wild animal, I ran up the path, the others struggling to keep up behind me. My heart was thumping fast enough to tear through my ribcage.

I guessed the direction of the path Antonis was supposed to be on and cut through the woods, sprinting through the tall firs to get there faster. I prayed I was going in the right direction.

I froze when I heard a second gunshot, closer this time. Faster, harder, I jumped over rocks and fallen tree trunks, unconscious of the branches tearing at my clothes and scratching my face and arms.

Abruptly, I came to a small clearing, and gasped at the sight before me. A man holding a rifle stood over a motionless body. Beside the body, a white stone was splattered with red drops. Tears filled my eyes as I approached the man on the ground. It was Antonis, lying on the blood-soaked grass.

My scream echoed all the way down the valley as I fell to my knees. Unable to understand what was happening, I hugged his body. I felt the faintest pulse throb in his neck. His blood warmed my hands as I cradled his head, desperately beseeching him to talk to me. The stranger came near me, but all I cared about was trying to understand how seriously Antonis was wounded.

Suddenly, I started to cry out for help, as if I were all alone. Everything around me turned dark, and I only raised my head when I sensed the others approaching. In shock, I asked the man with the gun what had happened, but he stood there motionless, unable to utter a word.

My father and the ranger hurried to my side, and with their help we lifted Antonis off the ground. "The vehicles aren't far," the ranger said. "We need to get him to the hospital."

"Quickly," I urged. "He's badly wounded."

"He'll be all right, ma'am," the ranger said, without much conviction.

The man was now crying out that he was sorry. His whole body shook as he explained he'd heard a sound and, turning in a panic, had fired his gun by accident. I ignored him, trying to keep my calm and thoughts in order. The clock was ticking against us, and all I cared about was saving Antonis. His blood filled my palms as the shrapnel had filled his head and his neck.

As we stumbled up the path, carrying Antonis between us and trying to jostle him as little as possible, I turned to look at the man who had shot him. He was nearly in tears now, and panting as he held up Antonis's right shoulder.

We pushed our way through the ferns. Soon, we arrived at the parking area, where the pickup truck, my car, and the ranger's van waited for us. "Take my truck," the man who'd shot Antonis said. "We can stretch him out on the bed." His voice was distorted through a haze of guilt and agony.

He and his partner hastily emptied the truck bed, and then helped us placed Antonis inside in the recovery position. I clambered onto the truck bed with my father, who was trying to tend to Antonis's wounds. The poacher who had shot Antonis took his seat behind the wheel, with one of the rangers sitting beside him. The other man was with the second ranger; they would stay behind and wait for the police to arrive and take their statements.

As we drove along the bumpy ground, Antonis's blood continued to flow, thankfully more slowly than before. I stripped down to my undershirt and used my blouse to make a rough bandage for his head. We drove over the bumpy ground, our bones jarring with every jolt. Holding Antonis's bandaged head in my hands, I looked at the stranger, who kept glancing at me through the rearview mirror, white-faced. I couldn't stand the sight of him, no matter how much he protested that it had been an accident. He had shot the man I loved more than anything in the world. I looked down at Antonis again, stroking his head and trying to revive him.

The ranger finally managed to get through to an ambulance on his phone, and arranged to meet them on the road to the hospital in Edessa. Antonis remained unconscious despite my efforts, but I could still detect a pulse, although weak. The minutes it took us to reach the main road felt like centuries.

Finally, the truck burst onto the asphalt, and the spring breeze turned into a gust of cold wind that made me shiver in my thin camisole. My father immediately pulled off his jacket and wrapped it around my shoulders. I remembered then the day Antonis had saved my life, carrying me on his back through the snow. I remembered how I had hoped I would be able to repay him someday. I wished I could now breathe into him the life he had gifted me with his kiss. Just the thought that he might not make it sent daggers through my heart.

I had lost all sense of time, but the blare of the ambulance siren gave me a flicker of hope that we might make it. A police car followed closely behind. All I wanted was to get into the ambulance and reach the hospital quickly.

We pulled over so as not to waste time. My father agreed to stay behind to escort the police to the clearing in the forest. The ranger came with us, sitting beside the ambulance driver, while I climbed into the back with Antonis and the paramedics.

They gave first aid to Antonis and tried to stop the bleeding as we drove off. One of the paramedics pulled an oxygen mask over Antonis's face to help him breathe. Antonis was paler than I'd ever seen him, and looked oddly peaceful, like in the mornings when I would wake up before him and gaze at him. The only difference was that by now he would have opened his beautiful eyes and smiled at me...

Evora

TIME WAS GUSHING past us like a landslide sweeping up everything in its path. We arrived at the hospital in Edessa, where the ER was on standby. The paramedics, who never stopped tending to Antonis, didn't look optimistic. They evaded my relentless questions and just advised me to be patient.

It was evident that the hospital had been briefed on our arrival, and a handful of people in medical scrubs were waiting at the drop off bay. Swiftly, they placed Antonis on a stretcher, and we all dashed through the doors, a doctor hurrying along beside the stretcher and shouting at everyone to clear the way.

They entered a surgery suite and told us to wait outside. A nurse pushed the swinging doors shut, but they did not close fully. Through the crack, I could see the medical staff prepping Antonis for surgery. The ranger and the man who had shot Antonis stood behind me. I hoped the poacher understood the enormity of what he'd done today, what havoc his thoughtless, selfish actions had unleashed on us.

The doctor's sudden shout made me jump. He was asking for the defibrillator, saying he could not detect a pulse. I felt my legs shake, ready to give wake. Someone closed the doors properly, and I lost all contact with them.

People were coming and going, but time stood still for me. In vain did I try to detect through the tumult what they were saying. I felt a hand on my shoulder, but when I saw it was the poacher, I shook it off. I had nothing to say to him. I just wanted Antonis, alive.

While doctors entered and left the room, I paced the corridor outside, trying to think of what I should do. The ranger walked up to me and handed me a phone to talk to my father. I struggled to keep my cool, but I could hear the shakiness in my voice as I told him what had happened since we'd left in the ambulance. He told me the police would be arriving shortly to arrest the man who had shot Antonis.

I glanced at the man as I spoke. He was sitting on a bench, elbows on his knees, holding his head in his hands and staring at the floor. He appeared to be in despair, but I had no space in my heart right now for empathy; all I felt was rage when I looked at him.

I answered my father's questions mechanically, then hung up and handed back the ranger's phone. A minute later, a nurse hurried out of the room. Unable to take the uncertainty anymore, I stepped in front of her, blocking her way. "Please, tell me what's happening," I pleaded.

"He's stabilized," she said, and I nearly collapsed in relief. "The doctor will brief you shortly. We will probably have to move him to the hospital in Thessaloniki."

At least he was alive.

Evora

"How serious is it?" I asked anxiously.

"The doctors will brief you," was all she said.

I stood there, watching her walk down the corridor. The air in the hospital was stifling. I walked to the windows to catch a breath of fresh air. As the minutes slowly ticked by, I felt my anxiety mounting, knowing that this hospital was not equipped to deal with such serious incidents.

My legs still shook with shock, and I decided to sit down. I walked to the bench. The poacher was no longer there and the ranger, his back turned to me, was still on the phone. Had the man escaped while the ranger wasn't looking?

I felt my temples throb with rage. As if what he'd done was not enough, now he was trying to avoid arrest. I looked all around me, and I was just about to summon the ranger when I saw him coming down the corridor, two bottles of water in his hands.

I calmed down a little. He handed me a bottle, and I reluctantly took it because my mouth was dry. Although I had been wrong in thinking he had run away, bottomless fury still raged inside me at the very sight of him.

We sat on opposite benches, an awkward silence between us while I thought of what to say. "How did it happen?" I finally asked, as I placed the half-empty bottle on the floor.

His eyes full of tears, he looked at me and pulled his chair closer to the table separating us.

"It was an accident. I'm so sorry. I was walking through the trees when I heard a noise and turned around abruptly. Before I could see what it was, I was so startled I pressed the trigger. It was so foggy I could not see him. It was all a blur." His eyes widened in terror. "I was so scared and could not tell what was happening. The rifle went off accidentally," he said with great difficulty.

"Guns don't go off on their own! You shouldn't have been there in the first place!" I spat out through gritted teeth. "You went to the forest to kill, in secret, knowing that hunting was prohibited. And now a man is at death's door because of your irresponsibility."

My loud, angry words caught the attention of everyone standing near us. I was so enraged I could have torn his flesh with my nails. The ranger came beside me and put his hand on my shoulder, trying to calm me down.

"You are right, absolutely right. I wish I could turn back time," the man said, bowing his head.

Although he looked remorseful, I could not accept what he had done. It made no difference to me; it was as if he had murdered Antonis in cold blood.

Just then, two policemen approached us and, after a quick word with the ranger, came to stand by the man.

"Did you shoot the man in the forest?" one of them asked.

"Yes, but it was an accident."

"What's your name?" the other policeman asked in a stern voice.

"Pavlos Lambrakis," he replied.

Before he could say anything else, the policeman took him by the arm and forced him to stand up. "You are under arrest, sir. You can tell the public prosecutor the rest. Follow us." Then, turning to me, he added, "You'll need to come to the station with us to make a statement, ma'am."

I shook my head. "No, there's no way I'm leaving right now. My partner is fighting for his life as we speak. I can't abandon him. Your statement will have to wait."

The policeman didn't look pleased about this, but the ranger had some quiet words with him, and eventually he gave me a curt nod. The police put the man in handcuffs and placed him between them as they walked toward the exit.

The poacher looked back at me imploringly, as if asking for my help. I turned my back to him and walked towards the door of the ER. At that moment, I did not care about statements or what would happen to Pavlos Lambrakis. He deserved everything that was happening to him.

I asked the ranger if I could use his phone and called Eva. My father had notified her, and she was on her way to the hospital. I asked her to drive carefully because I did not want another tragedy to befall us.

A few minutes of indescribable angst passed until the doctor attending Antonis finally stepped into the corridor. "Good afternoon," he greeted me solemnly, and came closer. "What is your relationship to the patient?"

I felt my knees buckle again. "I am his partner," I answered in a shaky voice, sensing that he was not bearing good news.

"We managed to stabilize him. That's the most important thing right now. That he made it here alive is a sign that he is fighting hard. In a few minutes, a special ambulance will carry him to Thessaloniki. His condition is critical. Unfortunately, we can't do anything else for him here. When they told me that we were receiving a patient with a bullet wound to the head, I asked for a special ambulance immediately."

"How is he, though? Tell me! Will he make it?"

The doctor looked around us, and lowered his voice. "As I said, his condition is critical. His most serious injury is the one to the head. There is a piece of shrapnel we were not able to remove. We were able to tend to everything else. I hope he improves."

He turned to walk away, but I blocked him. "I want to go with him. Can I?" I implored, knowing that whatever the answer, I would follow them anyway.

"That will be up to the doctor with the transit unit. Someone also needs to inform his family, because they will need to decide..." He seemed to regret speaking, and fell silent, turning his eyes to the floor.

"Decide what, doctor?" I asked, and gripped his hand in fear, waiting for his answer.

"I'm afraid I can't tell you more. We need to get him ready. The special ambulance will be arriving any minute now. Let's take it one step at a time. As no one else is here, the nurse will bring you his things. It would also be useful to arrange for a blood donation. He will need it." He gently removed my hand and returned to the ER.

I suddenly felt as if everything around me had gone dark. My brain refused to accept that things were so serious. I remembered that someone needed to notify Antonis's parents. I did not have their number, and I wondered how I could contact them.

A nurse approached me, holding a bag with Antonis's blood-stained clothes. A smaller bag contained his phone, which was smashed—either from his fall in the woods, or when we put him up on the truck bed, I didn't know. I desperately looked around for the ranger, hoping to borrow his phone again, but he was nowhere to be seen.

In the distance, I made out a figure hurrying towards me. Like a guardian angel, Eva was rushing towards me down the corridor. I fell into her arms, and she hugged me, crying and asking me what happened. I tried to explain as calmly as I could, but I did not have a chance to say much before the doctor came out again to inform me they were ready to transport Antonis. He was already on his way to the ambulance, which would soon depart. I was not allowed to ride with him.

I grabbed Eva's hand, and we both ran to the exit to get in her car and follow the ambulance. We almost missed it in traffic, but we finally made it. Soon we were driving right behind them. Luckily, the other cars parted as soon as they heard the siren. Keeping our hazard lights on, we finally reached the highway and sped up.

Eva drove, and I thought more about how to contact Antonis's parents. Knowing their name and address, I found their number, and when I called, I tried to sound as collected as possible. A long time ago, Antonis had skyped them, and we had met that way. When I told his father what had happened, he seemed unable to believe it. I finally managed to convey the severity of the situation to his mother. I wished I did not have to reveal the whole truth over the phone, but every minute counted.

We hung up soon after, as they needed to get down to the ferry dock on the little island of Thasos where they lived before they missed the last boat to shore. Then I started calling all my friends to ask them to donate blood. Most of them had not heard the news, and I had to repeat my story often. I desperately tried to sound calm. I also called his work in Thessaloniki and informed his colleagues. No one wanted to believe it was true, but they all wanted to help any way they could.

Evora

The scene on the road was touching. The cars, hearing the sound of the siren that split the air, pulled aside to let us through, both on the highway and in the city.

It took us more than an hour to reach the hospital. Everything there happened so quickly I barely caught a glimpse of Antonis as they moved him inside. I ran ahead, hoping to at least touch his hand for a moment, but it was not to be. They indicated where we should wait, and we reluctantly went to the waiting room outside the operating theatres.

I was exhausted, but could not sit down. I had a bite of something Eva had brought, and began the torturous wait for news. His parents were already on their way. We received dozens of well wishes on Eva's phone. I could only hope the outpouring of love would be enough to turn the tides of this horrific day.

The thoughts swirling through my mind were a tangled web I could not order. I asked a nurse where the blood bank was. A few minutes later, I was sitting in an armchair being prepped by a nurse. I mechanically answered all her questions, as my thoughts wandered over the most beautiful moments Antonis and I had shared. I had not realized how much I loved him until I found him lying wounded on the forest floor.

The prick of the needle in my arm brought me back to the present. I watched my blood fill the vial, and hoped with all my heart and soul that Antonis would recover.

"All done," said the nurse, tidying away her instruments.

"Can I give more blood if need be?" I asked, despite knowing that was not possible.

She looked at me and smiled. "This will do for now. I wish everyone donated blood even once in their life. Few people know how much life just one vial of blood can give someone who needs it."

I felt guilty because I had not donated blood for a long time. We forget how precious such a small act can be for some people. Luckily, many friends and acquaintances had responded, so there should not be any problems as far as Antonis was concerned. Leaving the blood bank, I promised myself to donate blood at least once a year, hopefully more.

Eva had also decided to give blood, and I hugged her before she went into the clinic. "Thank you, sis."

"Everything will be fine, Ariadne. We must be strong now," she said, stroking my arm before she stepped inside.

I sank into a seat and held my head in despair, waiting for Eva to be done. Just that morning, we were enjoying our peaceful life at Evora, and now we were sunk in the depths of a nightmare. I called my father on Eva's phone and asked him to bring me some clothes. My trousers were stained with mud and Antonis's blood. I would need them in any case because something told me we would be here for a while.

As soon as my sister left the blood bank, we went back to the sitting room outside the operating theatres in case there was any news. The room was full of people waiting to hear the fate of their loved ones, anxiety etched on their faces. I felt as if we were all one, and the glances we exchanged said more than a thousand words could have.

I leaned against the head of the armchair and briefly closed my eyes. Eva, always by my side, held my hand and tried to give me courage. I thought I was strong enough to handle stressful situations, but everything that had happened exceeded my reserves of strength. Worry, guilt, and fatigue were all sabotaging my efforts to be strong. I must not give up. I struggled, in vain, to convince myself that everything would turn out fine.

A few minutes later, I opened my eyes when I heard the voice of a doctor looking for Antonis's next of kin. I jumped up and went to explain that at present I was the only one there. Eva came to stand beside me and squeezed my hand.

"His condition is critical," the doctor informed us, evidently troubled. "We have managed to stabilize him, and that's something. But he lost a lot of blood and is very weak. Our colleagues in Edessa removed all the shrapnel except the fragment at the back of his brain."

"Which you will remove. Right?" I said, and held my breath.

The look that came over his face was like a punch to the gut. "One of the fragments is lodged close to the cerebellum and appears to have caused considerable damage to it. It is impossible to attempt to remove it at this stage. His body is so weak, it could not withstand such a long operation."

"So, what's going to happen?" I asked shakily.

"I wish I had an answer for you. We will monitor him, and then a decision will have to be made by his family."

I faltered. My mind refused to understand what the doctor was trying to tell me.

"What kind of decision, doctor?" Eva prompted.

"I understand that you are worried, but at this stage, I would advise being patient and seeing how his body reacts. Then we can discuss it again. I should stress, however, that his condition is extremely serious."

It was one of those moments where every cell in your body refuses to accept reality. The doctor walked away, and I felt as if he were carrying all my hopes with him. My sister gently pulled me back to the bank of seats against the wall. My mind was in turmoil, pandemonium, and I did not know how to react. On the one hand, I had to be strong, but on the other hand, I wanted to scream in despair, give voice to the rage choking me. Something inside me was howling in pain, but I would not let it come to the surface, maybe because I was still hoping that someone else would turn up and tell us everything would be fine.

I was desperate to see Antonis, but the doctors would not let me. The head nurse made me understand that the Intensive Care Unit was overwhelmed with other severe cases too, and they had suspended visiting hours. I tried to find out if there was a hospital that would be better suited to his needs, but any thought of transporting him had to be given up due to the fragility of his condition. His body could not withstand being moved again.

Later, some of his colleagues and my friends arrived to donate blood. Eva was always by my side, giving me courage. I saved every ounce of strength left in me for the moment I would meet his parents. If I felt this way, how would the people who had brought him into the world feel? Earlier, they had called to say that they had arrived at the port of Kavala and were on their way to Thessaloniki. They had also contacted his sister in France, and she would be catching the next flight to Greece.

It was nearly afternoon, and unfortunately we had no more news. In the meantime, my father had arrived, and I could finally change clothes. I gave my father my clothes to carry back to Avgerinos, along with the bundle of Antonis's things.

Eva booked us a room in a nearby hotel, although I knew there was no way I would be leaving the hospital until I had at least seen Antonis. As the person closest to him, I wanted to be calm, but something had shattered inside me, and I knew an outburst would come sooner or later. In this kind of situation, you always wonder how it could be happening to you, but nothing could change what had happened.

The police in Edessa had arrested the two men. My father told me that they had appeared before the public prosecutor, and were now being held in custody. They would appear before the examining magistrate the following morning. Everyone involved in the circumstances leading to the shooting had to give a statement to the examining magistrate, as would the doctors attending Antonis in Edessa and Thessaloniki. I did not know much about the law. From what my father told me, the two men would have to convince the magistrate that it had been an accident and that Lambrakis had no intention of shooting Antonis.

Somewhat calmer, I thought about the way Lambrakis had reacted to what had happened, and despite my anger, I could see how worried he was and how he had tried to help as much as he could. As much as I wanted to hate him for what he'd done, it was becoming more and more clear to me that there was a good chance it really had been an accident. It wasn't as if he had a reason to shoot Antonis.

It was time to meet Antonis's parents. His mother could barely stand while the doctor in charge informed them about his condition. The look in her eyes as she listened to him pierced my heart, and I turned my face away to hide my tears. I tried to console them, and it felt like a struggle to give myself courage, too. His father appeared more in command of his feelings, and my father was talking to him, trying to alleviate his fears. Both his parents were elderly and thankfully had family in the city.

A little later, a doctor informed us again that due to some problems in the Intensive Care Unit, we would be unable to see him. All visits had been suspended for today. I could see the agony of a mother wanting to see her child, and my heart broke alongside hers. After the shooting, I'd thought no one else could be suffering as much as I was. The moment I held his mother in my arms, however, I understood how terrible it is to fear for your child's life. That love is probably the deepest bond ever created by nature.

She reminded me so much of my mother, never dropping a single hint that she might consider me responsible in any way. She could have easily said that it would all have been avoided had we let the authorities do their job, but she said nothing. Even when I said something along those lines, she blamed it all on an evil twist of fate. Maybe she instinctively sensed how much I loved him and that I, too, was now suffering. I pulled away, unable to hold back my tears.

Seeing the anguish in her eyes, the hope that Antonis might gain even one more day of life, I thought that a mother is not merely the person who brings a child into the world. A mother is a woman who will not hesitate to shed her blood for the child, who will set ego aside so that the child's self might flourish. She is love personified, because she can love a child in the purest and strongest way. She is the woman whose life becomes more beautiful after the child's birth. She will never tell her child how much pain she felt, what tears she shed. She is the one who soothes her child's every pain in a magical way, telling him how everything will be all right, even while her heart is breaking. A mother is not the woman who gives birth, but who acts guided by her love.

We decided after some time that there was no point in his parents spending the night waiting at the hospital. His mother was adamant that she did not want to leave. I finally managed to persuade her to go by reassuring her that I would not leave the hospital, not even for a second. I promised to stay until the following morning, when I would have to see the examining magistrate in Edessa. They agreed to leave with their relatives, and I promised to keep them updated on any news.

My father had to return to the village because there was only one waitress at the restaurant. Not that anyone really cared about that at the moment, but several other matters had to be settled, and I saw no reason for him to remain at the hospital. Eva tried to stay with me, but I insisted she go to the hotel and get some sleep.

Night was falling by the time everyone left. I was just settling in for the evening when the head nurse approached me. "Things have calmed down in the ICU, so later I might be able to let you in to see him for a couple of minutes."

It was the first moment of joy I'd felt after a long while, but before I could get too excited, she added, "Please, don't tell anyone else. I'll tell the other two visitors waiting here, but no others. We have had many problems at the unit today, that's why we suspended visiting hours, but now things are starting to calm down. I expect I'll be able to let you inside in a couple of hours, but I'll let you know closer to the time. You can go outside and get some air, if you like. You've been here for so long."

I struggled to find the words to thank her. "Thank you. I appreciate your thinking of me. The truth is that I want to see Antonis more than anything in the world."

"I understand. Believe me," the nurse replied, and squeezed my hand before walking away.

The idea of taking a walk in the fresh air was tempting, but I couldn't shake the fear that, if I left for even a moment, I would miss the opportunity to see Antonis. I needed to hold his hand, to let him know I was there for him, to infuse him with all the strength inside of me. Looking around me, I decided to stay put.

I made a quick trip to the cafeteria to get a juice and a sandwich. I had hardly had a bite to eat all day. I hurried back to the waiting room and began pacing as I made nervous calls to check in on everyone. Eva was safely in her hotel room, about to turn in for the night. Antonis's parents were at their relatives' house. And my father had made it back to our village with no problems, although he noted that no one had seen Voras since noon. I told him not to worry—Voras tended to wander, but he always came back before too long. We agreed to talk the following morning to arrange our meeting up in Edessa to give our statements.

Phone calls completed, I sat down on a hard couch, then stretched out in a less-than-comfortable resting position. But I must have underestimated how tired I was, because the next thing I knew the nurse was gently shaking my shoulder to wake me. "I'm sorry it took so long," she said quietly. "You can see him now."

I immediately sprang to my feet, exhaustion banished from my mind, and hurried after her. Following hospital procedures, I pulled on an isolation gown, mask, gloves, and shoe covers. Then we went through a wide double door into the intensive care unit. I kept my eyes on the nurse leading the way, averting my gaze from the patients on either side of me. The sounds of medical machinery disturbed the hushed atmosphere. Behind me came the few other people who had waited with me to see their loved ones.

When we reached the end of a long corridor, the nurse came to a stop and pointed at Antonis, intubated on the bed. I'd thought I would be strong, but I was wrong. Seeing him pale and immobile, I froze, unable to take a single step.

"If you are not feeling well, we can go back outside," the nurse whispered.

I shook my head. "No, I'm fine," I stammered with great difficulty, and pushed past her.

Timidly, I reached out to touch him. I wished I did not have to wear gloves so I could feel his hand against mine, his skin for just one second. His head was bandaged up, and so many tubes were attached to his body.

"Antonis," I whispered, even though I knew he was probably unable to hear me.

The nurse discreetly moved away to give me some time alone with him. I gently stroked his hand, the way we did every time we met. Except that now all I could feel was the harsh coldness around me and the monotonous beeping that was a constant reminder that Antonis's breathing was not his own. I so wanted to start talking to him in the hope that he could hear me and take heart from my presence, find the courage to fight his way to recovery. I could not. All I could do was gently stroke his hand and his forehead, praying for the slightest reaction.

From the corner of my eye, I saw the nurse approach and realized it was time to go. I wished I could spend the night lying down next to him, to sleep beside him and wake up together the following morning, to the sound of the mockingbirds singing outside our window...

I couldn't have slept for more than an hour on the couch in the waiting room. My inner turmoil, the shock of everything, and the noise of people coming and going made any sleep impossible. Although I was not really supposed to be there—visiting hours were officially over—no one said anything. Maybe they sensed that they would have to physically remove me. This was the place nearest to Antonis available to me, and I wasn't leaving until I had no choice.

Morning arrived far too quickly, and as much as I wanted to ignore the police's summons to Edessa to give my statement on the incident, I knew it was something that had to be done. I waited for Antonis's parents to arrive and take over my vigil before leaving for Edessa. They arrived with his sister, who had just flown in from France.

A quick meeting with the doctors before I left made us realize that there was not much more that could be done at the moment, medically speaking. At least his parents would be able to see him for a few minutes during the next visiting hours.

Evora

EVA AND HER BOYFRIEND drove me to Edessa, leaving early in the hopes of getting back to the hospital as quickly as possible. I sat in the back, exhausted, and thankfully managed to sleep during the entire drive. My father was waiting for us outside the building where I would make my statement. He had just finished giving his, and I followed him to the office of the examining magistrate.

A few minutes later, I was called in. I was impressed by the magistrate's appearance. I had expected to see an elderly man or woman, conservatively dressed. Instead, a relatively young, smartly-dressed woman was seated behind a desk, sporting a haircut that reminded me of an 80s pop star. She smiled at me and pointed to a chair opposite her desk. I sat down and narrated everything, exactly as it had happened.

I had been describing our arrival at the hospital in Thessaloniki when she interrupted me. "Everything you have said points to the defendant being constantly willing to help."

No matter how angry I was with Lambrakis, I had to tell the truth. "Yes, from the start, his actions indicated it was all an accident. He declared his remorse up until his arrest by the police. He was also willing to help. But he will be punished for what he did, won't he?"

"That is for the court to decide," she replied rather abruptly, without looking at me.

She then asked me more questions, such as whether I had seen the man before, and if there was any chance that Lambrakis and Antonis knew one another. "I can't think of any reason they would know each other," I told her.

"Had you met the defendant before yesterday?"

I was perplexed by the tone of her voice.

"No, never," I answered, trying to understand why she was asking me that.

She scribbled something on a notepad, still avoiding my eyes.

"The others stated that they heard two gunshots, a few seconds apart."

"That's right," I interrupted her before she could finish her thought. "The moment I heard the first gunshot, I started running, until I arrived at the spot where he'd shot Antonis."

I could tell that she was troubled, because she was rifling through her papers, searching for something. A thought crossed my mind that sent a chill through my heart. "Did he shoot Antonis twice?" I managed to ask her in a shaky voice.

"Ballistic analysis will give us a definite answer. The defendant claims that the first shot was directed at something he'd spotted in the forest. Please describe your exact relationship to the victim."

It was so hard to find the words that would capture the relationship between Antonis and me, the love between us. I gave up and settled for a brief description. "We've been together for almost a year."

"Do you live together?"

"Yes, for the most part."

"I understand this is difficult for you, but if you recall any details that might be escaping your notice right now, I would like you to contact me."

This time her voice held more warmth. Maybe she saw how overwhelmed I felt. She then asked me about Evora, and whether there had been any other poaching incidents in the past. I filled her in as best I could, and she took diligent notes as I spoke.

"When will the trial take place?" I asked, when her questions came to an end.

"You will be notified in time," she said, reverting to her formal tone. "Thank you. I hope your partner recovers, and all goes well."

I stood up and shook her hand warmly. I turned to go, but hesitated. "Could I ask you another question?"

"Certainly," she said, stretching.

"Will the man who shot him go to jail?"

"As I already said, that is for the court to decide. It's too early to draw any conclusions."

I said goodbye again and left the room. Outside, the doctor from Thessaloniki who had attended Antonis, was waiting to give his statement. He smiled and told me he would see me back at the hospital.

Evora

EDESSA WAS NOT FAR FROM AVGERINOS, so I decided to pop into the village and pick up a few things I needed and then drive back to Thessaloniki in my own car. I did not want to depend on my sister or my father, or to give them all this trouble, even though I knew they never minded helping me.

I had missed the morning visiting hours, so while my father drove us back to the village I called Antonis's parents to check in. They had been able to visit him, briefly, but nothing had changed since last night. I didn't know whether that was a good sign or a bad sign.

During the drive, my father informed me that Voras had not been seen since the previous day. For the first time, I felt worried. He had never gone missing for so long in the past.

When we arrived in Avgerinos, I asked my father to drive me straight to Evora so I could return to Thessaloniki as quickly as possible. As we crossed the village, a basketball rolled out in front of the car outside the gym. My father stepped on the breaks, allowing a little girl to pick up the ball. She cuddled it and stepped aside to let us drive through. Her grateful smile filled me with optimism. I watched her wave at us until we were out of sight. A wave of nostalgia swept me back to my childhood, and I saw myself in the girl's face.

"Don't you think you should spend the night here and get some rest, sweetheart?" my father asked, as we pulled up outside my home. "You can return to the hospital tomorrow morning."

We both climbed out of the car and faced each other in the garden.

"No, dad. I'll sort some things out and be back by lunchtime. I can't stay far from him."

"This is all my fault!" he suddenly exclaimed. "If I hadn't called you about the poachers, none of this would have happened." His voice was filled with guilt and despair.

I wrapped my arms around him. "It's not your fault. Those two monsters are to blame. Just them. No one else."

Leaning my head against his shoulder, I saw Voras slowly approaching in the distance. I instantly fell to my knees, opened my arms wide, and called him. He came to me, but not with the same joy he'd always shown after a long absence. I cupped his head and looked him in the eyes, telling him how much I missed him. He seemed strangely sad, as if he could sense what had happened.

I reassured my father I would call him if I needed anything, and said goodbye. Accompanied by Voras, we walked to the house. Terrible loneliness seized me. The sun shone, but inside me, I felt swamped by all the gloom in the world. Voras was whimpering sadly and only seemed to perk up a little when I filled his dish with food.

Evora

I stepped back inside the house to take a shower and quickly get ready to return to the hospital. I decided to cancel all my sessions for the rest of the month. I doubted I would have the stamina or presence of mind to focus on my work, and I preferred not to have to think about it while everything was still up in the air. I did not even know how long I would have to stay in Thessaloniki.

In the blink of an eye, everything had changed. I trembled at the thought that the phone might ring at any moment to give me the dreaded news. How wonderful it would be to hear Antonis's voice again and wake up from this nightmare.

I stepped into the shower and, as the water gushed down my back, I leaned against the stone wall and began to cry. I could not hold back my tears and sobbed for a long time, venting the pain I had struggled to keep buried inside me.

A few minutes later, calmer, I stepped out of the shower and hurriedly started packing. I picked up my phone and added the numbers of Antonis's parents and sister to my list of contacts. All my appointments were in my calendar app, and I now had to notify everyone that their sessions were canceled.

The road out of town took me past Eva's restaurant. My sister insisted on accompanying me, but I assured her I was fine on my own, and would call her if I needed anything. I kissed Voras, who was pleading with me to take him along, and handed him to my father, who had to restrain him to stop him from following me into the car.

Back on the highway, my anxiety returned. The last time I'd driven this route, it was chasing after an ambulance carrying the man I loved as he lay injured and bleeding out. Everything was so similar, I could almost hear the ambulance siren. I stopped at a traffic light and looked at my phone, which was blinking. Eva had sent a message. "I love you, sis. Don't ever forget that."

Even though my mind was elsewhere, Eva's words gave me strength. Feeling the support of my family at this moment was so important, sensing the protective embrace of their love.

As I drove, I began to remember everything that Antonis had done for me. Over the years, I had realized that everyone expresses their feelings differently. Knowing how much love there was between us, we had set our egos aside. We made no compromises or sacrifices. Usually, people who love each other push away the thought that their relationship might end one day. It is impossible to let yourself go and surrender to the wonder of love if you think of its end from the start. Love does not end; randomness, and not necessity, is what determines its hold over you. Our random meeting had been colored by moments of tension and anxiety from the start.

It is easy to give without love, but almost impossible to love without giving. The experience of loving is the greatest reward in itself. I was so grateful for that. Antonis filled every void inside me, and I still could not believe that our relationship would end this way, so suddenly and tragically. Before Antonis came into my life, I had been under the illusion that I could tread my life's path on my own, experiencing love in its more platonic forms, even when it culminated in carnal pleasure. People try to find an ideal other half, but are not willing to work to create their ideal love. We might not be perfect, but our love can be. It is up to the individual to decide whether they will unconditionally surrender to its magic or not.

For Antonis and me, every day was a new start. There were moments when I felt that he had gathered all my pieces and laid them out in the right order. Inside me, I begged that his recovery would be swift, that it would be a new start that would make us even stronger.

I arrived at the hospital in the early afternoon and immediately made my way to the waiting room. Exhausted, Antonis's parents and sister had left to get some rest. I made my way to the doctors' consultation rooms to find out if there was any news. The doctor who had attended Antonis the previous day had just returned from Edessa, where he had gone to make a statement.

It did not take me long to understand that the news would not be good.

"How is he today, doctor?"

"There's been no change. I briefed his sister earlier, as we agreed not to tell his parents the whole truth. Especially his father, who has heart issues." He stopped to consult some medical charts, then looked at me again.

"I would like to know the whole truth," I insisted.

I could not live in ignorance. Whatever the prognosis, I wanted to know so I could better manage both my feelings and the feelings of those around me.

"As I said from the start, this is a complicated case. The shrapnel has caused extensive brain damage. The part of the brain where the fragment is lodged puts any attempts to remove it out of the question."

"You can operate later, though, right? When he is stronger?"

"We are not considering that option."

"Meaning?" I asked, as his words hammered my mind.

"Our hands are tied."

"I'm not sure I understand. Are you telling me that nothing can be done for him?"

"I'm afraid so."

"So, there is no hope of recovery?"

"Medically speaking, and based on all the test results, it would be a miracle if he recovered."

I froze. "How is that possible?" I stammered, looking away.

I refused to accept that all hope was lost, that he would never speak to me again, never look into my eyes.

"I wish things were different. I'm so sorry," I heard the doctor say.

Rage and despair bubbled inside me, making me want to scream. I choked the emotions down and struggled to collect myself. "So, what happens next?"

The doctor hesitated, but I was staring at him with such force that he had to give me an answer. "We are doing everything we can to keep him alive. He still responds to some stimuli."

Refusing to accept it, I still hoped that Antonis might make it deep inside me. Seeing my devastation, the doctor continued. "We will give him the necessary medication to protect him from any other complications."

"Until?" I prompted.

His eyes gave me the answer that I did not want to hear. My body suddenly grew heavy, as if weighted down to the chair by thick chains. I could not move.

"I understand how difficult this is for you," he said sympathetically. "I wish there was something we could do, some way we could help him recover. You said you wanted to know the truth, so I need to tell you that, medically speaking, there is almost no hope."

"How long will he stay here?" I asked in a shaky voice.

The doctor raised his palms, and I thought I heard him say, "Until the end."

Summoning every ounce of strength in me, I stood up and turned to go outside and wait for the next visiting hours.

"There is something else I would like to discuss with you," he said, before I could step outside.

"Please do."

He seemed to regret having spoken, and made a reassuring gesture. "It's not urgent. We can talk in a couple of days, when we have a clearer view of the situation."

There was no way I could leave his office now without finding out what he wanted to say. Any chance of an improvement glowed like a glimmer of hope, so I pressed him to go on.

"This might be a little premature," he said, "but as the unexpected can happen, it would be good if you spoke to the family about the possibility of donating some of his organs. If and when that comes to pass."

His words stabbed me like a knife. I almost doubled over in pain. I was angry that this man dared to raise this issue while Antonis was fighting for his life. I felt like screaming at him, "He isn't dead yet!"

Everything had happened so fast that I refused to consider such an outcome. I had become an organ donor many years ago, but making the decision for someone you love is very different. I immediately realized there was no reason to be angry with the doctor. He was just doing his job and showing concern for others who might be saved.

"Ok," I managed to utter. I thanked the doctor and walked back to the waiting room.

As I moved down the corridor, my eyes pierced the floor as if searching for a way out. I had no hope left. Everything indicated that this terrible prognosis was final and irreversible. Two sets of feet blocked my way, and I raised my eyes. The bright faces of Yiannis and Myrto standing in front of me gave me courage. We hugged before we could say a word, trying to hold back the tears. Joined as one body, we walked to the couches and sat down. I spent some time recounting everything that had happened in the woods. Then, summoning all the courage I had left in me, I informed them about his condition.

"I don't know what to say... it's such a shock," Yiannis stammered and squeezed me in his arms, cursing Pavlos Lambrakis under his breath.

It was impossible to express all the despair and rage overflowing inside me. I was still trying to come to terms with reality, to understand that I might never see Antonis walk and talk to me again. While my two friends searched for any words that might soothe my pain a little, I shared the doctor's exact words, extinguishing their hopes in turn.

"What's going to happen now?" Myrto asked me, her eyes brimming with tears.

I opened my mouth, but no sound came out. The despair I felt would give her the answer through my expression. I gritted my teeth; I had to be strong and accept reality, which was inconceivably tragic, first and foremost for Antonis, and then for all of us.

"I don't know... I really can't think. Between the doctors and Antonis in the ICU, I can't... Damn it..."

I leaned against Myrto's chest as silent sobs racked my body. Every effort on my part not to break down was futile. I was with friends who loved me, and I let my feelings flow freely.

I stayed in her arms for some time, until I roused myself and wiped my eyes dry. Antonis's family would be arriving shortly, and they should not see me in this state.

Myrto and Yiannis would be staying for a couple of days at a friend's house. Yiannis offered to take leave from work and stay longer, but I could not see a reason for it. Antonis's parents, sister, and I were the only people allowed to see him, so I urged them to go. Their downcast faces forced me to take on the role of supporter and try to give them courage.

As we waited to be called in to see Antonis, I motioned to his sister that I wanted to speak to her in private. She seemed on the verge of collapse, and I decided not to mention anything about organ donation. At present, her emotional state was so fragile, she could only be shocked at the prospect. It upset me to think that we had to consider that, too, amongst everything else that was happening.

We decided that we had to tell Antonis's parents more about his condition, to prepare them. No one and nothing, however, had prepared me for this outcome. I was not ready. I would never be ready to part from him in this way. The man who had saved my life was now locked in an unjust and unequal battle to save his own. And I stood on the sidelines, unable to help him.

Eventually, we all stepped inside the ICU unit and walked to Antonis's bedside. We stood around his bed, and the tragic figure of his mother broke my heart. She was murmuring, almost to herself, and the few words that reached my ears were her pleading with him to wake up. I touched his hand again, trying to sense the slightest reaction, but in vain. He felt colder today.

I looked at the monitors behind his bed as if they could tell me more. The mechanical beeps were the only signs that there was still some life in Antonis. To be precise, they were all that was keeping him with us.

There were times when time flew by and times when it crawled past as if the whole universe had slowed down. I had lost all sense of time, all my bearings. I felt like one of those dolphins that become stranded on the shore, and someone must soon return them to the sea so they don't die. The air that I breathed felt thin, as if someone was snatching it from me. Everything inside me was like an hourglass, the sands trickling inexorably down and running out.

When night fell, his family left, as I would be spending the night at the hospital again. I was hoping that later, when everyone was gone, I would be allowed to go back to Antonis.

My father called to check in, and I numbly told him the prognosis. He was deeply upset. Ever since Antonis had saved my life, he had thought of him as a son. He had been overjoyed when we'd become a couple. Maybe he saw the son he had always wanted in Antonis.

Like a little girl, I waited for the nurse's signal to go see him. Just before midnight, the nurse came and called me. As we entered the room, I saw a small armchair had been placed next to his bed. "So you can sit down, Ariadne," the nurse said with a smile.

In the bleakness, people were showing me love in their own way. I thanked her, then sat beside Antonis and looked at him. The lights had been dimmed, and he looked as if he would wake up if I nudged him.

A few seconds later, I lowered my head until my cheek was gently brushing his hand. I desperately wanted to feel the slightest reaction, a sign that he was aware of my presence. My breath caressed the skin of his arm. I closed my eyes and remembered his smile. What I would not give for one more night with him, one more smile from him as we woke up in our slice of heaven.

I must have fallen asleep, because the next thing I felt was the doctor's hand on my shoulder. "You need to step outside now," he whispered apologetically.

I looked around blearily and realized that at least an hour had passed since I had entered the room. "Thank you," I said, and gently squeezed Antonis's hand before standing up. "I really appreciate what you are doing," I said, meaning the fact that they let me spend more time with him than was strictly allowed.

"I know what you are going through is unbearable, and I wish you could spend more time with him," the doctor said. "But we have already broken some rules, and it's best to be careful. You, too, should get some rest. I was informed that you also slept in the waiting room yesterday. It's not the best place to spend the night. Is there somewhere you can go? A friend's house, perhaps, or a hotel?" he whispered so as not to disturb the peace that reigned in the ICU.

"I want to be near him as much as I can," I said, as I followed him out of the room—not before turning to cast one last glance at Antonis.

"I understand. But you need to look after yourself..."

I made to move ahead, but the doctor fell into step beside me. "If I may," he said quietly, "I would like to tell you something I saw a while ago, and which reminds me of what you are doing. It might sound a little unconnected, but I can't put it out of my mind."

"I'm listening," I said.

"I was watching a wildlife documentary. Part of it was about wolves."

I gave him a puzzled look, as I wondered why he was making such an association now.

"Should I go on?" he asked, seeing my bewilderment.

"Yes, of course," I said, sure that he could not possibly have known about the incident in the woods.

"When one of the members of the pack is sick or injured, the others look after it and rarely abandon it. After that documentary, I can tell more easily which of our patients were members of a pack, and which weren't."

I nodded but refrained from telling him about my encounter with wolves. I could understand why he'd made the association. "You're saying we are not that different from animals as we like to think." We are not that different from animals in many aspects," was all I said.

"We all need our pack. I'm sure yours is worried about you, and if you are unwell, it affects them too. I understand that you love Antonis, but you must take care of yourself. If you wish to leave for a few hours, you should do it. The moment something happens, for good or ill, I will let you know. That is my promise to you. Now, please—go find a bed, and get some rest."

"Thank you, doctor, I appreciate it," I said, and he walked off down the corridor.

I returned to the waiting area, which was empty, and sat there by myself. I replied to some text messages, set my phone aside, and thought about returning to my hotel for a few hours. The hotel was close to the hospital. The idea of leaving Antonis's side was unthinkable, and yet I know I had to rest if I was to stay strong. Decision made, I left my phone number with the nurse in case there was any change, then departed for the hotel.

The truth is that I really needed those few hours of sleep. There are times when even your spirit will succumb to physical fatigue. The hotel was not anything out of the ordinary, but it was still better than the couches in the waiting area.

I had been put through the wringer these last two days and, returning to the hospital the next morning, I was seized by a strange feeling of optimism. I hoped it was an omen of good things to come.

Antonis's parents, sister, and I made our way to Antonis's bedside to see him during visiting hours. When the visit was over, a doctor invited us into his office and more or less repeated what we already knew. He mentioned something else that troubled me. Antonis might be moved to a ward for coma patients, as the demand for ICU beds was very high. I did not understand what the repercussions of that would be, and although I pressed him with many questions, I received no reply.

There was some upheaval at the hospital, due to the many incidents that the ICU unit had to handle. I thought how terrible this constant back and forth at the hospital was for Antonis's parents, now that they knew all hope had been lost. But what could I do, besides be there for them?

We stepped out into the corridor where Eva and my father were waiting for us. A few minutes later, I escorted Antonis's parents to the exit. We hugged and promised to meet again in the afternoon, and then I returned to the waiting area, which had become my base.

"I just got a call from Edessa," my father said when I sat down beside them. "Lambrakis is out on bail until his trial. There are some conditions attached, but he is now walking free."

"When will the trial take place?" I asked, gritting my teeth.

"In a few months, they say... If I understand correctly, Lambrakis will be charged with involuntary manslaughter and won't spend a single day in prison. Especially now that we know who he is..."

"What do you mean?"

"He's a rich kid," Eva said sourly. "His family is wealthy, owns factories across the Balkans. He had three lawyers representing him in Edessa."

"What does being rich have anything to do with it? A person's actions are not defined by their financial situation!" I snapped, and instantly regretted it. It sounded like I was telling her off.

My father pulled me into his arms and stroked my hair soothingly, and I could see from Eva's expression that she didn't hold my outburst against me. "Nothing changes what happened," I whispered, looking at them both.

"Let's go to the cafeteria," Eva suggested, stroking my hair. "I brought something for you to eat."

Soon we were seated in the hospital cafeteria, where I mechanically ate what Eva had brought with her, not tasting any of it.

"Do you need anything else?" my father asked me, while my thoughts wandered aimlessly.

"No, Dad. Thank you for coming, but there's really no reason to stay. Go back to Avgerinos, and I'll call you if I need you. It's not like you live nearby..."

"Why don't you come with us for a while? You said that Antonis's condition won't change while they're keeping him in intensive care."

"It's too soon for me to even consider it. I want to see what's going to happen about moving Antonis to another ward, so I'm not going anywhere," I said in a tone that brokered no argument. "If it was me in that hospital bed, would you leave?" I asked, my eyes filling with tears.

"No, Ariadne, I would not leave you," my father said, bowing his head.

It was my turn to hug him. "I love him, Dad. With all my heart. And I will stay with him till the very end. Even if I have to set up a tent in the waiting room."

"Follow your heart, sweetheart," he said, and kissed me on the cheek.

"We support you, whatever you decide," Eva affirmed.

I escorted them to the front of the hospital, where we stood on the front steps to say our goodbyes.

"Just look after my dog, please..." I said.

"Do you think we ever get to see him? He's disappeared again since you left," Eva said. "But of course I'll keep putting out food and water for him."

I would not have been surprised to see him looking for me in the hospital forecourt. He was capable of coming all the way here because he had undoubtedly sensed that something terrible had happened. I said goodbye and stayed in the hospital forecourt for a moment. The weather was dull. Clouds pregnant with rain covered the sky. After they left, I paced around for a while, trying to order my thoughts, until the first raindrops began to fall.

The rain was getting heavier. I had to go back inside. The sound of footsteps coming towards me made me pause. I turned around, and my mouth twisted in an ugly grimace as I came face to face with Pavlos Lambrakis.

"Good afternoon," he said.

I did not reply. If I opened my mouth, everything I wanted to say would come gushing out. I tried to guess what Lambrakis was doing here. As I stared at him in silence, he awkwardly shifted his gaze towards the dull sky.

"I would like to talk to you about something, please."

"If you've come to apologize again, there really is no need. You could come inside intensive care and see the result of your actions and then, if you wish, apologize to Antonis. Except he can't hear you. Because he can't hear any of us," I snarled, and made to push past Lambrakis.

I felt his hand on my elbow, trying to stop me, and I wrenched my arm out of his grip. "Don't touch me."

"Please, I'm only asking for a minute of your time. This is what I want to talk to you about."

I stopped and turned back towards him. The rain was growing stronger, but I didn't care. A bit of water was the least of my concerns right now.

"I can't take back what I did," he said. "But I can help, if you agree."

Our faces were now drenched with thick raindrops.

"I'm listening," I said, looking him squarely in the eye. I wanted to force him to stay here until the rain chilled him to the bone, just like the chill inside me.

"I just found out about your boyfriend's condition. I'm truly sorry. I already spoke to the hospital director and, if you agree, we can move him to a private clinic where he would receive better care."

It was the last thing I'd expected to hear coming from him. More than anything, though, I was impressed that he did not seem to mind having this conversation in the pouring rain. Perhaps he really did feel as guilty as he was making everyone think he was.

"Why would you do that?" I asked, wiping the raindrops trickling down my face.

"Because I am to blame for everything that happened," he said flatly.

Notwithstanding that I could not stand the sight of him, his offer took me by surprise. The image of Antonis lying on the forest floor, injured by the shot fired by the man standing across me, flashed through my mind just then.

"Come back this afternoon and tell it to his mother. Look her in the eyes and tell her. She will decide whether to accept your help."

"Yes, I'll do that," he said and took a step closer. "Do you think she'll accept my offer?"

"I have no idea," I said. "But even if she agrees, it won't change anything. The doctor says he'll die if we try to move him to another facility. That means no private clinic, no better care."

"But—"

"Don't you understand what you've done?" I shouted, no longer able to contain my rage. "You killed him! He is more dead than alive. He will never recover, in any hospital in the world, so get away from me!"

I was screaming the words so loudly that faces appeared at the windows, looking down at us. I turned around and hurried away. Without glancing back, I could tell that Lambrakis was dumbstruck, standing still in the pouring rain and watching me as I disappeared inside the hospital.

I was still struggling to regain my composure when I called Antonis's sister and told her what had happened. I was surprised by her reaction. I had expected her to turn down the offer, but she said she would talk to her parents about it.

I received another surprise when the head nurse informed me they were planning to move Antonis to another ward—not at some vague point in the future, but in the next few days. She tried hard to convince me that the move would not change anything, but I knew it meant Antonis was no longer a priority for them. They would not be moving him to the coma ward if they thought there was a chance his condition would improve.

Discreetly, I asked her opinion about moving him to a private clinic, and she immediately stressed both the exorbitant costs and dangers of such a move.

Exhausted and soaked, I ended up back in the waiting room once again. There, my mind grappled with a torrent of tormenting thoughts. I knew that life was intertwined with loss by default. I had already lost my beloved mother; the scent of death was familiar to me. I knew full well the sense of loneliness you feel when you realize you will never see someone you love so deeply again. I was not ready to accept that my life would go on without Antonis. All my dreams of a life shared with him had come crumbling down. His absence had released a strange kind of pain inside me, had ruptured the continuum of life, the shared life we would never live. I stood helpless before reality, and nothing could soften my sorrow.

Despite my friends, despite my family, I felt all alone and denuded, desperately searching for something to hang on to. That gunshot had split time in two. The past had become frozen, and the present did not seem to want to give way to the future. Suddenly, the gloriousness of the world I had created began to shrink, to diminish, not just in terms of time but as if someone was pulling earth and sky together. I fed the guilt I felt, and it festered. How different everything would be if we had never left our home that morning...

The next day, Antonis's mother and sister returned for another visit. I went to meet them, and they informed me that his father was not feeling well and had decided to stay with the relatives who were accommodating them. We moved towards the intensive care unit, and when we reached the doctors' offices, I saw Pavlos Lambrakis talking to one of them.

Once again, his presence made my blood boil. When he noticed us, he stopped talking and opened the door wide. I will never forget what followed. Without hesitation or fear, he revealed his identity and begged Antonis's mother and sister for forgiveness. They looked at him expressionlessly, surprised by his reaction. Antonis's mother, her voice breaking with emotion, spoke first. "You caused my family the greatest harm conceivable. No matter how many times I forgive you, my child will never wake up again..."

"You are right... About everything, you are right," Lambrakis said. "I'm here because I would like to help you any way I can. There's nothing I wouldn't do."

She held his hands and looked him in the eyes. "Then go wake my child and bring him to me so I can hug him one more time."

Everyone—doctors, nurses, cleaners—froze. The silence that followed her words made us all shrink to insignificance before her. I struggled to hold back my tears, just so she could not understand how weak and helpless I felt.

"I wish I could do that, but it can't be done," Lambrakis said. "However, there is a private clinic we could move him to, entirely at my expense, of course, and—"

She put her hand over his mouth, forcing him to stop. "My child is gone," she said simply. "We will stay here until the very end."

Without giving him the chance to say another word, she moved towards the ICU doors. Pavlos Lambrakis was looking at her, lost in thought. I glared at him and then followed the others. For a moment, I had believed it would be better to move Antonis to another clinic, but in the end, I agreed with his mother.

Just before we reached Antonis's bedside, the hospital director caught up with us and told us that, for the time being, Antonis would remain in intensive care. Maybe he, too, had been moved by the courage of a mother who had expressed everything that could be said in a few simple words. She also had a surplus of love inside her, the same as her son, and did not let hatred guide her actions or words.

A few hours later, as night fell, everyone left. I felt a strange sense of relief at finding myself almost alone in the waiting room. Maybe because it helped me think more clearly. The nurses had given me to understand that I would not be able to see Antonis again tonight, so I decided to return to the hotel. I would snatch a few hours of sleep and then return to the hospital. The hardest part was not being away from Antonis. It was the fact that there was no hope, nothing to hang on to and draw strength from.

Days and nights felt so alike, so unchanging, that it was as if I was suffocating. I walked to the exit to pick up my car. The smell of rain drying on concrete flooded my nostrils. I thought of the scent of the first raindrops on the soil in my garden, and felt even more melancholy. The rain had stopped, and the patches of sky I could see looked clear. Slowly, I walked on the pavement, my mind swamped by dozens of thoughts.

Lost in the drone of the city's sounds, I thought I heard someone call my name. I turned around, puzzled, my eyes scanning the pavement to see who had called me. In the distance, I saw Lambrakis step out of his car and start to walk towards me.

I turned in the direction of my car and picked up my pace. He kept calling my name, but I did not look back and moved faster. Instead of giving up, his footsteps became quicker. I broke into a run until I reached my car. Quickly, I turned on the ignition and turned the engine on. With a start, I saw him standing in front of my windscreen, motioning at me to stop. His eyes glimmered with the reflection of my headlights. For the first time in my life, I thought about stepping on the gas with no regard for the consequences for either one of us. I stared at him fiercely as I thought about how I could avoid him.

A car was parked behind mine, so the only way out was forward. Misinterpreting my inaction as hesitation, Lambrakis stepped closer and gently touched the hood of my car, then walked around towards my window. Without a second thought, I stepped on the gas and pulled out, the side mirror swiping his hand as I passed him by.

I gritted my teeth as I drove back to the hotel. I was frightened; for a split second, I had seriously considered running him down. I did not know such feelings could even exist inside me.

Everything I had spent my whole life teaching now took on an altered hue, now that I was experiencing it myself. It was easy to advise someone to conquer their rage and anger, but at this moment, it was I who could not control such feelings, despite seeing Lambrakis contrite and eager to help. For me, he would always be the man who took the love of my life away.

There was no traffic, and I reached the hotel in no time. Back in my room, I called my sister and we spoke for some time. I told her what had happened in the parking lot. She tried to calm me down, repeating everything I used to say to my students. I had to rein in my hatred and my anger, or else I risked becoming a worse person than he was.

As soon as we hung up, I pulled open the balcony doors and stepped outside to get some fresh air. The din and noise of the city made me feel worse, and I wondered how all these people could live in their bright yet prison-like apartments. I knew that most of them had chosen to live in the city while trying to find some time in their busy schedules to return to their villages or close to where they really belonged: nature.

These thoughts carried me away for a moment, but the sound of an ambulance brought me back to the present. I felt chilly and thought it was the fatigue, but I had forgotten that I was drenched, and my wet clothes had been drying on me. I stepped back inside, firmly closing the doors and drawing the curtains to shut away all these annoying sounds. A few minutes later, exhausted, I stretched out on my bed and tried to chase away the image of Lambrakis running after me.

A few days later

I OPENED MY EYES and looked at the crack in the hotel room curtains that allowed a thin ray of light to creep through and light up the opposite wall. Three more days had gone by, and they had been identical: sitting outside the ICU from dawn till dusk, seeing Antonis whenever I was allowed, putting on a brave face when the doctors told me his condition remained unchanged.

His sister had gone back to France for a couple of days and would return soon. His parents came to see him once a day, accompanied by some nephews and nieces who were accommodating them. The doctors had made them understand that, at their age and with their fragile health, they should not expose themselves to hospital environments for long. It was particularly dangerous for his father, whose heart issues were flaring up.

The most pressing issue for me was to decide what I was going to do about work. At the moment, I was just canceling one session after the other. Everyone was telling me to go back to Evora, but I could not, not while Antonis was fighting for his life. My thoughts kept returning to what the doctor had said about wolves, about how they looked after the sick and helpless members of their pack. Antonis was my pack. I couldn't abandon him now.

I did not know how long I would be able to keep up this pace to stay by his side, but at present, I could not even stand the thought of staying away for more than a day. For the time being, I was the one who was looking after him more than anyone else, and I did not plan to stop.

I rose from the hotel bed without feeling particularly rested. I was not eating well, and I was not sleeping well during the few hours each night that I returned to the hotel. I had a bath, and prepared to go. My eyes felt heavy, as if I had been sleeping for years. I glanced at my reflection in the mirror, and I no longer recognized myself.

I reached the ground floor and made my way towards the exit, but, seeing Pavlos Lambrakis waiting in the hotel lobby, I stopped. He stood up and walked towards me with an awkward smile.

"Good morning," he said.

"Good morning," I reluctantly replied, and prepared to turn my back on him. Was there even a point, though? He'd made it clear he was willing to chase me down to make me listen. Perhaps I should call the police. It might be the only way to make him leave me alone.

"Please, hear me out for a minute," Lambrakis pleaded. "I promise never to bother you again."

I wavered for a moment, but decided to listen to what he had to say, on the off-chance he would actually keep his word and disappear from my life for good.

He led me over to the hotel's restaurant, where he indicated I should sit down, and then hovered above me as he called the waiter. "What will you have?" he asked, looking down at me.

"I won't have anything. I have to leave in a couple of minutes," I told the young man who had come to take our order.

"Please, have something," Lambrakis insisted.

"Fine," I relented. "I'll have a fresh orange juice. Now, say what you came to say. " I said, hoping that this way, he would cut to the chase. "I'm listening. Please be quick; visiting hours start soon, and it might be the last time I see him alive..."

The waiter made a discreet exit with our menus as Lambrakis exclaimed, "What do you mean? Has something happened?"

"Nothing more than what you did. Now every time I see Antonis could be the last time." I tried hard to appear calm and collected, but it was impossible.

"Everything you say, everything you feel, you are right," he admitted, looking straight into my eyes. "You might not believe me, but my life has been hell since that day.

Everything happened so quickly, and I wish I had reacted differently."

"Let's start with why you went hunting in a prohibited zone, outside of hunting season."

"But, we weren't going hunting..."

I scoffed. "What were you doing in the woods, then, carrying hunting rifles and hounds with you?"

"Give me some time to explain, please. I have told the examining magistrate everything too."

Without offering any encouragement, I just stared at him.

"My friend, who was with me, had told me about this great Valley, and I really wanted to see it. He insisted it was a place worth investing in. We decided to go, but my friend insisted we bring guns and his dog with us for protection— he'd heard there were wild animals in the area, and that a wolf pack had attacked a group of hikers." He paused, as if not sure if he should keep talking. "I later learned that you were in the group of hikers who encountered the wolves."

He stopped expectantly, as if waiting for me to confirm what he was saying, but all he got from me was an angry scowl.

"We weren't going to shoot any animals," he insisted. "I'm not that kind of person, believe me. We were carrying guns for protection. I thought I saw a wolf in the trees, and shot at it because I was scared. I was already on edge and frightened, and when your boyfriend appeared behind me, I panicked, thinking it was another wolf. I swear, I didn't realize it was a person. I would never have fired if I had. I've never even been in a forest with a gun before!"

"And the first time you decided to do so, you killed the man I love!" I shouted, outraged.

"Yes, and I will have to spend the rest of my life living with what I did. Believe me, it is difficult for me, too. I wish there was something I could do to change it all."

The waiter carrying our drinks interrupted us. I checked the time, and started to stand, intending to leave. Lambrakis leaned toward me, wide-eyed with sincerity. "Please, accept the offer I am about to make, and then talk to his parents about it."

"His mother has already given you an answer," I said curtly, and pushed my chair back.

"I'm not talking about that. Since I can't help him, I would like to make your life and the life of his parents easier. For as long as you need to stay here."

"I don't understand what you mean. Our lives would have been fine if you hadn't shot Antonis."

He shook his head again, disappointed.

"Please, hear me out. The nurses told me how difficult your daily life is, what with all this coming and going. There is a house near the hospital that you could use instead of the hotel. You could get to the hospital on foot, as could his parents. It's got two floors, so you would all three be comfortable and have your own privacy. The house is at your disposal for as long as you need to stay here, along with a housekeeper who will cook for you and assist you. I am offering it for purely practical reasons."

I stood up, ready to refuse his offer, but he spoke before I could say anything. "There is no point in going through extra hardship, especially his parents, who are elderly. Call me any time of day or night, and I'll make arrangements for you to move there immediately."

He placed his card near my handbag, which was resting on the table. My feelings were in an utter state of confusion.

"Thank you for the juice," I said. Then I picked up my handbag, leaving his card exactly where it was, and walked briskly to the exit.

Lambrakis called after me, but I did not turn back. If I delayed my departure any longer, I would not be able to see Antonis. And right now, all that mattered to me was being by his side, not staying in a better house.

I had been right to be concerned about the time—my late departure, combined with the heavy traffic, caused me to miss the morning visiting hours. Antonis's mother was there when I arrived, and a brief chat with her was enough for me to see that she was exhausted. Her relations lived on the other side of town, and the back and forth to the hospital was laborious and time-consuming.

Lambrakis's offer flashed through my mind. I hated the idea of accepting anything from that man, but Antonis's parents were suffering enough as it was. I also knew that my finances would not allow me to stay at a hotel for much longer, and I absolutely did not want to ask Eva or my father for financial assistance. So, I decided to talk to Antonis's mother about the house Lambrakis was offering us.

When I was done, she looked at me and gripped my hands. "Ariadne, what you are doing for Antonis shows how much you love him. I do know, though, that you have given up everything to be here. And if this house makes it easier, you should go to stay there. We are fine staying with our relatives. You should go, dear, to save yourself all those expenses."

The only reason I was even discussing this with her was to make their lives easier. If she wouldn't accept Lambrakis's offer, then neither would I. "I don't think I can stay there... You are leaving now, right?"

"Yes, my niece is waiting for me downstairs to take me back home. I think we will try to come back in the afternoon, too."

"I'll be here. Don't you worry," I said, and escorted her to the car.

I decided to go for a walk around the neighborhood and get something to eat. Food options at the hospital were limited, and not really to my taste. I contented myself with buying some fruit and slowly walked back to the hospital, munching on an apple. I was thinking about driving to Avgerinos after visiting hours were over in the afternoon. Just to spend one night there. I missed the feel of nature. Mostly, I was missing Voras, who by the sound of it had fallen into a depression. I had deterred my family from coming all the way to Thessaloniki, so it would also be a chance to see them.

Not too far from the hospital, I came across a pretty coffee shop and sat down until it would be time to return. I spent most of my time on the phone with Yiannis and Myrto. They were planning to come up to Thessaloniki for the weekend again. I also spoke with Eva, who was happy to hear I would be spending the night with them. They were expecting me for dinner. An hour later, I decided it was time to get back.

As soon as I reached the doors to the ICU, I saw the head nurse give me a glance, as if she had been on the lookout for me. A terrible premonition twisted my guts when I saw the compassion in her eyes. We had spoken often during Antonis's stay, and were on somewhat friendly terms. "I've spoken to his parents, and I was just about to call you, Ariadne."

"What happened?"

She motioned for me to enter an office, prolonging my agony. She closed the door, and I saw the clinic director waiting for me. The looks on their faces made me want to scream.

"Miss Nastou, I'm afraid his condition has taken a turn for the worse..."

"Meaning?"

"There have been a few complications in the past hours. A sudden fever leading to serious edema. We have asked for a neurologist to..." He seemed to hesitate.

"To?" I demanded.

The doctor looked at the head nurse, and sighed. "We knew how things stood from the start, but I don't think there could be a worse complication for a person who is still alive. Up till now, there was some reaction, albeit minimal. The neurologist will determine whether he is brain dead."

Speechless, I stared at him in dismay. I knew there was not any hope, but hearing it confirmed was still difficult to bear. "What does that mean?" I asked, even though I knew the answer.

"We will, of course, wait for our colleague's diagnosis, but it is evident that the brain damage is irreversible. There is a permanent loss of all brain functions. I am very sorry, although I think you knew that sooner or later things would lead to this... outcome."

I nodded in agreement as I was unable to utter a single sound.

"We have called his parents to come here, so you can all decide how we should proceed."

"What do you mean?" I asked, suddenly starting to shake.

"We could keep him on mechanical support for some time so you can say goodbye. If the parents agree to donate his organs, then we will definitely keep him breathing to preserve all the organs that can be used."

"Let me see if I've got this right. If Antonis's parents do not want to donate his organs, you will take him off life support tonight?"

"I think we should have this conversation once the neurologist has made a conclusive diagnosis. Then we can talk and make final decisions. I am so very sorry."

The doctor touched my shoulder compassionately, and left in the direction of the ICU. Although I had known Antonis was lost to me, the fact that he was still alive, even in this way, had given me a glimmer of hope for a miracle. The miracle would now never come to pass.

"Can I see him?" I asked the head nurse.

She nodded, and asked me to follow her. I dressed in the protective gear, and we entered the ICU. As soon as she left me alone with Antonis, I moved to his side with tears in my eyes. He looked so peaceful. I reached out and touched him. Instinctively, I pulled off one of my gloves. Finally, after so many days, I could feel his skin without the interference of the plastic.

He was warm, probably due to the fever, but this warmth made our contact more intense than ever. I stroked his hand gently, then his forehead. I was well aware that this might be one of the last times I would get to see him with the tiniest flicker of life inside him. I stayed there, beside him, picturing us doing the things we loved.

I had dreamt of us sharing so many things, so many experiences, and now the bitterest feeling I had ever experienced seized me. I would have given anything just then for one more smile from Antonis, like the smile he'd given me before our paths parted in the forest.

I squeezed his hand and kissed his forehead. Then I heard footsteps approaching, and rose from his bedside. The neurologist was here to examine Antonis and certify what was evident. I slowly backed away, my eyes on Antonis, as if I were still expecting one last reaction. In vain. With heavy footsteps, I now walked away, knowing that I was leaving behind the most beautiful thing I had ever experienced. The most real.

Kostas Krommydas

Thasos

WE HAD JUST SAID GOODBYE to Antonis on the island where he was born. All the people he loved were here. There was a strange beauty to the day. The sun had been battling the clouds since dawn, continually shifting the hues of the island's landscape. It was nearly noon, and the only false note in the serene atmosphere was a breeze that rustled the leaves on the trees and made them whisper strange sounds.

In my efforts to support his parents, particularly his mother, I had not had time to come to terms with many things. Other than my love for him, I discovered what a great man he was and how many he was a friend to. In the crowd, I spotted his ex-wife, who had come to say goodbye to him. Under other circumstances, I might have felt bad towards her, but now all of that seemed small and insignificant. In the shadow of death, reality assumes its proper dimensions. I tried, to the extent my emotional reserves allowed, to appear strong.

When it was all over, people began to depart, but I decided to stay. I wanted to say goodbye more quietly, more personally, away from the ceremonial aspects of a funeral. His parents were surprised at my wish to be alone, but I asked them to go ahead without me, and reassured them that I would be joining them shortly.

When they left, my eyes sought the distant horizon. It was some comfort to know that Antonis was being laid to rest somewhere so beautiful. Every time I would think of him, I would remember this image of the horizon. We had not had enough time to go sailing as we had dreamt. Now, I imagined the two of us on the open seas, sailing from port to port, going wherever the wind blew us...

Everything had happened so quickly that day at the hospital. When Antonis's parents were informed that their son was brain dead, they broke down in sobs, and it took some time before they could recover from the shock. Initially, they were reluctant to donate his organs. But when I told them that Antonis would keep living in another person's body, in a way, they decided to give their consent. It was a courageous decision on their part. Not many people could get over the initial shock and accept to donate the organs of their loved ones.

Antonis was kept on mechanical support for three more days. Once everything concerning the organ donation was in place, they turned off the machines, and he left us peacefully. I was there the whole time, holding his hand. I will never forget the moment the machines fell quiet and he stopped breathing. It was one more way of experiencing the process of saying goodbye.

I knew well that the value of life is greater than that of death. Everyone tried to dissuade me from being there right then, but there was no way I would leave the man I had loved, and who had saved my life. It was the second time we found ourselves in proximity to death, except this time, he had irreversibly crossed to the other side.

As we were making our way to the funeral, I inadvertently overheard two women comment that luckily we were not married, meaning that I would suffer less for that, as if marriage made mutual love a certainty. Whatever might happen from this day forth, I would never forget him, even if, at some point, I managed to love someone else.

A cool breeze as gentle as a caress filled me with peace. It was nearly summer, and everything on the island was a vibrant green. After so long away from home, I yearned to return to Evora and take stock of everything. More than anything, I wanted to avoid all the clichéd expressions of compassion. I yearned for the words of those who loved me and gave me strength.

My studies had taught me that life was intertwined with death. I vividly remembered my mother's last words to me. She said that someone only truly dies when there is not a single person left to remember them. For as long as I lived and remembered, Antonis would also exist.

Walking down the slope to the cemetery exit where I'd left my car, I watched those coming to visit the graves of their loved ones. Some looked after the graves meticulously, holding on to the illusion that they were looking after something belonging to the departed. I remember we had done the same for my mother's grave, in the first years after she passed. Even if you accept the person you love is gone forever, you still try to prolong the special contact you had with them. That is what usually happens when you lose someone suddenly and unexpectedly. The pain of the separation is unbearable, and sometimes never fades away completely.

I stopped outside the car, tormented by a sudden thought. I did not want to join everyone else at the restaurant where they were holding the wake. I felt the need to travel, to go on a long drive and lose myself in my memories. I called my father, and after I told him, I asked to speak to Antonis's mother. She encouraged me to listen to my needs. She seemed so grateful, and she never stopped showing her gratitude.

My father and sister had driven here with me, but luckily there were others here who could give them a lift home. I decided to set off on my own. I really needed it, after so many days of extreme stress and pressure. I got inside the car, impatient to reach the mainland, and from there, move on to wherever the road may lead me. I could wander aimlessly for days.

I arrived at the port of Thasos, bought my ticket, drove my car aboard the ferry, and then made my way up to the passenger deck. I watched from the railing as the island slowly disappeared into the distance.

How I would have loved to have him standing at the port, waving to me as I floated away, secure in the knowledge that he would be there when I returned. I imagined him standing there until we both became distant dots. To always have the prospect of meeting again, instead of a permanent parting.

I sat on one of the benches, my body still turned towards the shore. I closed my eyes and turned my face to the sky. The midday sun caressed my face with its rays. My black clothes absorbed the heat, warming my whole body. Sensing something blocking the sun, I opened my eyes. Someone was standing in front of me. I shielded my eyes to see who it was. Pavlos Lambrakis stood before me, offering his hand for a handshake.

"Please accept my condolences..." he said, while I tried to recover from the shock of seeing him here, on today of all days.

"How did you get here?" I asked coolly.

He let his hand drop by his side, disappointed. "I came for Antonis's funeral, and now I'm on my way back. I did not want to disturb you during the funeral. I decided to give you my condolences now, in a spur of the moment when I saw you on the deck. I apologize. I should not have."

Lambrakis walked across the deck and turned to the right and out of sight. He was the last person I'd expected to run into. He must have some nerve to appear at the funeral of the man who had died because of him. Just when I was starting to feel a sense of peace, his presence had disturbed me.

I had learned that the examining magistrate had recalled him after Antonis' death to announce manslaughter charges. Not that it would change anything until the trial took place. As I had just found out, he was still a free man. On the other hand, if I had caught an earlier boat, I would not have met him. In any case, it was still a strange coincidence.

I knew that I had been rude, but I could not behave any other way towards him. Every time I saw him, I thought of Antonis's blood seeping from his wounds into my palms. From the corner of my eye, I spotted Lambrakis on the other side of the deck, leaning against the railings and looking out at sea. He did look remorseful, but I could not change my stance towards him. In vain did I try to put our encounter out of my mind. I wondered whether it was not so random, after all. I would not put it past him to have followed me.

When the ferry arrived, I went down to the cargo area to retrieve my car and ran into him once again. He was parked beside me. Another strange coincidence, or deliberate design? Head bowed, shoulders slumped, Lambrakis did not even turn to look at me. For the first time, I felt that he might be genuinely sorry.

I had not learned to shy away from facing matters head-on. I walked towards his car, and, when he saw me approach, he rolled his window down with a look of surprise. Before he could speak, I announced, "You must understand that it is impossible for me to just draw a line under everything that happened and forget."

He opened his mouth to speak, but I did not let him.

"I can't forgive you. I don't intend to hide every time I see you in order to avoid you, either. So don't expect anything else from me. Not now, not in the future. Perhaps today's meeting was... random, but please, don't ever contact me again."

I turned away to return to my car, and heard him call out after me, "I would be feeling the same way, Ariadne."

I did not react. I kept going until I left the boat. I drove carefully while the street was narrow, but once I hit the main roads, I picked up speed, as if I wanted to escape him. I kept checking my rearview mirror to see if he was following me, but as far as I could tell, none of the cars behind me looked like his. I needed to step on the gas, to drive fast, as if that way I could outrun all the bad memories, leave them behind to scatter, like dust rising and falling back to the ground.

The air gushed in through the open windows as I sped down the Egnatia highway. I looked at Thasos on my left, knowing that Antonis would be on that island forever. I also knew that I could never be at Evora without feeling his presence everywhere.

I turned on the radio, hoping to distract myself, and flicked through the stations. A jazz melody instantly reminded me of him. It was like all the music in the world had been written to say goodbye to him. I turned the volume all the way up. Anyone driving past me would think I was celebrating. I didn't even notice how the tears began to run down my cheeks. I made no move to wipe them.

It was finally time, away from everyone and everything, to mourn the man who had entered and left my life so unexpectedly. There was nothing to stop me and no one to judge me. Remembering the moments we'd shared, I sobbed and sang along to some of the songs, as if my mourning could fill all these verses. I drove and cried and sang all the way to the outskirts of Thessaloniki. Now all I wanted was to get home before dark and take Voras for a walk in the woods. Walk as far as our feet could carry us until nightfall.

When I entered the house, I hurriedly changed my clothes as if I were late for something. The fresh air instantly made me feel better. Voras was wagging his tail ecstatically to show me how much he'd missed me. Despite the joy my beloved dog felt at seeing me again, he could sense my sorrow. For the first time, as we followed the path up to the cabin, Voras did not veer from my side for a single moment.

Dusk had fallen, and a plane crossed the sky over our heads, leaving a droning sound in its wake. That noise always reminded me of travels, of those departing on a journey somewhere beautiful. When we neared the cabin, I could see that a number of people were already there, possibly tourists here for their vacations. I hesitated while Voras stood still beside me, looking at the brightly-lit building. The guests were obviously enjoying their stay. Their laughter resonated from the open windows. I crept past the cabin without them sensing my presence, absorbed as they were in their conversation.

We wandered all over the village until night fell, eventually ending up at the café-restaurant. By then, everyone had returned from Thasos. Luckily, not many people were there. Grabbing a bite with Eva, we could forget ourselves for a moment as we discussed changes she was considering for the restaurant décor. My family knew me well and did not persist in their efforts to console me. I felt intensely that once this day was over, my life would radically change. Everything would be different as of tomorrow morning. Although I shuddered at the thought of the loneliness awaiting me, I knew that only by looking ahead did I stand any chance of moving forward.

I intended to resume coaching sessions the following week, but I did not want anyone to stay at the guesthouse for the time being. I would book a comfortable room at the village hotel for anyone coming. Eva offered to spend the night with me at my house, but, despite all my love for her, I wanted to be alone. I bid everyone goodnight and slowly set off towards home, Voras impatiently waiting for me outside the restaurant.

Although it had gotten very dark, I chose to take the footpath back to the house. I knew the lay of the land like the back of my hand, and it was the fastest route. It was a cold night; Voras's beloved wind was blowing. I loved to feel the night chill against my skin. In the distance, lightning lit up the sky, but I could tell the storm was not headed this way. Once again, it had been a while since the last rainfall.

Just before we reached the house, Voras dashed ahead as if he had sensed something. He growled, but I did not pay much attention. He often growled when he spotted a weasel or picked up the scent of some other dog wandering in the village or the fields. Dogs' quests to mark their territories were impressive.

He stopped on the edge of the footpath facing a cluster of trees across the creek that flowed between the path and the forest. I could not make anything out in the darkness, so I walked ahead and called Voras to follow me. I took a few more steps, but could not hear him trot after me. I turned around and called his name more loudly. But he stayed there, gazing unflinchingly in the same direction and baring his teeth in a low, angry growl.

I turned towards the same direction, and this time saw the two eyes glinting in the dark. Under other circumstances, I would not have paid any more attention. But Voras was insisting. I walked towards him and grabbed him by the collar, forcing him to move. He reluctantly obeyed and walked ahead, straight for home, making strange sounds along the way.

I looked at the cluster of trees beyond the creek, and the eyes were still there, in the foliage, watching us. For a few seconds I stared back, until slowly the creature, whatever it may have been, pulled back into the darkness. I turned around carefully so as not to lose my footing and walked on. What I needed right there and then was to burrow under my bedcovers, not deal with the animal stalking us in the night.

On my way to the bedroom, I noticed Antonis's belongings that were in my house. Some of them I would have to return to his parents. I did not have the strength to grapple with any of that right now. I would keep avoiding the task for as long as possible.

Eva had placed his bloodstained clothes from that fateful day in a blue box next to the bookshelves. Some of Antonis's other personal belongings were there, as well as his phone. I would probably never open that box. If Eva had not done it already, I would probably never have washed my clothes that his blood had soaked.

I took out my planner before going to bed. I carefully removed the note Antonis had handed me that morning at the Armchair. I smiled bitterly as I read it, and returned it to its place before turning out the light. I felt a tear trickle down my cheek before I closed my eyes.

Voras, whom I had allowed to sleep beside my bed, sighed. I mimicked him, releasing all the tension that had gathered inside me. He let out another sound, something between a growl and a complaint, as if he felt sorry for me. I did not need to hear more. I called him to jump up and, with a leap, he settled at my feet.

He had not slept with me since the first evening I had brought him home. Then, he had slept on a rug beside me. After that, I taught him to sleep on his mattress. Most of the time, he preferred to stay outside the door, like my guardian angel.

I raised myself in the dark and gave him a tender pat. It was just the two of us once again. Voras had been the one to bring Antonis into my life. I stopped thinking, my eyes heavy with tears and tiredness. It was time to rest. The following day loomed like the beginning of a new life...

Evora

IN EVORA TIME FLOWED very differently to any other place in the world. Here, I sometimes had the illusion that I could even control the hands of the clock. My day always started early, regardless of what time I had gone to bed the previous evening. There was nothing more revitalizing than catching the sun's early light.

I had watched hundreds of sunrises from many different locations in the area, as well as all the places I had traveled to around the world. I loved watching the sun climb up the sky from a mountaintop. Sunrise and sunset at sea were also beautiful, but when you gaze at the sun from high up, it's a different experience. You can almost believe that you are standing at the same height. It feels like you are measuring yourself up against the sun, especially during those moments when the first rays line up with your eyes and warm your face. Then, you are present at the birth of a new day, the birth of life which relentlessly pursues its journey, indifferent to mankind's concerns.

That is more or less what I had decided to do with Joanna. She had arrived the previous afternoon to spend a week at the village and participate in my program for the second time. I had decided that the first person to come after the loss of Antonis would be one of my old students, so we had kept in touch during my time at the hospital.

Today, then, we woke up very early, intending to watch the sunrise together. As soon as Joanna arrived at dawn, we went for a walk with Voras to gather fruit from the "stray" trees of the village. Joanna had struggled with depression for a large part of her life. From what I could gather, her depression had worsened due to her crazy working hours and her lifestyle in general. Lately, however, she had managed to find some kind of balance and, most importantly, stopped medical treatment, as she no longer needed it. I was glad her experience at Evora had helped her. Now she was back, looking better and evidently feeling better, both mentally and physically.

Depression is a devious illness of our times. A large part of the Earth's population suffers from some form of depression, and a whole industry has grown around it. I had read enough about depression and talked to many specialists, so I knew that the real causes of the illness were not clear. Most believed that it was probably caused by a combination of genetic changes and external factors, such as certain experiences or events. In other cases, it was the side effect of a physical ailment. I had a very different approach to most doctors, who quickly resorted to medication as a solution. I respected their work, but I believed that in many cases, an improvement could be achieved through meditation as well as other activities.

Moreover, people could be helped by friends and family. It was beneficial to have someone, even just one person, who they could really talk to, and who would also genuinely listen to them. Of course, I never asked anyone to stop medical treatment, nor did I question doctors' work. They did their job, and I did mine.

Joanna had come to Evora almost a year ago with a diagnosis of acute depression. Everyone thought Joanna had a happy life because she was professionally successful, but they did not understand what was happening deep in her soul. When Joanna began to experience some strange symptoms, she realized that something was amiss. She felt permanently tired, had trouble sleeping, and suffered from various inexplicable aches. What also harmed her was that she sought cabin in food, trying to suppress the negative feelings that swamped her with eating. The problems that started creeping up in her relationships isolated her even more, and she struggled for a long time to find some kind of balance.

Before returning to Evora, she had managed to sort things out, and now she was feeling much better. She, too, had discovered how beneficial it was to live close to nature. In the months since her last visit, she had cut back on her working hours. She often retreated with her boyfriend to a house by the sea, which she loved, away from the noise of the city. What had made the greatest difference in her life, however, was the fact that she had managed to limit what I call pointless and harmful interactions—in other words, people who are full of immorality and envy. Although I never spoke the words out loud, I thought of them as the living dead. Their body might be functioning, but their soul was dead, as their only concerns were meaningless and hackneyed. All these people achieved was to hold others captive to their own misery.

I was happy for Joanna because she had managed to break such ties. And, even though it seemed simple enough on the outside, it had been no easy task. Even those ties she had to maintain, due to family or professional obligations, she now dealt with differently. She adopted a new perspective, forbidding them from intruding into her daily life. She had worked hard on herself because she had learned to listen to others. That was a crucial step, as that was the only way she could build meaningful relationships.

I had chosen to return to work with Joanna because I feared that the intense emotions still churning inside me would not allow me to truly listen to anyone coming here for the first time, no matter how hard I tried. Therefore, Joanna, as an old student, had been a perfect choice.

After our short walk, we returned just before sunrise, and now, seated under the chestnut tree, we turned our gazes to the point where the sun would soon be making an appearance.

"How are you?" she asked me, and when I turned to look at her, I realized I had lost myself in my own thoughts again.

Although we had spoken the previous day briefly about what had happened, I had avoided dwelling on the subject, trying not to transfer my feeling onto others. Joanna, noticing my long silence, looked sorry to have asked. It was evident that her concern for me was genuine. I did not want her to regret expressing it, so with a small sigh and, turning my eyes towards the sunrise, I replied.

"I really don't know how I feel," I said. "There are times when I forget what has happened and I think that the door will open and he'll come inside. Then, my soul is filled with despair when I realize that it won't happen. I thought that I had experienced the greatest sense of loss already with the death of my mother."

I felt her intense gaze on me, and turned to look at her. Her eyes were filled with the sweetness of someone listening to a beautiful story. I turned back to the rising sun, determined to go on. Usually, she should be the one doing the talking, and I should be listening to her, but unexpectedly the roles had been reversed.

"It is strange how a single moment can change your whole world. Small decisions that we make, or don't make, can determine the outcome of our lives so dramatically. That morning, I made a choice that took away the person I had loved more than anyone else. Everything is still so fresh in my mind, so raw."

Joanna took my hand and squeezed it. "As you told me the last time I was here, what really matters is moving forward and appreciating the gift of life."

"That's right, Joanna... On the one hand, I feel so lucky for everything I shared with Antonis. On the other hand, the bitterness I feel for his sudden, unexpected loss still torments me. I will feel like this for a very long time. Maybe because I know how rare this relationship was. Antonis was not just my lover, he was my best friend, my family. Everything I teach about love, I experienced in this relationship. So simply, unconditionally, with no selfishness or obligation. I wish for you to experience it someday..."

Hearing myself talk, I understood that I was not ready to leave my painful feelings behind. Maybe because I was trying to keep all the beautiful moments we had shared alive. I did not want time to fade them in any way.

Just then, the sun appeared, drenching our faces with soft light which gradually grew more intense. A brand new day was at our doorstep.

"Just think that, at this very moment, some people on the other side of the world are watching the sunset," I said, turning towards her.

Joanna, her face glowing with pleasure, sighed.

"Tell me about yourself now," I said in a more cheerful mood. "I'm glad to see you are doing so much better."

Then she spoke to me in detail about everything she had decided to put behind her. She exercised more regularly and devoted more time to her current boyfriend. We spent a long time talking, her sharing her new plans with me, and later decided to make lunch. Our plan for the afternoon included some meditation exercises I desperately needed, too. We had arranged to make pancakes with Eva the following day, using the raspberries we cultivated on our land. That was a culinary event in itself. There would be nothing left by the end of the day, and we would all be filled with guilt. Of course, I called it "happy guilt," as everyone has the right, every now and then, to deviate from their routine.

Kostas Krommydas

Evora

IN A SPORTS CENTER outside Thessaloniki, Pavlos Lambrakis was playing tennis with a friend. All the courts were full, and many people were watching. The match ended with Pavlos hitting the ball forcefully and winning the game. A sparse round of applause followed, and the two players shook hands over the net. Pavlos and his opponent returned to the chairs at the side of the court, dripping with sweat from the exertion.

"Good game today, Pavlos."

"Thank you. I have been agitated recently, and it's obviously coming out in the way I play," he answered, wiping his face with a towel.

"Whatever it is, it's helping your game," the friend replied.

Pavlos gave a bitter laugh. "I wish I lost because I felt calmer," he admitted.

"As a friend and your lawyer, I advise you to relax a little. The court case will take place soon, and then it will all be over."

"I can't get over it. I wake up with a start in the middle of the night. I keep having nightmares."

"It's still fresh in your mind, that's why. I think your mood will change after the trial."

"Are you sure everything will be okay?" Pavlos asked.

"Worst case scenario, in my view, will be a suspended jail sentence of a few years," the man replied with certainty.

Pavlos looked pensive for a moment, and then lowered his head. "The point is, though, that I have caused great harm."

"We have gone over this so many times. It could have happened to anyone. Given the circumstances, no great harm was done."

"What do you mean?"

"Well, that there is not the slightest shred of evidence against you, and…"

"Yes, I know all that," Pavlos interrupted, raising his hand. "I am talking about the harm I caused to him, first and foremost, and his family, but mostly his girlfriend…"

"Ariadne…"

Pavlos gave him a look of surprise. "Yes," he answered drily.

"As your lawyer, my job is to do everything I can to win the trial ahead. Which won't take much, really. It will be a formality. As your friend, however, I must say that I have noticed your interest in that woman."

"I accidentally killed her boyfriend. Should I not care?" he asked, kicking his sports bag.

"No, that's only human, my friend. And any other kind of interest you may feel is also human. Just remember that it is probably a case of your need for forgiveness clouding your judgment. Forgiveness that I don't think she will give you."

"I honestly don't understand what you are getting at," Pavlos cried out, and he stood up, annoyed. "I have no interest other than the responsibility I feel for everything that happened!"

"Don't get mad at me, I'm on your side. I should tell you, though, that your parents have noticed it too."

"Noticed what, exactly?"

"I'm not saying you are doing anything wrong. Ariadne is a very attractive woman, and anyone could feel... captivated."

"So, what's your problem?" Pavlos spat out angrily.

"I guess you think of me as your enemy."

"Right now, you are my lawyer. You should concern yourself with the trial. My personal life is none of your business."

"Not if it can affect the judge's decision," the lawyer snapped. He looked around, making sure everyone was out of hearing.

"I don't understand what you are implying..." Pavlos said suspiciously.

"I think you understand what I'm saying, Pavlos. The slightest suspicion that you have feelings for Ariadne could change everything. Don't you understand that it could be used to prove that you had a motive for the shooting?"

"But I did not even know her when I stepped into the woods," Pavlos replied after a pensive pause.

"Why put us in a position of having to prove that? Don't forget that you are not the only one affected..."

Pavlos, trying to order his thoughts, returned to his chair and flung his towel around his neck.

"In any case, I don't have feelings for her, so there is no point talking about this."

"Fine. Just remember that the trial is approaching, and only once the judge declares you innocent of all charges will this whole thing be over."

The next two players appeared at the edge of the court, so the two men interrupted their conversation. They rose, gathered their things, and left the court.

"I'm going to take a shower. Are you coming?" the lawyer asked.

"No, they're waiting for me at home. We'll talk tomorrow morning at your office at nine o'clock."

"Ok. Goodnight, then."

Without returning the greeting, Pavlos turned away. He crossed the tennis club lobby, hurriedly greeting acquaintances, before heading to the exit and then the parking lot. He took out a t-shirt and replaced the sweaty one he had on. He threw his bag in the back seat of the car and sat down behind the wheel. Before switching the engine on, he took out his phone and began searching for something.

Before long, Ariadne's Instagram account appeared on the screen. If it were not for her name, the photo with Evora's logo could have been misleading. It did not mislead him, though. He checked her profile all the time for any new posts, which had stopped a few days before he shot Antonis in the woods. Scrolling further back, he located the only picture where Ariadne appeared, seated on the grass with her dog, Voras, gazing at the sunset beyond the lake. He brought the screen closer to his face. No matter how many times he looked at that photo, he could not get enough.

His ringtone—a fire alarm—went off, and the picture of the woman calling him appeared on-screen. He swore and then took the call. "Babe, I'll be there in ten minutes. I'm just leaving the club."

A dry "Okay" was heard through the car speakers. As soon as the line went dead, he gunned the engine on and set off.

A few days later

I WAS PACING UP AND DOWN the garden, trying to calm myself, because I was expecting Pavlos Lambrakis's visit any minute now. He had called me the previous afternoon and pressed hard for a meeting. Although I initially refused, he would not give up, saying that he needed to discuss a serious matter concerning the village, Avgerinos, with me. I did my best to convince him to tell me what it was about over the phone, but he insisted on meeting me face to face. I was already regretting succumbing to his pressure, but I did not intend to allow him to stay long. I asked him to come to the house because I did not want to be seen in his company in the village.

As soon as I heard the sound of the car, I went to the garden gate and stepped outside through a small side door, keeping the large gates closed. There was no way I was letting this man set foot on Evora. Voras approached me, trying to understand what I was doing, but I left him locked behind the gate. If Voras picked up on my emotions, as he so often did, he was liable to attack Lambrakis when he arrived.

It was noon, and the sun was burning, so I stood under the shade of a large oak tree. When Lambrakis drove up, I motioned for him to stop in the middle of the road, making him understand we would not be going inside. He stepped out of the car and walked up to me, holding his sunglasses in one hand.

"Good afternoon, Ariadne," he said, offering his other hand.

"Hello," I said, and reluctantly shook it.

"I would like to thank you for agreeing to see me. I know how difficult this is for you, but if you hear me out, you will see that this is for the greater good."

"I will be honest with you. I already regret agreeing to meet you, so I have to ask you to be brief."

He looked at the door as if expecting us to move inside, but I did not budge, not even a centimeter. His sigh evidenced his disappointment.

"Although I can't get a good look from here, it seems like you have a beautiful home."

I did not say one word. I just stared at him.

"I was not expecting a warm welcome. I understand how you feel."

"Trust me, you don't," I interrupted him, feeling my anger rise, as he was not getting to the point.

He raised his palms and instantly changed the subject. "The reason I wanted to see you was because I wanted your permission for something my family and I are planning for your village. We could go ahead and do it anyway, but I would rather have your endorsement."

"I'm afraid I don't understand you."

"Fine, then, I will get straight to the point. I feel responsible for Antonis's death, and would like to do something to commemorate him. We've decided to renovate the playground and the gym and name the new buildings after him. It is the least I can do, Ariadne, and I beg you to agree."

It took me a while to grasp what he was saying. His offer had taken me by surprise. I glared at him, and he lowered his eyes as if in fear. The man who stood before me seemed remorseful and, if his actions had not upturned everything in my life, I would have treated him with more compassion.

"Why don't you do something in your own village? It won't change the meaning of the gesture."

"You are right, but I spoke to the mayor of the region and found out about the needs in Avgerinos. I thought it would be better to offer something to a place he had lived in, albeit briefly."

"Then you should talk to his parents on Thasos. I am sure the island has many needs, too."

"Ariadne, the place does not really matter. Avgerinos is where the accident happened, and I would like to make something to commemorate him so you and the people who loved him can remember him."

I had mixed feelings, and struggled to find the right words. "If you were in my shoes, how would you react?" I asked him angrily.

"I can't imagine what it must feel like to be you right now. All I wish to do is ease everyone's pain by building something for him that will help the village and the children growing up here."

"You have caught me off guard, and I don't know how to respond. Why do you need my agreement on something like this? I am not the president of this community, nor the mayor of the region. You should put this proposal to them."

"The mayor has already been informed, and thinks the council will have no difficulty in approving this decision. I have not spoken to your father, who is the president of the village, because, without your approval, I will not go ahead. I will donate the money I intended to spend on another cause."

I really did not know what to say. I watched his eyes, and he seemed to mean every word he said. Solemn and humble, he stood before me fully aware of the consequences of his actions. I took a deep breath, thinking that this was something I needed to discuss with my family.

"I must confess that I am surprised by your proposal. However, as it is for a good cause like you said, I would like to discuss it with my family."

"Yes, I don't need an answer right away. Think about it. Also, think that this is a chance for something good to come out of the terrible harm I have caused."

For the first time, I felt my feelings soften a little. It's not like I suddenly liked Lambrakis, far from it. But I did start to believe that he genuinely felt bad about what had happened. Indeed, he seemed tormented by guilt. I remembered how willing he had been to help, in the days after the incident, showing his remorse. He could have done none of that and simply waited for the trial, where my understanding was that he would have got off lightly.

Voras, who had been silent all this time, now whimpered softly. He evidently wanted me to open the door, so he could come closer. His intervention, however, seemed to trigger all my memories of the day Antonis was shot by that man.

"I am going to ask you not to contact me again," I told Lambrakis coldly. "I will inform my father about your proposal, and any further discussions will have to be with him."

He looked at me in despair. I don't know what he was expecting from me, but I did not intend to become his friend. My father could decide about his offer.

"Fine then," he said, in a voice hoarse with disappointment.

"I have to get back to the house now," I said, and turned to go.

I saw him stay there, rooted to the spot, and went to close the door behind me, but Voras dashed through the gap and ran towards him. Convinced my dog was going to attack him, I followed after him, calling him to come back.

But Lambrakis simply took a step back and calmly stretched out his hand. Voras stopped in his tracks, then sniffed his hand. I had been so sure Voras would bite him, because I thought he sensed what that man had done to Antonis and to us. However, none of that happened, and my dog kept examining Lambrakis as if he were another animal and not a human being. In fact, he sneezed loudly, but never stopped sniffing him.

"I was scared he was going to attack me," Lambrakis said, "but I guess he can smell my dog on my clothes. I have a Rottweiler."

Lambrakis stretched out his hand and petted Voras, but my dog paid him no heed. I gripped him by the collar and pulled him behind me, telling him to follow me. Voras reluctantly obeyed. We stepped into the garden, and I slammed the door shut.

I cast a quick glance at Lambrakis, who stood there watching us. He raised his hand to wave goodbye, but I turned away. Voras tried to return to him, but I stood in front of him and put him in the living room the moment we reached the house. Just then, I heard Lambrakis's car pull away.

I approached my mother's photo in the hallway and touched the glass. "What would you do if you were in my shoes?" I whispered.

I turned to the kitchen, convinced that with her infinite kindness, she would have forgiven him from the start. Wouldn't she?

Evora

I sat with Voras under the chestnut tree and listened to the sounds of the panegyri. For the first time in years, I had not gone to the restaurant or the party that took place in the village on this day every year. Yiannis and Myrto had just left. They had insisted they stay and keep me company, but I refused, saying that there was no reason for them to miss out. I had decided to stay here, and I persuaded them that I would be okay with Voras keeping me company.

I did not do it to show others that I was still grieving, but because I found dealing with everyone who wished to express their condolences hard. I was neither hiding from the world nor seeking interaction with it. They had arranged a hike for the following day, as was their yearly custom, but I declined to join them. I preferred my solitary walks with my faithful friend.

When I took a break from holding sessions with my students a few days ago, I visited Thasos. I had only returned to Evora the day before yesterday. I was upset because Antonis's parents did not seem to be coping well with their son's death. It was as if not a day had passed for them. I, on the other hand, was beginning to resume my everyday life, without ever forgetting.

The trial date had been set for mid-September. In the meantime, Lambrakis had started turning the offer he had made into reality. About a week ago, works on the gym and the surrounding area had begun. My father said it was a significant expense which had been entirely covered by the Lambrakis family. I didn't want to admit it to myself, but I did feel glad, despite my bitterness, that the children would have a new space to exercise and play.

Lambrakis kept trying to engineer a meeting with me, but I assiduously avoid him, referring him to my father. If everything went according to plan, the new spaces would open next spring, bearing Antonis's name. It was a consolation of some sort, even though I did not need a plaque with his name on it to remember him.

I picked up a glass of wine and clinked it with a half-empty glass that stood on the table. I felt sure that if there was some kind of life after death, Antonis would find a way to be here. In our slice of heaven, as he always called Evora.

Evora

EVERYTHING WAS SET for Pavlos Lambrakis's trial to begin. If it were up to me, I would not be here. I would rather stay away from this soul-sucking experience. After a family meeting, we decided not to be represented by a lawyer. As there was no question of malicious intent, we did not want to prolong this painful process for no reason. We just hoped that Lambrakis would be punished for his mistake.

After all these months, not a day passed that I did not think about everything that had happened. Not a day passed that I did not wake up thinking of the morning that had changed our lives. Walking into the courthouse and seeing all those people who had been present during Antonis's last moments, the painful memories that had only just started to fade resurged. The faces of the doctors, the face of the man who had accompanied Lambrakis in the forest...

Antonis's parents were also present, despite the hardship that travel presented for them. So were his sister and her husband and elder daughter, who loved her uncle very much, as she told me when I'd met her earlier that day. Yiannis and Myrto were also here, having made the long journey from Athens to be by my side.

We all gathered outside the courtroom, and at some point they let us inside. A few moments later, the three judges, the jury, and the public prosecutor took their seats. The hearing began with witness testimonies. I had never been in a courtroom before, and everything was different from what I expected. The building's exterior was a mess, sprayed with graffiti. Inside, the rooms smelt moldy. It reminded me of an old hospital rather than a courtroom. I could feel Lambrakis's eyes on me, but I avoided looking at him.

After some consultation among the judges on the bench, the presiding judge called my name and asked the other witnesses to step outside. I was surprised he was starting with me. I stepped onto the witness stand and, when instructed by the judge, started to calmly describe the events that unfolded that day, from my father's first phone call in the morning to the moment we arrived at the hospital.

When I finished, the presiding judge said, "All the statements so far indicate that you saw the defendant for the first time in your life on the day of the incident. Is that right?"

"Yes," I answered, trying to understand what he was getting at.

"And you have been in contact with him ever since?"

He was looking at me inquisitively, as if trying to discover something. I had nothing to hide, so I summarily reported all my contact with Lambrakis. The judge interrupted me often, asking for more details, such as how long we spoke or where we met. I felt as if I were being interrogated, but then he thanked me with a smile.

The public prosecutor spoke next. "What was your relationship to the victim?

How poor and inadequate words seemed when it came to describing the love Antonis and I had shared.

"We'd been together for the better part of a year, and mostly lived at my house in Avgerinos."

"And how long had you known each other?"

"A little more than a year," I replied in a shaky voice.

"I understand this is a difficult process for you, so this will be my last question."

I looked at her, wiping away a tear.

"In all this time, have you ever thought, even for just a second, that the defendant shot your partner on purpose, for some reason that we might not know?"

I mechanically bowed my head. My eyes focused on a loose plank along the bench. When I lifted my head again, that first and final "I love you" Antonis had said before leaving my side flashed through my mind. I tried to reply, but my voice seemed stuck in my throat as if my vocal cords had been twisted into a painful knot. I brought my hand to my mouth.

"No, I don't believe he saw him and fired on purpose. He had no reason to. Only a psychopath would shoot someone for no reason," I managed to stammer. "But, it could have been a child playing in the woods instead of Antonis," I said more forcefully, my blood starting to boil. "It could have been you or me... The danger he caused, carrying a gun in a peaceful place, firing without looking at what he was shooting..." I was beginning to lose my cool, and forced myself to stop talking.

Now it was the turn of Lambrakis's lawyer, who expressed his condolences yet again. "Miss Nastou, when you arrived at the scene, what condition was Mr. Lambrakis in?"

"He was shocked, but when I realized that Antonis had been injured, all my attention was on him and trying to help him."

"My client, as you have previously stated, helped you until you reached the hospital. Is that so?"

"Yes..."

"So, you too observed a man who, fully aware of his mistake, was trying to help in any way possible..."

"If you look at it that way, yes. As I already said, he showed his willingness to help from the very first moment." I paused, feeling that any minute now, we would be heaping praise on Lambrakis for his actions. "However, none of that changes what happened. I have been walking through these woods since I was a young girl, on my own, and I don't even take a stick with me for protection..." I breathed deeply. My voice was about to crack with emotion.

"Why did you go to that part of the woods?"

I took another deep breath before replying. "Antonis, my father, and I went there because we had been informed that poachers were in the area. Not only was it not open season, but the forest is also a protected nature reserve. We love our forests and would never consider leaving them unprotected, not for a single moment. And yet, our love turned against..."

I had become so emotional that I could not go on. I thought I was strong enough, but my eyes had welled up, and my voice had dwindled to a hoarse whisper. "I'm sorry, I can't," I said, bowing my head.

I heard the presiding judge advise me to sit down. I returned to the bench beside Eva. I had not expected to be so affected by this. I thought I had the strength to remain calm and control my reactions. My heart, however, was doing as it pleased and refused to set boundaries to what I was feeling.

As they called the next witness, I observed everyone else in the courtroom. Lambrakis's parents were here, sitting at the back, their eyes fixed on me. Antonis's family sat across the room. They all looked at me warmly, tears in their eyes, trying to give me strength. His mother's eyes pierced my heart. She exuded serenity and incredible courage. I noticed some of the people from the village in the room, and many people I did not know.

Eva gripped my hand in her lap. I gave her a smile, and then turned my attention to the judges' bench.

The presiding judge had called Lambrakis's friend, Archontis, to testify. He described more or less everything that had happened, and then spoke of meeting us in the Valley.

When he finished, the judge asked, "How long have you known the defendant?"

"We met a short while before the incident. My wife's family owns a share of the land we visited. We met through a mutual friend to discuss whether Mr. Lambrakis would be interested in purchasing the whole of the land."

"So the land does not belong to your wife?"

"No, she owns one-fifth. The rest belongs to relatives."

"Were the other owners informed of your initiative?"

"No, we wanted to see if he was interested in buying, and then we would approach them with the offer."

"You say you split up in the woods because the defendant wanted to visit the footpath and see whether it could be turned into a road."

He nodded. "That's right."

"Do you not think it strange to split up instead of staying together, if you were worried about being attacked by wild animals, as you claim?"

"Yes, it's just that Mr. Lambrakis also wanted to..." Archontis hesitated, and turned to look at the lawyer, who nodded at him, encouraging him to go on. "Let's just say that nature called, and he had to answer."

Someone in the audience laughed, and I turned angrily around. I recognized the man who had laughed, and he froze when he saw my expression. Lambrakis also seemed annoyed, because he turned around and spoke sternly to the man. The presiding judge asked for the man to be removed from the courtroom. Then, he called for quiet in the courtroom. I turned back to face the bench, still seething at the laughter.

The public prosecutor spoke next, looking down at some papers spread out before her. Without raising her head, she asked: "You have testified that both guns belong to you, is that so?"

"Yes, that is correct."

"You knew you would be together the whole time. You also knew that the defendant was unfamiliar with guns, so why did you take a second gun with you? Did you not worry that an inexperienced man with a gun could cause an accident?"

"That was a grave error of judgment, which I truly regret. I had the guns in my car before we met up, and I encourage him to pick one up. I, too, had been frightened by rumors of wild animals and did not want anything to happen to us. I pressed him to also carry a gun so that we could be safe. I did not imagine anyone else would be in the area."

"How many times have wild animals attacked people in your area?" the public prosecutor asked, and he hesitated before replying.

"Other than the attack on Miss Nastou and her friends, I think it happened once before, a long time ago. I had heard of the attack and thought it prudent to take precautions."

I suddenly felt as if I was waking up from a dream. I wanted to speak up, but did not know if it was allowed, so I kept quiet. I wanted to clarify that the wolves had not attacked us that day, that it had been the deer they were after.

One of the other judges spoke next. "Did you and the defendant have any other kind of connection?" he asked.

"No. As I said, we only met shortly before the incident."

The presiding judge looked up from a paper he was reading and addressed Archontis again. "Is it true that when you met Miss Nastou and her father in the forest, you told them that you were alone?"

"Yes, but I meant alone in the Valley. I did not realize that they were asking me whether I was accompanied overall."

Archontis had just lied. I remembered that morning clearly, and he had claimed there was no one else with him, at all. But it was a small lie, and I did not see how it could matter, so I said nothing.

The presiding judge looked at Archontis for a moment, then asked if there were any more questions. None of the other judges replied, but the lawyer asked to address the witness.

"When Pavlos Lambrakis took the gun you had placed in his hands, did he seem to be at ease with it?"

"No, he only took it because I insisted. I showed him how it worked. I wish I hadn't."

They then asked Archontis some questions about his ties to the village, and what he did for a living. The presiding judge then asked my father to take the stand. He, too, described what had happened from his point of view.

At the end of his testimony, the presiding judge asked him, "Do you and the other villagers take a gun into the woods for protection?"

"Never. No one I know does that, sir," he replied.

Then everyone else testified one by one, from the two rangers to the doctors. I was surprised to hear the doctor from Edessa report that Lambrakis was persistently asking about Antonis's condition from the start. The doctor from Thessaloniki took the bench last. He said that, by the time we had arrived, it was all over for Antonis. Then he analyzed the bullet wounds in great detail.

I looked outside the window at a pigeon, perched on the ledge as if it were trying to see what we were all doing in that room. My anger had subsided. I knew that being permanently enraged would not change anything. I wished

I never had to set eyes on that man again. He was a constant reminder of those terrible moments. I wondered when this soul-crushing process would end.

Just before the doctor stepped down from the stand, the lawyer asked him, "Did you know the defendant, doctor?"

"I met him at the hospital two days later, when he came to find out about the victim's condition."

"And was there any further contact after that?"

"Yes, every day. He would either come to the hospital, or contact a colleague or me by phone. He wanted to know about the victim's state of health."

"You also spoke about something else, right?"

"Yes. Mr. Lambrakis asked whether his condition would improve in another hospital. We excluded that from the start. When there was no longer any hope of recovery, he offered to move the patient to a private hospital, but the patient's family declined the offer."

"In your opinion, did the defendant show genuine concern for the victim's condition?'

"Yes, absolutely."

"Thank you. I have no further questions," the lawyer said. He cast Lambrakis a satisfied glance and returned to his seat.

I had no idea who the next two witnesses were. One spoke about Lambrakis, describing him as a law-abiding citizen who was also an active philanthropist. I wondered what the point of it all was, but it was evidently a part of the lawyer's defense strategy.

The other witness was a policeman who spoke about the ballistic report, as there was some doubt about whether Lambrakis had shot Antonis once or twice. Their investigation had shown that the first shot had been fired towards a totally different direction to the shot that had ultimately killed Antonis.

I was starting to feel exhausted in this dingy room, where even the thought of resting your hands on the bench was repulsive. A woman at the back shouted out something, but they asked her to keep quiet. She was complaining about the heat, and she was right. There was not even a ceiling fan to move the stifling air around.

Lambrakis was the last to testify. "When you realized you had just shot a man, what did you do?" the presiding judge asked.

Lambrakis sighed. "Initially, I did not even realize I had shot someone. The fog and the dense foliage prevented me from seeing much. I told you I cried out before firing, but I heard no reply. I was convinced it was a wolf, so you can imagine my horror when I discovered a man on the ground, bleeding. I hurried to him immediately, to see how seriously he was injured. When I realized he was unconscious, I moved to call for help, but I heard someone approaching just then. It was Miss Ariadne Nastou."

He gave me a sideways glance, and then continued narrating what had happened from his point of view until we reached Edessa. He also answered questions about his business activities.

The presiding judge spoke again. "There is a small detail arising from the ballistic report. It states that the cartridges from the rifle hit Antonis Stavrou at an angle. Two superficial wounds to the ribs and neck, and a serious wound to the head, close to the ear. Can you explain how that could happen, given that a man walking in a straight line towards a gun would sustain injuries at the front, and not the side, of his body?"

Lambrakis did not seem at all surprised. "As I said before, I had not seen what was approaching when I fired the gun. I thought that an animal was coming towards me to attack me. In both cases, I fired to scare the animal off rather than to hit a target. The terrain is very rough. It's possible that he momentarily turned sideways to approach from another direction. It was also a little foggy, which made things even more difficult. So I couldn't distinguish his position when I shot him."

"Except that this time you did not fire in the air like you did the first time. You fired aiming to hit what had frightened you, as you say."

"I was not aiming in a particular direction, if that's what you mean. I was confused and overwhelmed and had no time to think. I had been affected by the stories of my companion about wild animals, and I thought that something was attacking me. Both times I fired instinctively."

He paused briefly. His voice was steady, but there was a sense of compassion in it. He wiped his forehead with his palm.

"I don't know what it feels like to lose a loved one so unjustly. No sentence, no apology, can bring back a man who everyone agrees was an exceptional person. I will carry the burden of having taken a life for the rest of my days. I am trying... My family and I are trying to somehow soften the pain of their loss and ease the burden of my soul. I will accept any sentence the court deems just, and will do what I can to ensure such an accident never occurs again, to anyone. Thank you."

Lambrakis returned to his seat, looking at me all the while. The presiding judge whispered something to the other judges and the public prosecutor. Then he gave the floor to Lambrakis's lawyer. He cast a quick glance over the room, greeted everyone, and prepared to deliver his closing argument.

"After everything we have heard here today, I would like to ask the bench to show clemency in its judgment. The defendant has always been a law-abiding citizen with exemplary conduct. In essence, he is a victim, too, although, of course, he is fully aware of the consequences of his actions." He buttoned up his suit and continued after a brief pause. "Before I say anything further, I would like once again to express my own sorrow and the sorrow of my client in particular, for the terrible loss of Antonis Stavrou. A terrible misfortune was the cause of his death. I will go on to set out events exactly as they happened that day."

He turned towards me. "But let us start at the beginning. Some time ago, Pavlos Lambrakis was informed of the beauty of the wider region. He had been on the lookout for land that could be developed for tourism. Mr. Panagiotis Archontis accompanied him that day to an area in the woods known as the Valley, wanting to propose its purchase for that purpose. Given the previous wolf attack at a nearby location, Mr. Archontis brought two rifles with him, solely for their protection. They also took his dog with them for greater safety. My client had no knowledge of the two rifles until they arrived at the Valley. Not only that, but, as Mr. Archontis testified, he objected when his companion proposed that they enter the forest armed. Mr. Archontis's insistence, along with the recent wolf attack, led to my client being forced to take the gun with him. A gun which, I must stress again, did not belong to him."

The lawyer took a sip of water before continuing. "Shortly thereafter, my client, following his companion's suggestion, took a different path to the Valley." He cast a fleeting look at Lambrakis. "He wanted to see whether a road could be constructed to the Valley on that side, as well as attend to...

biological matters. Before they parted ways, Archontis further increased my client's anxiety about wild animals by advising him to fire in the air if he noticed anything amiss. Please let it be noted that my client has never been a hunter and knows nothing about guns. He has not touched a gun since completing his military service. I would also like to stress that, as others have testified, the area was covered in fog that day. The fog not only restricted visibility greatly but increased, if you like, the sense of danger lurking in the woods."

From the corner of my eye, I caught Lambrakis looking at me, but turned my attention back to the lawyer, trying to ignore him.

"Then, when he was on his own, he heard a rustle in the leaves. He called out, asking who was there. Instead of a reply, he heard the roar of an animal. Frightened, he fired in the air to chase the animal away. Indeed, whatever it was, it ran away. However, it left my client terrified. He tried to make his way back. Confused and entirely unfamiliar with the area, he decided to retrace his steps. That's when he heard another noise. With terrible visibility, and believing that the same wild animal was approaching with hostile intentions, he called out again. Again, he received no reply and, convinced he was about to be attacked, he took a blind shot towards the trees. He never had the time to understand that the noise had been made by a person.

"Unaware of what had actually happened, he stayed rooted to the spot at first, frightened. Then, he slowly moved in the direction of his shot and, to his horror, realized what had happened. Before he had a chance to call for help, Miss Nastou arrived on the scene. Together with her father, one of the rangers, and Miss Nastou, they carried the injured man as quickly as possible to the hospital in Edessa in my client's car.

"Up until the moment of his arrest, Mr. Lambrakis stayed with the victim's friends, trying to help them, fully aware of his actions, which bore no malice but had taken place under the extraordinary circumstances I just described. Later too, after he was released, he kept trying to assist the victim's parents and partner, to the point where he offered them accommodation at a house near the hospital. He also provided the authorities with all the information they needed, never hiding anything. As we speak, the gym and surrounding area of Avgerinos are being renovated with funds provided by my client and his family. Indeed, it will bear the name of the deceased, honoring an exceptional man whose life was lost so needlessly."

The heat and tension I felt had soaked my shirt with sweat. While the lawyer delivered his speech, I kept thinking back to the events of that day, reexperiencing them with all my senses. Lambrakis was hunched over, holding his head with both hands. His lawyer was not done, however.

"What the evidence shows is that my client had absolutely no ties to the victim. The tragic accident that took place was just that—an accident. Their unfortunate meeting was the first and last time that the two men had come across each other. They never spoke, never argued.

"Before concluding my speech, I would like to mention the donation that the family's company has made to the organization where the deceased worked, and which is dedicated to investigating climate change. I would like to enter the organization's letter thanking them into the court record."

He took a piece of paper from the defense table and handed it to the judges. Then he turned to the audience and, in a melodramatic tone, said, "Of course, none of this can bring back Antonis Stavrou. It will possibly alleviate some of the burden Pavlos Lambrakis carries. In this manner, he wishes to preserve the memory of the man whose life he accidentally took. You should also know that my client has never had any run-ins with the law. He is a law-abiding citizen, a member of a respectable family whose charity work is well-known. For this reason, he asks the court to take all the mitigating circumstances into account before delivering its final verdict. Thank you."

The lawyer turned away and, before he could even sit down, the presiding judge said, "Madame Prosecutor, you have the floor."

The court-appointed prosecutor removed her glasses and stood as she spoke, twirling a pen between her fingers. "This is not the first time a young person meets an untimely and needless death. This is also not the first time someone takes a life. Whether it happened intentionally or not will determine the sentence, but not the outcome of the act. Antonis Stavrou was a conscientious citizen, and it is evident from the witness testimony that all he wanted to do that day was to protect the forest from poachers. He did not set off to go into a confrontation, but into the woods. Guns, however, when they fall into the wrong hands, can become the most murderous instrument.

"Children have inadvertently become murderers in the past, as they had no awareness of the dangers a gun holds. Here, however, we are faced with two adults who carried rifles into the forest under the pretext of a potential wildlife attack. Suddenly, the Greek mountains are presented like the jungle. The evidence and witness testimonies indicate that there was no intention to kill, I am convinced of that. The arrogance and recklessness which underpinned the actions of both adults, however, are undisputed. They led to the untimely death of a young man. Pavlos Lambrakis may not have intended to kill Mr. Stavrou, but he was in full command of his faculties when he decided to pick up that gun—a gun he did not own, a gun he was not licensed to use.

She closed a lever arch file that was open before her, and, turning to look at Lambrakis, spoke loud and clear. "For all of the above, I recommend that the court find the defendant guilty of involuntary manslaughter."

The presiding judge declared the court adjourned. "We will reconvene tomorrow morning to deliver our verdict," he announced, and with that it was all over.

I was taken aback—not at the abruptness of the ending, but because I had assumed a verdict would be reached at the end of the session. I had expected everything to be over before the end of the day. I wanted this chapter of my life to end more than anything else. I wanted to resume my daily life without the pending case hanging over my head. I was impatient for the trial to end, and yet I had to be patient for one more day.

I avoided talking to anyone in the courtroom, and slipped out with Eva and my father. Accompanied by Antonis's family, we made our way back to the café-restaurant, Yiannis and Myrto following in their own car. During the drive, my father kept commenting on how well-prepared the defense had been, having an answer for everything. For my part, I found it only natural, thinking that anyone would do the same to get the lightest sentence possible.

After dinner, I bid my dear friends goodbye as they departed for Athens, and promised to call them the following day when Lambrakis was sentenced. I accompanied Antonis's family to the village hotel, and we agreed to talk later. Then, I returned to the restaurant and took the footpath that led back to my house with Voras, who had been patiently waiting for me.

The sun had almost dipped below the horizon. The sweet quietness of nature was disrupted by the voice of a huckster advertising his wares through the loudspeakers attached to the roof of his car.

I stopped on top of the hill for a moment to look at the works taking place at the gym and the surrounding area. I was surprised to see someone wandering among the machinery. I took a closer look and instantly made out the figure of none other than Pavlos Lambrakis.

I was perplexed by his behavior and his actions. Watching him move across the building site, I wondered whether his intentions were sincere. Were they just part of a plan to get off as lightly as possible, to earn the clemency of the judges with a display of great remorse? Even then, it was perplexing, as no one had accused him of intentionally shooting Antonis. His whole attitude made me feel ill-at-ease, as I had no intention of allowing him further into my life. Once the trial was over, I hoped never to see him again. I did not hate him. I felt something very strange towards him, as his presence forced the memories of those painful moments to the front of my mind.

I turned away, seeking Voras, who had pushed further ahead. I lengthened my strides to catch up with him. As soon as I entered my house, my eyes fell on the blue box with Antonis's things. I had promised myself I would open it when the trial was over. Walking past it, I stroked the box in silent promise. Tomorrow.

Next week I had booked back to back sessions, and I also had to prepare the guesthouse at some point. Tonight, however, I was determined to get to bed early. The following day would be an equally hard one...

Evora

I AM WALKING THROUGH THE TREES. My clothes are dappled with the dew from the bushes as I brush against their leaves, pushing ahead. The land is misty, and the sun's rays creep through any gap they can find, lighting up chunks of the trunks, making them appear like small islands of light. The birds are dashing to hide, tweeting anxiously as if they are afraid I will harm them.

I bend down among the ferns and pick the first wild strawberries of spring. I close my eyes in bliss as my mouth is filled by their fresh, intense flavor. I keep as many as I can in my palm to slowly savor them as I wander through the tall fir trees.

The trampled grass ahead betrays the footsteps of someone who has been here before me. I follow their tracks, careful not to make a sound and startle whatever may be walking ahead. A small squirrel hurriedly climbs a tree and skips far away, hopping from branch to branch. I hear the gurgle of the spring's water on the hill and desperately want to quench my thirst. With great difficulty, I grab onto the thin trunks and pull myself up the slope.

A strange noise forces me to stop and look around. It sounded like the caw of a bird, or the sound of an animal rooting for something in the undergrowth. The sound echoes for a moment until it is lost in the distance, allowing me to move on. I am not afraid. I feel at one with the forest as I now wander over familiar ground.

Soon, I arrive at the small opening where, from the depths of a rock, spring water surges forth and is lost among the stones. It is as if the earth is gifting it briefly to whoever wants to drink before swallowing it back up. I approach, thirsty, desiring to sink my head in the water and enjoy its crisp freshness.

Suddenly, I hear someone whisper my name. Startled, I turn around. I wonder if it was the rustling of the wind or an actual human voice. Large clouds suddenly cover the sun and a veil that dims the colors of nature descends, making them seem lifeless. Everything suddenly falls silent...

All that can be heard is the water gushing from the spring. I slowly turn around and bend down to assuage my thirst. Startled, I jump back and fall on the ground. In the place of water, red blood is flowing, like the blood that first springs forth from wounded flesh. The flow keeps getting stronger like lava from a small volcano, moving towards me. I try to run, but my feet are stuck to the ground. With superhuman effort, I cry out...

I sat up and opened my eyes. I could still see the red of the blood in the nightmare that had just woken me. Beside me, Voras stood up and started to lick my hand. I slowly leaned back against my pillow, trying to chase the last images from my mind. The early light of dawn timidly crept through the windows. Another day without him beside me.

THE FOLLOWING DAY FOUND US in our seats at the courtroom early in the morning. The judges arrived soon after, and, once we were all seated, the presiding judge spoke first. "The court finds the defendant guilty of involuntary manslaughter. Madame Prosecutor has the floor."

"I recommend a prison sentence of three years."

I was surprised to hear that. I thought Lambrakis would receive a suspended sentence. The way I heard it, it sounded as if the prosecutor was recommending that he spend three years in jail. Then the judges and everyone else began to speak softly amongst themselves. The judge to the left of the presiding judge handed him a piece of paper. As soon as he read it, he called for silence.

"The court, having examined all evidence and testimonies, finds Pavlos Lambrakis guilty of involuntary manslaughter and sentences him to a suspended prison term of three years."

I had not expected anything more or anything less. Of course, a short spell in prison would have done Lambrakis no harm, teaching him to resist the temptation to do something so reckless again. However, all I had wanted was for everything to be over and, finally, that moment had arrived. There were no remarkable reactions in the courtroom. Evidently, they considered this to be a fair punishment.

Noticing Lambrakis looking at me intently and moving in my direction, I turned the other way to avoid him. I asked my family to follow me outside. On the front steps of the courthouse, I said goodbye to Antonis's family with tears in my eyes, promising to visit his parents on Thasos soon. I had tried to persuade them to spend the night at my house, but they preferred to go back. His sister and her family would be departing for Strasbourg the following day, too.

Just before they left, his mother hugged me so tightly I could feel her heartbeat. "Take care, sweetheart, thank you for everything," she said, before stepping into the car with the others. I had to clench my teeth to hold back my tears. As the car sped away, I thought about the noble soul of a woman who could be thanking me when she had lost her child.

Once they had left, we made our way back to the village. I called Yiannis to tell him about the sentence. He did not seem surprised, either, and during our brief conversation advised me to put this whole experience behind me and get on with my life.

When we arrived at Evora, my father stepped out of the car and hugged me. "I know how difficult these past few months have been for you. Whatever you need, we are here for you."

"Thank you," I answered, and gave him a kiss on the forehead.

"Be grateful for the time you had with Antonis, even for a short while," he said, and got back inside the car beside Eva.

I watched them drive away and thought about what he'd said. How beautiful gratitude is. I turned towards the house and went straight to the chestnut tree. It was still quite hot, and its thick shade was soothing. I sat in my armchair, gazing at the horizon. This was my Evora. My own perfect time for gratitude.

Following Antonis's death, the question of why it had to happen to us constantly tormented me. I had told no one, but it was eating away at my soul. In the past, I had always cultivated the feeling of gratitude inside me. For a while now, though, I had forgotten it even existed. It is a feeling so strong that it can change not only the person who feels it, but the whole world. I was content with everything that I had before I met Antonis. I had learned early on to savor even the tiniest moments of happiness. Gratitude was not just a positive feeling; it made me a stronger person, too, as I could appreciate everything around me.

My teachers had encouraged me to write down a list of everything that made me grateful, and I encouraged my students to do the same. I asked them to write down on a piece of paper five things for which they felt blessed every day. It may sound easy, but people who have spent the greater part of their lives being ungrateful find it hard to change their attitude and pinpoint those moments. After some effort, however, they all discovered something that they could feel grateful for.

In my life, I had felt absolute gratitude when Antonis saved me from the frozen waters of the lake. Until I met him again, that feeling overflowed inside me unhindered, straight from my soul, and I wanted to share it with those around me. Because that is what happens when you express your gratitude. You transmit it to others, helping them change, even change their lives. It is wonderful to have the courage to say thank you. Not just voice it in words, but say it straight from the heart. When you cultivate gratitude, you gain spiritual balance. You set your ego aside and discover who you truly are. It is impossible to be selfish and grateful at the same time.

Here I sat now, in the shade of the chestnut tree, filled with the beautiful moments I had shared with Antonis as well as the perfect serenity of this hour.

I had been struggling to set aside my anger and the rage that often came knocking at my door. The time that flowed by relentlessly was an ally because it swept everything bad away. Because yes, time does heal everything, so long as you don't forget the things you should be thankful for. That is why I wanted the trial to be over. So that I could focus on the positive. This way, I did not only feel better, but I was learning to set aside the negative thoughts that could so easily trap you in a vicious cycle of hatred.

I was fully aware that if I wished to live my life guided by joy, I had to share this gift with those around me. This way, everyone could cultivate the belief that the world is not only filled with selfishness and unkindness. Besides, whether you believe people are good or bad is also a choice you make. I did not think Lambrakis was a bad person. Spoiled, maybe, unthinking of the consequences of his actions. Bad person or not, however, nothing could change what had happened.

Voras rubbed against my armchair, interrupting my thoughts. I gave him a smile and, for a moment there, he looked like he was returning it. What my father had said before leaving had spurred me on to remember how great it was to feel grateful.

I kissed the top of my faithful companion's head and stood up. I had decided to dedicate some time to my garden. Autumn was well on its way, and the first leaves had started falling from the trees. The circle of life in full harmony...

Kostas Krommydas

Evora

NEARLY TEN DAYS had passed since the end of the trial. My first student had just left the previous day. Having a free day before the next arrival, I decided to take a walk through the woods and visit the spot near the Valley where Lambrakis had shot Antonis. I did not tell anyone of my plans.

I had not been back since the shooting. In a strange way that I could not explain, I had been feeling the urge to return there these days. Also, I intended to open the blue box in the evening. Perhaps I should be sending his parents some of the items in there.

I stepped outside the house and sought Voras, but he was nowhere to be seen. I brought my fingers to my mouth and gave a loud whistle, and then waited for some time, sipping my tea.

The sun had already risen. The sound of machinery from the construction site the gym had become drifted up from the village. The school children carried fresh water to the workmen every day, who always welcomed them. The teacher had told them as a joke that if they helped out, the playground would be finished even sooner.

The sky was different today, and even though no rain was forecast, I had the feeling a storm might break out later. The microclimate of the region had become aligned with the overall climate change.

I finished the dregs of my tea and decided to set off on my walk without Voras. I placed a flask of water in my rucksack, a second t-shirt, and a snack for later in the woods.

I looked at the knife on the kitchen bench. I may rarely take my phone with me, but I always carried my knife. I put it in the inside pocket of my rucksack and prepared to set off. If my stamina held, I was sure I could reach the Valley in good time. Antonis, unfortunately, never had the chance to see this beautiful spot.

I took the path through the village in the hope of running into my dog, perhaps flirting with one of the female sheepdogs. I greeted everyone I crossed. One of Yiannis's aunts saw me from afar and called me to approach her fence. She handed me a slice of spinach pie, just like my mother used to make. Although wrapped up in wax paper, the scent of the freshly baked dough still filled the air. I thanked her and carefully placed the pie in my rucksack to savor later.

How wonderful to feel that the whole village was like one big family. It was not that common. In most places, people had serious arguments, and fights broke out frequently. In Avgerinos, we had worked out a way to get along, and tensions in the village were rare.

Just before turning off the main road and following the trail that would lead me to the footpath, I saw a car coming from the opposite direction. When I saw that it looked like Lambrakis's car, I broke into a jog and snuck into the forest. I had no wish to see him or talk to him. I heard an engine die down, and realized he had pulled over. Evidently, he had spotted me, but I kept going until I lost sight of the village. I decided to follow the dry riverbed and rejoin the trail later.

Eva had found out from the workmen coming to the restaurant that Lambrakis would still visit the works often to inspect their progress. In fact, he had joined the workers for lunch a few times, trying to engage my sister and my dad in conversation. The workmen, who were locals and had known Antonis, ignored Lambrakis entirely during his last visit, and he had not shown up in days.

Thankfully, he had not dared come to Evora again. I was convinced that he would have come back again, given the slightest encouragement. Actually, one evening last week, Voras started barking loudly, and I thought someone was standing at the other end of the garden. I could not be sure, however, so I did not pay any more attention.

Walking along the riverbed, I kept an eye turned to the sky, trying to guess the intentions of the weather. I tried to locate the origin of the sound reaching my ears, like someone gunning a motorbike. A little further up, I met the forestry workers logging with their chainsaws and axes. In the past, the sight of the tree stumps left behind used to fill me with anger. Then, a forester had explained to me that a proper scientific study would pinpoint which older trees needed to be chopped down. This would create space for younger trees to grow, thus renewing elderly forests. They carried the felled trees with mules because a truck could not easily reach many parts of the woods. So the mules did all the hard work.

The smell of chopped wood was intense. I greeted the lumberjacks, as most of them were from the village, and gradually I moved into the virgin forest where no human intervention was allowed. Even the land in the Valley, which Lambrakis claimed he was interested in developing, was likely to be protected despite being privately owned. It could possibly be farmed, but definitely not built on. My father told me Lambrakis would probably purchase it very cheaply from the owners and then try to develop it.

I took a shortcut by climbing over a small, steep hill and found myself close to the spot where we had left our car that day. The animal bells on the slope across sounded like a calming melody. Here, every sound arrived filtered by nature herself.

I listened carefully for a couple of minutes and then moved on. The path was overgrown with grass, as a sign that no one had been back here since then, at least not by car.

Ambling, I came closer and closer to the location where our paths had parted. I felt my trouser legs grow wet beneath my knees, and realized that they were getting soaked by the dew as I brushed against the undergrowth. I then remembered the nightmare I had had a few days ago. The thought made me shiver, but there was no way I would turn back now.

Following the same route, I finally reached the spot where the path split in two. I had been walking for over two hours and felt that I would be able to reach the Valley. I turned left, just as Antonis had done on that day, and walked on, admiring the beauty of the landscape. I greedily breathed in the clean forest air, feeling it purify everything inside me.

It did not take me long to spot the white stone and the spot where I had found Antonis on the ground. I slowly approached it and, with a quick glance, realized that nothing betrayed that my beloved had been shot here. The rain that had poured down from the heavens since then had washed away all evidence of his passage.

Exhausted from the hike, I sat down on the stone. I took out my flask and downed half the water in a single gulp, wiping the sweat from my neck with a handkerchief. I did not feel sadness. The dominant feeling inside me was undefinable, something between peace and loneliness.

I carefully took out the pie and the bread from my rucksack and set them aside. Before taking my first bite, I sniffed the pie again, because it awakened tender memories of my mother. Then I ate hungrily, and when the slice was gone, I realized that the bread would end up feeding the woodland critters. I chopped it up into small pieces and started spreading it around me. I was certain that in a short time, not a crumb would be left. Some ants were already carefully gathering the crumbs falling from my hands.

I stood up, stretching my back, and my eyes fell on some scattered stones. A thought crossed my mind, and I smiled. I pushed back my sleeves and set to my task. I had thought of making a small, impromptu monument around the large white rock with all the stones I could carry. Something to mark the spot where Antonis had died, to commemorate him.

My father had taught me well, and I selected stones with a flat surface, which could be supported one on top of the other. Carrying them was no easy task, as some of them were half-buried in the ground, and I had to pull them out with my hands or use a thick branch as a lever. I was placing them in a rough semi-circle, and would decide how to fit them together once I had collected enough.

I almost dropped a heavy stone when I heard someone speak.

"Hello, Ariadne."

I jumped with fright and quickly turned around. I stared at Pavlos Lambrakis standing a few meters away and, without returning the greeting, I wondered what he was doing here and why he had followed me. I let the stone fall from my hands and drop to the ground.

"I called out to you in the village, but you must not have heard me. I decided to come to find you afterward. I have wanted to come here, too," Lambrakis said, and moved closer.

"Why have you not come before? Why are you here now?" I snapped at him.

He looked taken aback, and sighed. "This is difficult for me too. I have seen this place in my nightmares countless times."

"You are not the only one," I spat out with a sneer.

I bent back down and started placing the rocks, without any idea of the shape I would be giving them. Concentrating was impossible after the upset his presence had caused me. Undeterred, he came and stood beside me.

"I was such an idiot that day..." he said.

I chose not to reply, so he could take my silence as agreement.

But he carried on, nonetheless. "We could construct something beautiful here if you wish..."

"Stop," I said, raising my soil-covered hand.

"What's wrong? Was it something I said?" he stammered, at a loss.

"I don't want you to build anything else for him. I need to make something for him that expresses me. If that's okay with you," I added sarcastically.

"Please forgive me. You are right, of course, I just don't know how I'm supposed to act."

"I want you to put yourself in my shoes for a moment and tell me how you would react."

"But you know that I can't..."

I interrupted him again, because I knew what he was going to say. "If the person standing before you were responsible for the death of the person you loved more than anyone in the whole world, what would you do?"

He looked at me for a moment, and then fell to his knees, head bowed.

"I honestly don't know," he managed to say in a trembling voice, avoiding my eyes.

I wanted to ask him to leave, but I also thought that perhaps he was in pain too, in his own way. I kept quiet and carried on placing the stones one on top of the other.

"If you want it to be sturdy, you need to place a big stone beside the white one as a base," Lambrakis said, looking around him.

Before I could reply, he hurried off and, pushing the grass aside with his feet, he bent down to lift a huge stone. I did not want him helping me, and was outraged that he was taking such liberties. When I saw him struggle to lift and carry the stone, however, I did not say anything and let him bring it over.

"I'll dig out some more stones for you to use as a foundation," he said, brushing the soil off the stone.

Again, I did not manage to say a word because he was off in a flash. All I had wanted was to come here and find some peace and quiet. Now, he had made it impossible. I thought about leaving, but I did not want to let him have that kind of impact on my life.

Stubbornly, he carried over a second stone, and another two he found later. I would not have been able to bring them on my own, and despite my anger, I could see that he was right.

"Now you can place the rest of the stones on top of them. It's a stronger foundation," he said, laying the rocks side by side.

He was kneeling beside me and then turned towards me, waiting for me to say something. I ignored him and started piling up the stones. Disappointed, he sat cross-legged on the ground.

"I know that Antonis saved your life by diving into a frozen lake," Lambrakis said, "and that the scar on your forehead is from your injury that day."

I looked at him inquisitively. I was trying to understand what he truly wanted from me.

"Do you know what they say about someone who saves the life of another person?" I asked him. He looked at me expectantly. "Saving a life is like saving the whole world..."

He nodded in agreement, but I was not done. "They also say that destroying a life is like destroying the whole world."

My words must have hurt him, because he instantly frowned.

"I wish I had not come here that day. I know this is very hard, but you must move on. You are young, and you must not allow what happened to break you. I wish we could turn back time..." he said, his voice choked with emotion.

I was impressed he was not trying to hide his feelings; it was unusual for a man.

"I am going to ask you for a favor," I said. "If you truly want to help me after what happened, don't come to find me again. Build what you want in the village and then go back to your life. Unfortunately, I can't force you to do this, but I am asking you to."

"I know you hate me, but..."

"You are wrong," I interrupted him, wiping the soil from my hands. "I have learned not to hate anyone. Hatred makes you worse than the person you want to hate. Yes, I am angry. I feel the anger inside me, I make no secret of it. Angry about everything we would have shared, and which you took away from us. But I don't hate you. If I did, you might not be here now."

My answer frightened me, as well as him. He gulped and looked away.

"What do you want?" I asked him, determined to put an end to whatever this strange game was. I sat back on my heels. "You have done so much already, but you won't stop. The court allowed you to continue your life. Why don't you return to it? Why do you keep digging up the past? Don't tell me you are doing it to preserve Antonis's memory, because I don't buy that."

He wiped his palms on his trousers and stood up. He turned to the side and took a couple of steps away from the makeshift monument.

"You're right. I'm not doing it just for him," he said, his words barely audible.

"Why are you doing it, then?" I asked, and stood up.

He turned to face me and looked at me raptly. I felt something move behind me like a shadow, and he followed my gaze.

"Is someone here?" he asked.

I shook my head. Whatever it was, it was gone. Maybe it was an illusion created by the shadows of the branches moving in the wind.

"I don't think so," I said.

"It's strange, talking about all this here," he said.

"You came here, I didn't invite you," I said flatly.

He took a couple of steps towards me but then hesitated, holding back. If he hadn't, I would have made him. He kept giving me an intense look. "Ariadne, I'm sure you won't believe me when I say it, but I have never met anyone like you before."

"You mean someone who did not try to punch you right there and then?"

"I wish you had. I deserved it. But you didn't, and that is a testament to your nobility."

"Is that why you're acting like this? Because I did not seek revenge?"

"Partly. There is also another reason."

I could recognize the look in his eyes. I was almost sure of what he was getting at. The signs had been clear for a long time, but I had refused to see them. It seemed so shameless that he would be trying to flirt with me.

"Watch your words, Lambrakis. There is a limit even to my tolerance," I warned him.

"I cannot stop what I feel for you," he said, and stretched out his hand to touch my face.

My reflexes sharp, I grabbed his hand. "What are you doing?" I shouted.

Undeterred, he gripped both my wrists in one swift movement and tried to pull me towards him as if he wanted to kiss me.

"Don't try to resist my love. You feel the same; I can see it in your eyes."

He moved nearer, and I struggled to free myself from his grasp. As he brought his lips even closer, with all my strength I jammed my knee between his legs.

Lambrakis staggered backward and doubled over, groaning in pain. I could not believe what was happening. The man must be insane; there was no rhyme or reason to his actions. He brought both his hands to his groin, his face twisted in pain, and began to curse me. A torrent of abuse fell from his mouth as he howled like a wounded animal, unable to stay upright.

I grabbed up a large rock and held it over my head, ready to defend myself if he tried to come near me again. It did not seem likely. My aim had been flawless. He tried to move toward me, but seeing me prepared, he stopped, grimacing with pain.

"Don't you dare step any closer!" I shouted, my mind racing as I considered the best way to escape.

Lambrakis, slowly recovering, straightened his torso and pointed at me. "You're lucky I don't have my gun with me! That would show you!"

He screamed, and then cursed Antonis and me in the worst possible way. I couldn't believe what I was hearing. I couldn't grasp why he was now acting in this manner. It was as if he had transformed into the most despicable beast. He sputtered words and sentences that made no sense, gesticulating wildly.

And then, just when I was ready to run away, he hobbled off, still limping from his injury. He moved downhill, screaming that he would put a stop to the renovations and never set foot here again. I could hear him shouting for some time, until the distance drowned out his voice. It was as if he was raging at the whole forest.

I had not taken a phone with me, so I could not even contact my family. Panting with anxiety and horror, I was rooted to the spot, stone in hand, trying to process what had just happened.

Once Lambrakis had vanished into the dense woods, I leaned against a trunk and hugged myself. I had not expected that kind of reaction. That was not the behavior of a healthy person, and I had every intention of reporting the assault, so he would not ever get the chance to do it again.

I looked around me, and my eyes welled up. Everything had happened here. Antonis's blood had flowed across this very soil, and yet Lambrakis had felt no scruples about making a pass at me in the most vulgar manner. I would not let this slide.

I decided to not even touch the stones which that monster had carried. He had defiled this place just by coming here. With a single kick, I brought down everything he had helped me build.

I decided to return along a different path to the one Lambrakis had taken. I had barely taken a few steps when everything around me went dark. Heavy clouds covered the sky, and a loud clap of thunder boomed. My heart beating wildly, I secured the rucksack on my back and moved quickly downhill, passing under the fir trees. I kept a careful eye around me. I did not put it past him to lie in ambush. If he did that, I was now determined to pull out my knife.

As I hurried along, the storm grew closer. The few raindrops that managed to find their way through the tree canopy splattered on the soil beside me. The whole place shook as lightning struck the ground nearby. Moving among the trees was not safe.

I quickly calculated that it would take me an hour to reach the outskirts of the village, given the distance I had to cover. I wondered whether it would be best to seek shelter somewhere, but I decided to keep going. I was still very shaken and wanted to get back as quickly as possible, even if it meant getting drenched.

A strange sound stopped me in my tracks. I pricked my ears, trying to gauge where it was coming from. It had sounded like a human cry, but the sounds of the forest were often deceptive. I made to move towards higher ground, hoping to get a better view.

The rain became stronger and soaked me from head to toe. Before I could reach the peak, I heard someone calling for help from the other side. It was coming from the direction Lambrakis had taken. I immediately thought he must have run into a flock of sheep and was being chased by the sheepdogs.

Serves him right, I said out loud, and made to turn back. But this time the cry was much louder and accompanied by howls. I was not sure whether it was his voice, but someone was desperately calling for help. That was not the cry of a person being chased by sheepdogs—that was the cry of a person in real fear for their life.

Without a second thought, I ran towards the cries. Once more, I was speeding through the same forest with a terrible sense of dread. Thunder shook the ground again, and the rain fell harder.

I started to climb the slope, moving as quickly as I could without slipping on the wet rocks. As I got closer, I realized that the howls came from wolves. My experience with the deer had seared their characteristic cry in my mind. Panting and following the sound, I realized I was close. In the distance, I could make out their shapes as they moved through the dense foliage. They had evidently cornered someone in the trees.

Instinctively, I began to shout loudly. I grabbed a sturdy branch and moved towards them. As soon as the wild animals sensed my presence, they moved up the slope. I could no longer hear the human voice. My heart beat frantically and irregularly, my breath coming in gasps. The rain had drenched my clothes, but I could barely feel it.

I kept moving closer, frantically hitting the ground and the tree trunks with the branch. It was the only thing I could do, hoping to frighten them. It seemed to work, and the wolves pulled further back. Something else was moving behind the fallen trunk of a large fir tree.

"Who's there?" I screamed.

I approached with trepidation, keeping a watchful eye. When I was closer, I saw a large black wolf slowly rise on his legs. He looked at me and gave me a threatening growl. His coat was dripping with rain. It was the same wolf that had stared us down on the path back then.

Seeing the blood dripping from his fangs, I froze. With a jump, he stood on the fallen trunk and seemed ready to attack. I held the branch in front of me like a spear and slowly stepped away until I felt my back brush up against a tree. As if the rest of the pack had been given an order, they started to surround me. Trying to frighten them away, I kept hitting the ground with the branch and shouted for them to stay back. I was already regretting coming here, but it was too late to run away.

The black wolf jumped down from the trunk towards me. Behind him, someone groaned—whoever they had attacked was still alive.

The animal, baring its teeth, moved closer. So did the others. I raised the branch and positioned it between us, screaming with all the air in my lungs to deter him.

I could feel its vicious eyes pierce me, and I gave a quick glance at the trunk behind me to see if I could climb it. I grabbed a nearby branch and prepared to throw my stick at the wolf and climb the tree as quickly as possible. Suddenly, as if obeying a secret, unspoken order, he moved around me and went to join the rest of the pack, which was still circling me. I braced my foot against the trunk so that I could swiftly push myself up to the first branch, at least, if they returned.

The black wolf moved on, the rest of the pack turning to follow. As soon as they were some distance away, I placed both feet on the ground, my senses alert for their return. My breath came in ragged gasps as I tried to calm down and recover from the anxiety and tension. When I saw the wolf and the pack pause a little further up the hill, I hesitated, too. He turned to look at me, and then began to pace left and right between the trees, followed by the others. Watching. Waiting.

I slowly moved to the fallen trunk and climbed over. Lambrakis was on the ground, covered in blood, and barely moving. I knelt beside him, and he grasped my hand weakly, breathlessly asking for help. The blood had soaked his coat, which lay in rags around him, torn by the wolf's fangs. He turned his face towards me, and I tried to raise him, putting my hand around his neck. He screamed, and I instantly released his neck, realizing where the blood was coming from.

"He bit me..." he managed to whisper.

I shot a quick glance around, fearing another attack from the wolves. But they kept their distance, as if waiting for something. "Stay awake," I urged Lambrakis. "Talk to me."

Evora

He was in a state of shock, his eyes unable to focus, his mouth unable to form the words to respond. I had to stop the bleeding from the bite.

I quickly removed my rucksack and unzipped it. The only thing inside it that could help was the spare t-shirt I'd packed. Time ticking by mercilessly and the rain drenching everything, I picked up my knife and tore it through the fabric to create strips of bandage.

Lambrakis's eyes bulged in terror when he saw the knife. The memory of the injured deer flashed before my eyes. I sharply chased away the terrifying memory and attempted to make a bandage. Then I tried to tie it around the wound, but it was impossible to tighten the fabric without hindering his breathing.

I pressed down on the wound as hard as I could and desperately tried to think of how I could get help, while also keeping an eye on the wild animals that continued to hover, waiting for a signal only they understood. The scent of the blood was intense, and I worried they might soon make another move. Or were they expecting me to do what I had done to the deer once again?

How could I go find help without abandoning Lambrakis to their fangs? With my free hand, I began to rifle through his pockets, looking for his phone, but found none. Then I spotted it on the ground, caked in mud and grass. I was amazed to find it still worked, but the screen was locked.

"How does it unlock?" I cried out in despair.

He tried to move his hands, but they were as stiff as pincers, and he could not even grip the phone.

"Face..." he uttered with great difficulty.

I hastily faced the screen of the phone toward him, praying it would unlock. After a few agonizing seconds, it worked. It was difficult to input my father's phone number, covered as my fingers were with blood and water, but I managed it. To my great surprise, I saw that the number was already stored on the phone as Her father.

The few seconds it took for my father to answer felt like years. I pressed one hand against Lambrakis's neck wound and held the phone with the other, desperately trying to explain to my stunned father what had happened and where we were. I could hear the terror in his voice when I told him about the lurking wolves. I also told him lumberjacks were nearby, and maybe one of them could get here faster. I explained that the phone might not work in a moment because he kept getting cut off. He promised to contact the police and an ambulance, and then hung up so he could make the calls.

I dropped the phone into my rucksack to keep it as dry as possible. When I raised my head, my eyes met the gaze of the black wolf, who was looking down at us angrily, as if waiting for me to leave so he could finish what he had started.

Lambrakis's eyelids fluttered as if he was about to fall asleep. He had a deep injury to the side of his neck. He gripped my hand and, with great effort, managed to slightly raise his head, wincing with pain. He looked at me and, for the first time, his gaze was lucid and able to focus.

"I'm sorry..." he whispered, and then fell unconscious.

His pulse grew fainter, and the bleeding from his neck would not stop despite the pressure I was applying. With as much calmness as I could muster, I tied the bandage around his neck and continued to press on the wound. I was desperate and did not know what else to do.

Suddenly, Lambrakis started to shake. He struggled to breathe, and his fingers dug into the mud. I grabbed his face, trying to help him, and he suddenly became still. Slowly, his body relaxed, as if exhaling his last breath.

I shook him, then pressed my ear against his chest. The rain splattered against my cheek as I desperately tried to listen for his heartbeat. I fumbled against his neck but could feel no pulse.

The wolves began to pace closer, perhaps sensing the life had left their prey. There was no way I was leaving him. As much as I despised him for what he had done, I did not wish him to die. I put my palms on his chest and started to give him CPR. Looking at his lips, I froze for a moment, but seeing him unresponsive, I bent down and gave him mouth-to-mouth, trying to revive him.

I fought to bring Lambrakis back, losing all sense of time, but always keeping an eye out for the wolf pack. Exhausted, my chest burning, I gave up after a few minutes. No matter what I did, the outcome would not change. Lambrakis was dead, and nothing could bring him back. I pushed myself back and howled in despair, my cry ripping through the forest.

The black wolf was only a few meters away now. Without a growl, he stared at me for a few more seconds. Then he turned back and moved away, the rest of the pack following him through the pouring rain until they all vanished into the deep woods...

Evora

JUST YESTERDAY, five days after the attack in the forest, the terrible process of the autopsy and inquest finally came to an end. Lambrakis's death had resulted from a wolf bite, which led to excessive blood loss and his death in my arms despite my efforts to save him. I felt strange when I realized that the police were looking into whether he had died in a different way to what I had initially reported. Some may have believed that I had done it to avenge Antonis's death. Luckily, that theory was discounted early on. The lumberjacks who had arrived at the scene that day, testified they had seen the wolves in the area earlier that morning. They also testified that when they had arrived, there was nothing more to do for Lambrakis than wait for the police and the rescuers to carry him away.

I told them that we had met by chance in the woods, and that Lambrakis had left on his own. I decided not to mention the assault. I told only my father, who agreed that I should stay quiet. I felt bad about everything that had happened, and there was no longer any reason for anyone to know about that incident. I only told my father, who agreed with my decision. He also said that the wolves had served him right, but I would not have wished such an end on anyone.

I had not slept a wink since that day. Gossip was rife in the region, and I did my best to avoid the journalists who had descended upon the village to cover the incident. They came all the way to Evora trying to get a statement from me, but I refused to comment. Voras served as my watchdog, barking at any who tried to trespass in my home. He alone was usually enough to deter them, although he rarely barked at anyone.

I had read many inaccuracies in these five days. People loved scandal, and many journalists gleefully fed the rumor mill. One of most widely spread theories was that Lambrakis and I were having an affair. There was nothing to prove this, as the inquest showed, but that did not stop people from speculating wildly. And Lambrakis's obsession with me did not help matters.

For reasons of his own, he had stored in his phone not only my contact information, but that of my family and friends as well. Using the renovations as an excuse, he would call my father often, although that had proved to be nothing but a pretext to get closer to me. I could see why the gossip mill invented an affair between us, but it frustrated me that they refused to accept the truth when it was put right in front of them.

It is challenging to try to understand the way some people think and reason. Lambrakis was one of those people. I may have sensed he had a crush on me, but I never expected he would have the nerve to make such a vulgar and inappropriate pass. Still, I was genuinely upset and felt some guilt over his tragic end, even if there was nothing I could have done to save him.

A price had been put on the heads of the wolf pack, as some believed that having killed a man once, they would do it again. Some said they should be put to death, others that they should be captured, and others still that they should be left alone. To my knowledge, no one had even managed to spot them so far, let alone get close enough to kill or capture them.

I, on the other hand, would wake with a start in the middle of the night thinking I'd heard the black wolf howl. I had not managed to understand their behavior that day. The strange connection that I believed had grown between us, especially the leader of the pack, frightened me.

I had so much to handle that I was in a constant state of turmoil. New feelings of guilt added themselves to the guilt I already felt over Antonis's death. At least the steady rainfall of the last three days gave me a chance to stay at home, away from all the clamor down in the village.

Curled up on the couch with Voras, I was trying to process what had happened. My life these past few months seemed more like an adventure movie rather than anything I had ever dreamed of. The worst part was that the life of my family had also been thrown into turmoil, and they did not deserve that.

I looked at the cloud-covered mountains across the valley and thought about the games fate had played with us. Two people had needlessly lost their lives. Of course, Antonis's loss did not compare to Lambrakis's, but my involvement in what had happened would not let me forget.

When all the procedural formalities were over, I intended to go on a long trip. I needed to get away for a while, travel to a place where I could become lost to everyone and everything. I was in no fit state to work, and my need to escape was stronger than ever.

While the rain fell in thick sheets outside, I turned my gaze to the shelf where I had placed the blue box with Antonis's things. I was expecting Eva and her boyfriend for dinner later, so now was the perfect time to open it.

I got up from the couch, and Voras, looking at me, moved to the door. I understood he wanted to go outside to play in the rain, so I let him out. Then I slowly walked towards the blue box and picked it up. I set it on the kitchen counter and opened it slowly, as if I was handling the most fragile object in the world.

I pulled out a transparent bag that contained Antonis's bloodied clothes and set it aside. Underneath, everything that Antonis had had on him that day, both in the car and at home, was lined up. His wallet, his keys, some papers, and his phone. A dark bloodstain was still visible on the cracked screen.

I picked the phone up and examined it. I remembered all the photos of us, which I had not had time to download. I tried to switch it on, but it was not working. I could not understand whether its battery was drained, or if it had been damaged.

Evora

I looked at the bookshelves and remembered that I had placed the charger in the laptop bag. I brought it to the counter and plugged the phone in. The phone still looked dead. Then I recalled that Antonis had set up his phone to automatically upload all his photos on a website for safekeeping. I carefully took out the laptop, plugged it in, and turned it on. The screen brightened and his desktop immediately appeared, as no password was required.

His wallpaper was a photo of Evora, with Voras and me in the distance gazing at the sunset. I sighed bitterly and started clicking on the icons. After examining the computer for a moment or two, I finally found the website where he stored his files. The password had been saved, and his photos filled the screen in no time. Also in the cloud storage were his messages, videos, and various other files he had stored there.

Tears welled in my eyes as I scrolled through the photos. I discovered how many pictures of me Antonis had taken without me being aware of it. Voras also held pride of place, of course. I wiped a tear from my cheek and moved to the latest photos he had stored. As I scrolled down, I noticed that the last image was a video. I pressed play.

Antonis's face appeared on screen, saying something. I brought my hand to my mouth in shock. I instantly pressed pause. It had been filmed on the day we had gone to the woods, when Antonis had been shot by Lambrakis. Not in the house, but in the forest itself—he must have taken the video after we'd parted ways to search for the poachers. These might very well be the last words he'd ever spoken.

My knees buckled, and I quickly sat down on a stool. I stretched out my hand to turn up the volume and pulled nearer, moving the cursor to play the video from the start.

"Ariadne, I don't know when I will show you this video, but a few seconds ago, I just managed to tell you those magical words. For the first time in my life, I feel like I truly mean them. You and your father are on your way to the Valley. I wanted to make a video, which I will show you many years later, to remind us both of this moment, the moment I told you that... I love you."

I hit the pause button. The screen had turned blurry as my eyes filled with tears. I had not even imagined he would do something like this. Now, it was as if he were standing before me, except that I could see him and hear him, but I could not touch him. He held his phone up as he walked through the woods, talking to me. I roughly brushed away the tears and pressed Play again.

"I like to think that you will hear those words from my lips many times, because I mean them from the bottom of my heart. I will never forget the day when your heart started to beat again... I would dive into a frozen lake for you a hundred times over..."

He brought the phone closer, and it was as if he was looking deep into my eyes. Then he turned it away towards the forest and kept talking to me, showing me the woods and his route through them. The mist had not lifted in some places, and the whole landscape looked like it belonged in a fairytale.

"I see all this beauty around me, and I wonder what I was thinking all those years of working nonstop and living a life I did not desire. You came into my life like a gift."

He turned the screen towards his face again, and a cheeky, conspiratorial look came over him.

"Don't let it go to your head, though, eh?"

I smiled at his funny grimace despite the tightness in my chest. He walked onward.

"I only hope I'm on the right path and don't find myself at the other end of the forest... Look how pretty it is," Antonis said, showing me the landscape. For a few more seconds, all I could hear was his breathing.

He suddenly stopped, and clumsily turned the screen around. "A deer..." he whispered.

He turned the phone the other way and zoomed in on a spot where the undergrowth was quite high. I could not make anything out when, suddenly, behind a towering fir, a beautiful deer appeared. "Isn't it gorgeous?"

I smiled bitterly, because I could sense the enthusiasm in the timbre of his voice. Suddenly startled, Antonis said something inaudible and turned the other way, focusing on someone aiming at the deer with a gun. I froze when I recognized Lambrakis, who seemed unaware of Antonis.

My hands gripped the kitchen counter as if I wanted to lift it up. Antonis lowered the phone by his side, and the image became blurry. His voice, though, came through loud and clear. "What do you think you're doing?" he shouted.

His words were interrupted by a gunshot. I could no longer see anything. It looked as if he had put the phone in his pocket, but it kept recording. I could hear Lambrakis's voice from a distance, and it was hard to make out what he was saying.

"Don't you know you're not allowed to hunt here?" Antonis was asking him angrily.

I faintly heard Lambrakis curse Antonis for startling the deer and making him miss his mark. I paused the video. I could not breathe. Like a loudspeaker in my head, I could hear his words at the trial, saying he had not seen what was there and taken a blind shot. He had lied. I dreaded what would follow. With great difficulty, I pressed Play to hear the rest of the recording.

"You should be ashamed of yourself!" Antonis shouted.

Lambrakis's voice now came loud and clear. He had moved closer.

"Who do you think you are, telling me what to do?"

Antonis let out a cry. "Put the gun down! Don't point it at me!"

There was the sound of frantic footsteps, and then Lambrakis shouting for Antonis to stay where he was. A gunshot almost burst the laptop speakers, and tore my heart to pieces. There was a small, faint cry of pain and a scratchy sound, as if Antonis was trying to grab his phone. The video ended there.

My tears had drenched the keyboard. The drone of a thousand bees buzzed in my head, and I tried to take deep breaths to stop myself from fainting. A voice inside me screamed that I must be mistaken. I moved to the sink and bent my head to the tap, gulping the water down. I wanted to scream. Everything I had seen and heard was so extreme, I wondered whether I was having a nightmare and would soon wake up.

I returned to the laptop and played the video again from the beginning. I must have been sobbing and shouting as I watched it, because Voras was knocking against the window, trying to get to me. The bastard had shot Antonis in cold blood, then looked me straight in the eyes and lied about it. If he had been standing before me right now, I would have torn him apart with my bare hands. Compared to my rage, the injuries inflicted by the wolves were nothing.

I kept playing the video over and over, unable to process what had happened, especially the last few seconds, as I could not comprehend exactly what had happened. From the snatches I could hear, I understood that Antonis had tried to run, and possibly tried to use his phone to call for help—or had he been trying to end the recording, to send it to someone so the world would know the truth? Of course, I was just conjecturing now, my thoughts spinning in my mind like a demented merry-go-round.

As I opened the kitchen door to let Voras in, I saw headlights approaching. It must be my sister and her boyfriend. I dithered for a moment about whether I would reveal everything I had seen and heard, but this was not the moment to make any kind of decision. I hurriedly stepped back inside, shaking, and replaced all of Antonis's things in the blue box and the laptop back in its case. As soon as I heard the garden gates open, I called out that the door was open and that I was going to the bathroom.

I stood staring at the mirror, like an animal about to attack. My hands still shook with the shock, and my eyes were bloodshot. I needed some time to decide what to do, and how I would handle this terrible discovery. I stayed in the bathroom as long as I could, trying to compose myself, and only when they called my name did I step out.

Despite my attempt at hiding my distress, my sister instantly understood I was not well. I excused myself, saying I was having one of those nights where I could not stop replaying everything that had happened in my head. Eva and her boyfriend had already started serving the food they had brought over. I picked up the glass of wine Eva handed me and downed it in a single gulp. Then we sat down to dinner, but my thought kept returning to the images captured by the video. I picked at my food and drank glass after glass.

"Slow down..." Eva whispered, and touched my wrist.

I felt as if I had been transported to an alternate universe. The wine was going to my head as I tried to talk to them.

Evora

The sound of Antonis's voice and his face in the video drifted in and out of my mind like a soft breeze.

Later, as Eva helped me with the dishes in the kitchen, she asked if I wanted her to stay tonight and keep me company.

"No, no, I'm just having one of those days," I told her. "I'll be fine. I'm sorry I was miserable company."

"Don't worry about us. Grigoris understands. He won't take it the wrong way... We'll let you rest, but please don't drink any more. I've never seen you drink so much. And if you need anything, call me, and I'll be right up. Promise?"

"Promise..." was all I managed to say. I loved her dearly, but I wanted to be alone.

I waved goodbye a few minutes later, gritting my teeth to stifle the scream in my throat. A whimper escaped my clenched lips as soon as they started to drive away. My back against the front door, I sank down to the floor and burst into tears. Voras curled up beside me, making sounds as if he were trying to console me. I have no idea how long I stayed there, curled up with my beloved dog.

At some point, I stood up and filled my glass with wine. I turned off most of the lights and picked up Antonis's laptop again. I sat on the couch and took a long gulp. I so wanted to rewatch that part where he told me in his sweet voice that he would dive a hundred times over to save me from the frozen waters. I wished he had never done it. Because then he would be alive today...

Autumn...

OCTOBER HAS ALWAYS been one of my favorite months. For as long as I can remember, the last few days of October always exuded a sense of tranquility that I sought no matter what. Tomorrow, the clocks would turn forward, signaling that winter was coming. This transition carried a sweet melancholy with it.

Seated with Voras in the garden, I was enjoying the sunset in his company. His face was turned sideways to better feel the breeze stroking his snout and making him happy. I wished there was some way to find out why he acted like this every time the north wind blew. I lifted my coat collar around my neck, feeling my body shiver.

Today was an important day, as a special guest would be arriving any minute now. I must confess that I was anxious about meeting her. I looked at a flock of birds flying over the lake as if dashing to reach the sun before it set. The mountain ranges across the valley, lined up against the backdrop of the horizon, looked like a painting.

So many thoughts jostled for space in my mind. Always dominated, however, by everything that had happened and the wreckage it had left behind. I kept trying to understand why it had happened, to no avail. Everything I had observed taking place in the world around me had taught me that a person's heart can become cruel, inhuman. I always believed that those who do great harm are the first to die inside, as they are now unable to save their own self. Whoever feels indifferent about the sanctity of life has no chance of choosing good over evil.

A person can often become a wolf towards others, ready to savage them at any moment. In the hardest, most tragic way, I had learned that the souls of some people, like Lambrakis, can harden after committing such an act, and then there is no way back. That is what his behavior had proved beyond doubt. He had chosen a curse over a blessing. Death over life.

Even today, nearly a month after his tragic end, I could not comprehend his actions and why he had shot Antonis in cold blood. I also could not find an explanation for his masterfully orchestrated performance, which he delivered daily. How can you kill a person in this manner and then pretend so convincingly that it had been an accident?

His behavior was not even guided by those primitive, animal instincts that can lead someone to commit a crime. In nature, you rarely come across a killing for no reason. Animals kill when they hunt or when they are in danger. Not only did he kill a man in the most cowardly manner, but then he went after his other half, convinced that I would respond to his advances. His sick, narcissistic mind did not allow him to confess or even stop after the court's light sentence. Free from the charge of murder, he could have moved on with his life, but he chose to desecrate Antonis's memory, going after me as a trophy. Only an insane man could act this way. The more I thought about it, the more I became convinced that he suffered from some form of psychosis that made him lose touch with reality.

I still mourned Antonis's death. I would mourn him until the end of my life, in my own way, invisible to those around me. The fact that Lambrakis murdered him with full intent did not change the outcome. Besides, he had been punished by nature herself, although I was sure that the alpha wolf had been responsible for that. Something strange and inexplicable now bound me to that animal. The court, even if it had found him guilty of murder by discovering his intent, would have sentenced him to many years in prison. But in ten, fifteen years at most, he would have been a free man again. Now he had paid for his actions with his life. Some would call it divine justice...

After serious consideration, I decided never to tell anyone about the video that proved beyond doubt that Antonis had been murdered. I saved it until the deer appeared and then deleted the rest, as well as the entire file from his account. It had not been an easy decision, and I had not taken it lightly. I was not interested in keeping any proof of Lambrakis's guilt, as he had already received his punishment. I kept that segment because the few minutes before his death were the priceless legacy that this incredible man had left me.

That short video would be my secret from now on. I promised myself that if I wanted to honor Antonis's memory, I had to keep living. To enjoy the gift of life daily, free from bitterness about everything that had happened, and free from rage and the desire for vengeance in particular. If I had discovered that Lambrakis had been lying while he was still alive, I do not know how I would have reacted. Fortunately, or unfortunately, I would never have the chance to find out.

The best revenge anyone can take in these circumstances is to keep on living and not grieve forever for someone who is never coming back. The people who have loved us and have departed would tell us precisely this if they could talk: spend every moment guided by love. Their memory lives through our own joy. I had found my Evora, and I was certain that if everyone took the trouble to search deep inside them, they would find their own Evora too.

For the first time in a long while, I posted something on my social media with a photo of the view from up here. This is what I wrote:

"Remember to smile at the simple things, because your smile makes you and the world around you prettier, and you know it. Love more, love louder, love truer, and say it often. Grab as much time as possible for yourself and all those you love. Give the precious moments you share with them the importance and the attention that they deserve, for as long as you have them in your life."

There were hundreds of comments under this post approving what I had written. The love I received from all these people filled me with hope.

Hearing the sound of a car coming up the hill, I took out the note Antonis had given me at the Armchair out of my pocket. I had read it so many times since that day and had felt sad every time, but not today. Not anymore.

When the car came up the driveway, Voras stood up and approached it, wagging his tail. My nervousness peaking, I stood up too. A young woman stepped out of the driver's side and moved hesitantly towards me, smiling. She had a strange beauty and was still pale, which was to be expected after everything she had been through.

As soon as the doctors had permitted it, she had arranged to come and meet me. We had spoken a few times on the phone, and some sort of familiarity was forming between us. We agreed that she should spend the week at the guesthouse so that I could show her the area and especially Evora, in all its glory. She had asked me if she could join my therapy program, but I suggested that we decide that together once she had settled in.

"You are Ariadne, right?" she asked in a soft voice, and I nodded, returning her warm smile.

I took another step towards her, and she did the same. Her eyes were shining, and I imagine so were mine. I was ready to hug her. I wanted more than anything in the world to feel, after all this time, Antonis's heart beating in her chest.

I opened my arms wide, and after we both took a few more steps, we were close to each other. Instantly, like a small bird, she crawled into my arms. We stayed like that for a while, like two people who had loved each other deeply and were meeting again after a long separation. She picked up my hand and placed it on her chest. I don't believe I have ever felt another heartbeat so intensely.

I wiped a tear with my free hand and led her to the edge of the garden, looking at the sun slowly disappearing behind the mountains. Voras came to stand beside us in his usual spot. I slowly pulled out Antonis's note and handed it to her. She looked at me, uncomprehending.

"The man whose heart beats inside you wrote me this once."

Visibly moved, she picked it up and read it aloud in her soft voice.

My heart will always beat for you...

A.

THE END

A word from the author

As with nearly all my books, the inspiration for Evora is based on actual events. In this case, a place and its people provided the foundation for the story of Ariadne and Evora. Although the plot of the book geographically takes place in the village of Panagitsa in Edessa, in Northern Greece, I altered the topography of the region and named the village 'Avgerinos,' a name that carries special connotations for me.

In this book, Evora is Ariadne's home and workplace, her 'slice of heaven'. In real life, it is a beautiful café-restaurant situated in the region where the story takes place. I altered the landscape to suit the purposes of the plot.

I discovered the real-life Evora after a message I received from Stavroula Parthenopoulou, who runs Evora, the café-restaurant. When she wrote to let me know how much she had enjoyed Lake of Memories, she could not have known that her Evora would become a protagonist in one of my following books.

The photos she posted on social media caught my eye to the extent that I decided to visit Evora. That visit reconfirmed my belief that contact with nature can be salutary. Panagitsa and Stavroulas' Evora became my slice of heaven too.

Having grown up in the countryside, I know first-hand how difficult it is to live there nowadays, leaving the noise of the city behind you.

Through Ariadne's eyes, I revisited my experience of growing up in a village and a life that I am still occasionally able to enjoy. I must confess I envied Ariadne's life, despite the tragic turn it took with Antonis's death.

I find myself on a quest for Ariadne's tranquility and serenity for myself more and more often. I envied that she lived in a place where every moment of her day could become her Evora.

All the characters and locations in the book are fictional, with the exception of Voras, who you can meet in Panagitsa. If you ever visit Evora there, ask to try their raspberry and chocolate pancakes. Just make sure it's early on in the day so you can walk it off afterward!

The scenery I describe can be found in my mother's village, Palaiochori of Kalambaka, in the region of Thessaly in Central Greece. That is where I hope to build the small stone cottage in the forest that I dream of. My own Evora.

Kostas Krommydas

About the author

When Kostas Krommydas decided to write his first novel, he took the publishing world of his native Greece by storm. A few years later, he is an award winning author of five bestselling novels, acclaimed actor, teacher and passionate storyteller. His novels have been among the top 10 at the prestigious Public Book Awards (Greece) and his novel "Ouranoessa" has won first place (2017). He has also received the coveted WISH writer's award in 2013 as an emerging author. When not working on his next novel at the family beach house in Athens, you will find him acting on theatre, film, and TV; teaching public speaking; interacting with his numerous fans; and writing guest articles for popular Greek newspapers, magazines, and websites. If you want to find out more about Costas, visit his website, http://kostaskrommydas.gr/ or check out his books on Amazon: Author.to/KostasKrommydas

More books by the author

Cave of Silence

A Love So Strong, It Ripples Through the Ages.

Dimitri, a young actor, is enjoying the lucky break of his life—a part in an international production shot on an idyllic Greek island and a romance with Anita, his beautiful co-star. When his uncle dies, he has one last wish: that Dimitri scatters his ashes on the island of his birthplace. At first, Dimitri welcomes this opportunity to shed some light on his family's history—a history clouded in secrecy. But why does his mother beg him to hide his identity once there?

Dimitri discovers that the past casts long shadows onto the present when his visit sparks a chain of events that gradually reveal the island's dark secrets; secrets kept hidden for far too long. Based on true events, the *Cave Of Silence* moves seamlessly between past and present to spin a tale of love, passion, betrayal, and cruelty. Dimitris and Anita may be done with the past. But is the past done with them?

Athora

A Mystery Romance set on the Greek Islands.

A tourist is found dead in Istanbul, the victim of what appears to be a ritual killing. An elderly man is murdered in the same manner, in his house by Lake Como. The priest of a small, isolated Greek island lies dead in the sanctuary, his body ritualistically mutilated. Fotini Meliou is visiting her family on the island of Athora for a few days, before starting a new life in the US. She is looking forward to a brief respite and, perhaps, becoming better acquainted with the seductive Gabriel, whom she has just met. It is not the summer vacation she expects it to be. A massive weather bomb is gathering over the Aegean, threatening to unleash the most violent weather the area has ever seen. When the storm breaks out, the struggle begins. A race against the elements and a race against time: the killer is still on the island, claiming yet another victim. Locals, a boatload of newly arrived refugees, foreign residents, and stranded tourists are now trapped on an island that has lost contact with the outside world. As the storm wreaks havoc on the island, how will they manage to survive?

Kostas Krommydas

Dominion of the Moon

Award Winner, Public Readers' Choice Awards 2017

In the final stages of WWII, archaeologist Andreas Stais follows the signs that could lead him to unearth the face of the goddess who has been haunting his dreams for years, all the while searching for the woman who, over a brief encounter, has come to dominate his waking hours. In present day Greece, another Andreas, an Interpol officer, leaves New York and returns to his grandparents' island to bid farewell to his beloved grandmother.

Once there, he will come face to face with long-buried family secrets and the enigmatic Iro. When gods and demons pull the threads, no one can escape their fate. Pagan rituals under the glare of the full moon and vows of silence tied to a sacred ring, join men and gods in a common path.

Lake of Memories

Based on a true story

In Paris, a dying woman is searching for the child that was snatched from her at birth over twenty years ago. In Athens, a brilliant dancer is swirling in ecstasy before an enraptured audience. In the first row, a young photographer is watching her for the first time, mesmerized. He knows she is stealing his heart with every swirl and turn, yet is unable to break the spell. And on the Greek island of the Apocalypse, Patmos, a man is about to receive a priceless manuscript from a mysterious benefactor. Destiny has thrown these people together, spinning their stories into a brilliant tapestry of romance, crime, and timeless love. How many memories can the past hold? Is a mother's love strong enough to find the way? Based on a true story, Krommydas' award-winning book firmly established him as one of the top Greek authors of his generation.

Kostas Krommydas

A Tuscan Night

A novel set in Italy and Greece

Some trips start with a suitcase in hand. Other, after a fight. And some when a new job forces you to drop everything and leave. Some journeys have been engraved in our souls. Because they hurt us. Because they made us hurt our loved ones. And some trips are governed by a crazy love. They make us forget what it's like to live and cause the pain of unrequited love. But the thing you may only realize when it's too late is that the best journeys are the ones you never made. The ones you never dared, the ones you never tasted...

My journey started on the day I was told that I only had a few months left to live... and it was the most beautiful I have ever made.

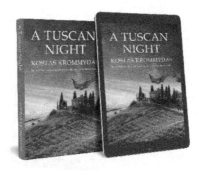

Evora

Very soon, more novels from Kostas Krommydas will be available on Kindle. Sign up to receive our newsletter or follow Kostas on facebook, and we will let you know as soon as they are uploaded!

Want to contact Kostas? Eager for updates?

Want an e-book autograph?

Follow him on

https://www.linkedin.com/in/kostas-krommydas

https://www.instagram.com/krommydaskostas/

https://www.facebook.com/Krommydascostas/

https://twitter.com/KostasKrommydas

Amazon author page:

Author.to/KostasKrommydas

If you wish to report a typo or have reviewed this book on Amazon please email onioncostas@gmail.com with the word "review" on the subject line, to receive a free 1680x1050 desktop background.

Translation: Maria Christou

Editing: Michelle Proulx

Cover Design: Marina Gioti

ISBN: 9798551578857

Thank you for taking the time to read *Evora*. If you enjoyed it, please tell your friends or post a short review. Word of mouth is an author's best friend and much appreciated!

Made in the USA
Las Vegas, NV
24 November 2023

81419977R00213